That Is SO Wrong!

An Anthology of Offbeat Horror Stories

Edited by Jan-Andrew Henderson

A Black Hart Publication

Scotland. Australia.

Offbeat.

Adjective. Unusual and strange and therefore surprising or noticeable:

Cambridge Dictionary

Horror is a reaction; it's not a genre.

John Carpenter

I'm so curious about knowing the unknown; it can be scary, but I see it as a game.

Hrithik Roshan

For Sammy

Note. Since the stories are from world-wide authors, this anthology uses both US and UK English spellings.

Introduction

When close friends and family are talking to me, I sometimes drift off and think to myself: *why do people like horror so much?*

There are many erudite and knowledgeable essays on that subject, so I thought I'd even up the score.

Horror is a mirror held up to society to society, they say. A familiar framework through which we can explore deeper social, psychological and cultural aspects of humanity.

Fair enough. The same used to be said of the western until stuff it couldn't handle - like social influencers and self-driving cars - came along. Then it simply hitched its wagon to sci-fi (Hello *Firefly*. I'm looking at you, *Mandalorian*). Horror can be even more versatile, warping and reconfiguring other genres, like Dr. Frankenstein on steroids. In this anthology, for instance, you'll find romance, psychology, social politics, family dynamics and a meth-dealing polar bear.

Others claim we like the experience of being scared while in a safe environment - but I'd dispute that. I'm not sure many people *do* like to be scared. Suppose I'm alone in a remote location with the wind howling. I start reading a horror novel (or watching a movie) about a remote location with the wind howling and a psychopathic maniac outside. If I begin to get really scared, what do I do? I put the book down or switch the TV over. Then I fetch my baseball bat.

Fear is not an emotion that can be equated with happiness, anger or joy. It's an atavistic fight-or-flight response. A mechanism for casting doubt on the stability of the edifice we call normality. And that *is* frightening.

The best horror stories don't necessarily scare us. However, they do linger in the mind. Then, in the darkness of night, they eat away at our confidence in reality. Unlike other genres, they make the reader their prey rather than an accomplice.

To some extent, recent horror has painted itself into the corner of a dark cellar. Slashers. Werewolves. Shapeshifters. Zombies. A dozen idiotic teenagers in some backwoods cabin. And don't get me started on vampires. Why are we even afraid of those sparkly munters? We now know every conceivable way imaginable to kill 'em.

These well-worn tropes are still popular but I've tended to shun them. This anthology does feature one vampire - but it's Hank Williams, so that's OK. Horror, after all, is in the eye of the beholder. Often taking the form of something pointy.

I used to jump out of the cupboard wearing a clown mask to amuse my 8-year-old son. Eventually, he stopped screaming and became rather blasé about it. So, one day, I jumped out and pulled off the clown mask - to reveal another clown mask underneath. Now he's back in therapy again.

That's when I hit on the secret of horror - and all it took was successfully traumatising a small child. We crave familiarity but we also *love* surprises.

That's where this anthology comes in. It's horror all right. Some of the stories are funny. Some disturbing or gory. But they're also an attempt to offer up fare that's a little different. Or a lot different.

So, follow the bloody footprints leading out of that corner and see where they lead. If you get too scared, you can always close the book.

Or will it be too late?

Jan-Andrew Henderson

The Stories

A Monster Circles the Wreckage

Jan-Andrew Henderson

Serial killers are not radicals: they have enthusiastically embraced the established order only to discover that it offers them no place they can endure. Encalculated with an ambition which they are either unable to attain or cannot feel at ease living.
Dr. Elliot Leyton. *Hunting Humans.*

I didn't think or realize I would ever do these things... I never really wanted to hurt anybody... what drove me to do this? I don't think I was born like this. Why did I start?
Albert De Salvo, The Boston Strangler.

"You know. There are two types of criminals." Miles Harrison was seated in the captain's chair, though the oxygen tank strapped to his back meant he had to perch on the edge. "Some think their biggest mistake was getting caught. Others believe it was getting born."

He glanced at Stuart.

"Aren't you going to take notes?"

"Oh, very droll." Stuart's arm was missing just above the elbow. "Don't worry. I won't forget this shit-show in a hurry."

A slow spiral of blood floated up from the ragged stump, diluted by water. From behind his mask, Miles could see the cabin had taken on a rose-tinted hue.

"Due to the circumstances, I'm going to be fairly direct," Stuart said. "I don't wanna... just circle the subject."

"Not like our friend outside, huh?"

As if on cue, a huge dark mass drifted past the window, momentarily blocking the weak light. Miles was almost out of air but he had no intention of venturing beyond the cabin while that creature lurked in the gloom. Stuart followed it with his eyes.

"Looks like this is your last chance to come clean."

"You want to know why I killed these women?" Miles thought for a while. "I think it was cause of a novel I was trying to write. Or maybe there wasn't much on TV these nights. In the end, all roads lead to Rome, Stuart."

He checked the cylinder gauge. Well below the caution zone. And he had so much to say. The two men obviously couldn't hear each other, yet communication didn't seem to be a problem. Maybe because of encroaching Hypoxia. Maybe because Stuart had died half an hour ago.

"Nazis!" Miles decided a tirade would be fastest. "Let me tell you about Nazis, Stu. Wore nice uniforms. Invaded Poland. What about those former blue-eyed boys?"

He put on a cut-glass English accent.

"How could the rotten Jerry persecute those poor homeless Jews? Bad form. Filthy Hun. Only Jews aren't poor or homeless anymore, says Facebook. No. Now they're controlling America or persecuting poor homeless Palestinians."

"That's Israelis. There's a distinction."

"Don't muddy the waters." Miles laughed mirthlessly. "Every man on the street knows, if we all gave an itsy bitsy, teeny weeny yellow polka dot bit of our wages to the Third World, we could wipe out famine. Cheese off our little suburban dicks. Do we do it?"

"I guess not," his companion admitted.

"Course not! We've endless excuses. I don't wanna be encouraging these people to have more kids - not with a global famine on! They overpopulate their world and, next thing you know, they're over here overpopulating ours. Turn back the fuckers' boats! Let 'em drown!"

He gave the instrument console a muffled thump.

"How do you think this nasty old tub ended up down here? It was already a grave before I discovered the wreck. I just added to it."

"How efficient of you. Also, a bit simplistic in the analogy department."

"Aw, don't tell me you people can't see the big picture. You're all sitting high enough up on white, middle-class picket fences."

"I wasn't going to," Stuart began. But Miles was on a roll.

"There's always a war going on somewhere, so you might have to become a Nazi, or you'll end up skulking in the ghetto. But you gotta be careful, eh? When a soldier fires at the enemy, he's a patriot. By the time the bullet has reached its victim, yet another ceasefire has been declared and he's a murderer. Ends up on death row, waiting for the state to execute *him*."

The oxygen gauge gave a bleep and Miles forced himself to calm down.

"We're allowed to kill, Stuart. I just didn't get the proper permission."

"Right. Thanks." Stuart's face remained impassive, but a slight eddy caught his wispy hair and wafted it upwards. It gave the impression he was horrified and trying not to show it. "I should have had you over for a Xmas lunch. Not just a provocative raconteur but an expert on carving. We could have eaten spleen with a nice bottle of Chianti."

"Call it the times, or genetics or our upbringing but we're as much a mass product as the processed meat on any supermarket counter." Miles ignored the sarcasm. "Future generations will probably look back on us eating animals with the same disgust we have for people who kept slaves."

"So... You were writing down your fantasies." Stuart refused to be side-tracked. "Then you acted them out. Would that be right?"

"No. Not at all."

"What then? Your pencil snapped and you did too?"

"Once things are down on paper, they come a little closer to being real, yes. But what I wrote didn't make me want to kill anyone. Course not. It just set my mind on a certain track. See, I stopped asking myself *what makes people kill* and started asking *what stops them from doing it*? Y'know? I seriously thought about it."

"And what stops them from doing it?"

"Circumstances mainly. And another reason."

"What's that?"

"They never seriously thought about doing it."

Outside the window, the leviathan made another pass, looking for some way to reach them. But the aluminium and fibreglass of the fishing boat's cabin had held up well, despite years under the sea, though the wooden panels were rotted and covered in barnacles. The compass was overgrown with moss and the steering wheel had fallen off long ago. It lay on the floor like a spiky tarnished halo.

"Awright." Stuart flourished an imaginary pen. "An awkward question. For an... ah... obviously intelligent guy. Well... your jobs..."

"Shit, huh?"

"Not exactly rocket science."

"I got bored easily. What's the difference between cleaning a toilet and curing cancer? One takes a lot longer. You never felt like that?"

"I suppose."

"Well, I'm more unsettled than you and you had a better job than me."

"I didn't, really." The man looked abashed. "I didn't make a lot of money."

"Shame. You would have, after this."

"What would you *like* to have done?"

"Avoided killing people, mainly."

"Ehm... apart from that?"

"I dunno. Something creative. Not writing, though. I gave that up. It's too cerebral. Too many notes, Mozart. That's why I asked you to tell my story."

"But you pinned your hopes on writing at one time?"

"I figured if I could get things published, that would set me up in a lot of ways. I could earn money and still not be stuck, y'know?"

"But you never got anything published."

"Nothing," Miles chuckled. "Not even my novel about a God-damned serial killer. Guess it didn't ring true."

His head had begun to ache, so he checked the gauge again. It was firmly in the red. His arms felt sluggish, though he was hardly in the same boat as Stuart. Then again, he was.

Miles began to giggle.

"Around the time you went... off the rails," Stuart said tactfully. "You were seeing a woman. Ally Stone. 28 years old."

He glanced at imaginary notes.

"Pretty young."

"Thank you. There were a couple of others, but they were casual."

"You shittin me?"

"I'd got that 'deep but fun' thing down pat. The 'hint of badness' that girls love."

"Yeah. If you're still living in the 1990s."

"Perhaps I was. Upshot of my environment and all that. Guess those girls didn't take the hint."

"I'm surprised you could get it up so often." Stuart's eyebrow arched and a couple of small bubbles drifted off, as if he'd had a cartoonish thought. "You could... couldn't you?"

Miles raised his own eyebrows in return.

"Forget it." Stuart grimaced. "I don't need to know every tiny little detail."

"Specially not if you're gonna phrase it like that. And don't be naive. My motivations were... complex."

"Was your sexual relationship with Ally a good one, then?"

"I'd say so."

"But... something must have been missing."

"You still think the adoring public has to know the size of my member?" Miles pursed his lips.

"No. You keep that under your hat, metaphorically speaking." Stuart gave an annoyed snort. "Besides, nobody's gonna read about you now."

Miles let the barb pass.

"I don't know. I guess sex was never a be-all and end-all for me. I mean, there's a brief period after the initial nervousness and the eventual... boredom, when screwing someone is great." He hesitated. "All right, boredom's too strong a word. Having nothing new to show them and them to show you."

He raised a hand to his brow, as if scanning unknown horizons.

"The first few times, you're both explorers. After that..."

"New lands to explore?"

"That's right. But I was getting old, Stuart. Way past my prime. A salty old dog with nothing but stories of previous encounters, slowly turning into a ruin of his former self."

"With a lover 20 years your junior." His companion sounded envious. "Doesn't sound so bad."

"She'd find a younger me, eventually. Too many wrinkles, Mozart." Miles patted his face. "Don't underestimate the call of the sea. Plenty more fish there."

"And what do explorers do when the only new lands left are hostile?"

"They attack and subdue them."

"Much as I appreciate these nautical metaphors, you gonna kiss and tell?"

"Nothing to say. I loved Ally and she loved me. She even asked me to go to America with her. But the age gap was huge and she wasn't the settling down type either. Then what? I... I... had a job here."

"That's right. You were head of Microsoft."

"In the end, she wouldn't want some old guy hanging on her coat tails." Miles flicked his flippers and rose a few inches, hovering over the seat. "You know what happens when you try to be Peter Pan? People stop believing in you and you fade away."

He sank back down and looked around. There were five female corpses in the corner of the cabin, weighed down by chains around their necks. Prey to every passing marine animal, none of them had faces. Miles tried hard to think but most of their names eluded him. Due to lack of air, he presumed. Or perhaps he had never known. His lungs were starting to hurt.

"Tell me about the women, Miles." Stuart broke into his reverie. "It's time."

"Let's see. If you took all the girls I slept with and laid them end to end, about a dozen would get run over on the highway."

"Being flippant isn't helping your case."

"I didn't mean to kill the first one, you know." Miles shrugged. "I was just getting my own back and it spiralled out of control."

"Getting your own back. You wanted revenge on society."

"I wanted revenge on *her*." Miles searched his memory. "I was at an ATM with Ally. She was being too slow or too flamboyant, I don't know."

"How can you be flamboyant at an ATM?"

"Ally could, trust me. Anyway, there were a couple of young girls behind us. Tall, blonde, out for the night. Cleavage like the Bermuda triangle. Started slagging Ally. Maybe it was the way she was dressed. Or just trying to cause trouble. I told one of them to shut it and, bang, the boyfriend was there - looking like he should've been on top of the Empire State building swatting planes. Right up in my face, he was."

Miles leaned forwards and rasped out a Brooklyn accent.

You looking at me, huh? You fuckin looking at me?

"You were attacked by Robert De Niro?"

"He's the only tough guy I can imitate."

"Did you get into a fight?"

"Nah. I hate violence. Anyhow, a couple of months later, I saw one of those girls again, going into her apartment. Then I knew where she lived. I kept watch on her house a couple of times, sort of like a game."

"A game?" Stuart frowned.

"I kinda thought I could use it as research for my book. To follow someone and secretly watch them? I wanted that novel so much to be a success. Thought I had a unique perspective."

"I'd certainly go along with that."

"I needed to really experience what a fledgling killer would. You're writing about me, after all. Don't you want to be accurate? But you won't understand how I feel, no matter how much I describe it. You'd have to..."

"Let's stick with the narrative," Stuart interrupted. "I'll live."

He glanced at his missing arm.

"That was a dumb thing to say."

"All right, maybe I was thinking of some way I could get back at her." Miles' face crumpled. "I only wanted to frighten her. Take some money. I was broke. She hurt other people without a second thought. Why shouldn't she have the tables turned? She gave up her right to safety, picking on Ally like that. I don't know. I had a million reasons."

"Too many notes, Mozart?"

"Yeah. Anyway, she came home late one night. Short skirt. Staggering a bit. I'd been drinking. She'd been drinking."

He clenched his fists and pounded his head.

"To this day, I still don't know where I found the nerve. I wish to God I hadn't. But I crawled through the window. Slammed into her coming out of the bedroom and there was no turning back."

He closed his eyes.

"I tied her to a kitchen chair and gagged her. I had a mask on and I went looking for cash. She was making whimpering noises in the next room, reminding me she was there. I only wanted to let her see what it's like to be threatened. I leaned over her, pretending like I was go-ing to do something to scare her. Moved my hands down over her breasts. To show her what it's like being abused by a stranger."

He looked at the floor.

"And... maybe cause I wanted to feel them."

"Miles..."

"I just... kept going." He raised his head defiantly. "You play dog eat dog and a bigger animal might just come along and gobble you up. Too many dogs, Mozart."

"Don't start telling me you ate your victims." Stuart looked dis-tinctly queasy. "I'll probably barf."

"Not at all. I always knew I wasn't quite right, though." Miles seemed properly reflective for a second. "I mean, I could act like the nicest guy in the world but my best friend might be pouring her heart out to me, and if there was a song I liked on the radio..."

"Half your brain would be listening to that."

"All of it. Then again, I'm a big music fan."

"And a complete sociopath."

"Well, duh! That's why you have to cover up your flaws." Miles gave a charming smile, though it was hidden by his mouthpiece. "No-body likes flaws. Everyone pretends, to some extent. No honey! You're not too fat... ya big sweaty beast. Of course, I wouldn't fuck your sister... unless she let me. We all think horrible thoughts and pre-tend we don't, so why not go for broke? Why not do exactly what we want to do and pretend we don't? Not hurting someone's feelings is much more important than truth."

"I'd say killing these women went a damn sight further than hurt-ing their feelings." Stuart was stone-faced. "Don't *you* have feelings to hurt?"

"I know how to feel lots of things," Miles retorted. "I know how to feel like an outsider. I know how to feel like a failure. I know how to feel incomplete. I know how to feel scared. I know how to feel use-less. I know how to feel cheated. I know how to feel lonely."

He grunted sourly.

"And I know how to pretend that I don't."

"You want to tell me about the other killings?" Stuart asked.

"Do I have to?"

"Yeah, Miles. It's sort of what makes you interesting to the general public."

"Shame, that, isn't it?

"Why victim two? Any particular reason?"

"I worked for her years ago. She was a complete bastard. I can honestly say the world would be better off without her. Eventually, I took her out."

Stuart looked astonished. Miles made a slashing movement with his hand.

"No. *Took* her out."

"What... eh... What... was it like?"

"I don't have words for it, Stuart. A feeling of absolute power. A release from everything that makes you human or, at least, part of the human race. It's disgusting. Sickening. But... your head spins."

Miles' head was spinning right now and he felt sick. He sat up straighter and sucked hard, trying to coax more oxygen from the tank.

"You'd have to try it to understand."

"I don't appreciate comments like that. I really don't."

"Victim three? I'd never seen her before. Aw, there were a thousand pretty girls passing me by on the street every day. Too many women, Mozart. I was getting older. My hair was thinning. My time was ending. But I couldn't let it be over. Picking up dames was the only thing I'd ever been good at."

"Why didn't you just..." Stuart began. But Miles wasn't finished.

"I saw a woman. She was young, beautiful. She'd never look twice at me now. Never try to know me. So, I decided I would have her. I could do anything I wanted. Why not? Why the fuck not?"

"Cause... it's horrible, Miles."

"I know. That's why I killed her afterwards." Miles levelled a finger at Stuart. "See... anything is acceptable as long as you don't have to stare it in the face. Like when you ignore those starving people all over the world. Or the ones risking their lives to get to another country."

Miles summoned a last burst of energy.

"Death. Taxes. Your life slipping away. The shit this world is in. The pointlessness of it. Your pointless, shitty, mundane little life, slipping away before your eyes. Anything at all. Don't you realise that? Anything is acceptable as long as you don't have to stare it in the face."

"No. No... no. I'm not taking that." Stuart shook his head. "I'm not taking that."

"Why? Cause it's not true or cause you don't fucking well want it to be true! If you're so squeamish, you're the wrong man for this job."

"I know the truth about you. You're a heartless killer."

"Simplistic! You realised that before you started! You were a struggling writer, just like me. And you jumped at the chance when I offered you the scoop of a lifetime. Believed me when I said I wouldn't harm you. That I'd show you where the bodies were."

"I wanted proof before I handed everything over to the police, you ass."

"I figured that. I didn't figure a fucking Great White was gonna tear your arm off on the way down to the wreck, then trap us here." Miles glanced at his watch. "I should be on my way to the bloody airport to catch a flight to the USA."

"I thought you might have contacted me because you secretly wanted to be caught. You'd have been tracked down if I'd survived. No matter where you went."

"I'm a master at hiding myself, remember? Maybe I just wanted to understand what it's like to be hunted. Give myself a scare, so I'd throw out the anchor a bit and get a grip."

Miles peered through the cabin windows. There was no sign of the shark and he assumed it had given up. He would have heaved a sigh of relief but couldn't spare the air.

"Let me ask you a question, Stuart." He decided to turn the tables. "Suppose there's someone you know and don't like. What stops you from killing them?"

"Some moral code, I guess."

"Would this be your own moral code?"

"Yes, it'd be my personal moral code."

Miles smiled thinly, ready to pounce.

"So, in that case... you could change your mind whenever it suited."

"Not at all," his companion protested. "I think we're also conditioned from childhood to adulthood, enforced with a decency the church or society, at one time or other, has put upon us."

"OK. Therefore, if you could get rid of the conditioning of church and society, your personal principles could be totally flexible. Wouldn't that follow?"

Stuart considered this before shaking his head.

"I think there is an atavistic fear in all of us about taking the life of someone else. We still subscribe to some arcane ideal we can't get rid of."

Miles leaned forward hungrily.

"Suppose you could take all the morals out of the world. Exorcise yourself from their hold. What would you replace them with?"

"Common decency?"

"That's a concept, Stu. Stop being coy."

"You'd replace them with the law of the jungle, I guess. Survival of the fittest."

"Dog eat dog." Miles shifted his gaze to the gauge. The tank was completely empty. "Thank you."

"Why don't you stop baiting me and fucking well ask them?" Stuart waved his good arm at the corpses. "You might get a different response."

One of the bodies lifted its head. The jaw was slack, held to the rest of the skull by a few loose tendons.

"My name is Jennifer Hillcross," it rasped. "I like typefaces and waltzing and drawing with fine art pens. I'd like to be richer; I'd like to be thinner. I used to live in Bundaberg but didn't like *that* much. I've got rats, three of them, though I don't keep them in a cage. They make me laugh. They do the funniest things. They were car sick last week because I moved to a new house. All three of them, holding onto the seat leather with their little claws."

She turned empty sockets towards Miles.

"I was looking forward to having my own place. I'd bought a new dress and was wearing it to a party when we met. Damn you to hell."

"I think this interview is over." Stuart sank onto his side.

"That's right. Cop out now!" Miles sucked as hard as he could, taking in one last lungful. "Where's the rule that says you can't do whatever you want? There's laws, sure, but why should you abide by a law if you don't want to? What if you don't want to do what other people tell you? There's no moral code out there in the ether everyone has to follow. There's no God and, even if there was, we don't have to obey him."

Both fists drummed on his knees

"What did I do? Eh? Eh? I want to grasp what I did that was actually wrong!"

The other women began to crawl towards him, pieces of flesh drifting from their decaying, bitten bodies.

"I didn't know you!" Miles tried to push them back. "You mean as much to me as these starving kids I don't send money to help. Yes, I'm filled with self-loathing. Do I hate myself? Too right, I do. But I try to find some fucking *rule* to condemn myself and I can't find one! There's nothing to actually stop me!"

"It's the way the world works." Jennifer rasped, clawing at his leg. "That's what stops you."

"*I don't like the way the world works!*"

Miles inched away from the advancing women.

"We're just dogs slavering and straining at our collars. Pavlov's fucking dogs, that's what we are. And I slipped my leash! Broke away! Bad dog. Slap his nose! Slap all our noses when we shit or fuck or act in any way that's not deemed acceptable. Eh? When we do what we want to do but we're not allowed!"

He slid off the chair and shook his companion, releasing another plume of blood.

"Maybe that's what we need. Maybe we need *more* training, *more* conditioning. But, for Christ's sake, we need to be taught to show affection, not attack. How many times do rabid dogs like me have to turn on people? How many of us have to be put down before we decide to just stop breeding them?"

He kicked out at Stuart's motionless body, but his flippers got in the way and all he could manage was a penguin-like slap.

"Maybe you should have written a book about dog training." Stuart opened one eye. "You are remembering I'm dead, aren't you?"

"Of course," Miles grunted miserably. "Surprise, surprise. I'm trying to justify myself to myself. Me, me, me, eh?"

"No, you moron. It means I don't need my air tank anymore."

Miles goggled at him. Then he struggled out of his harness and clumsily swapped the man's scuba gear for his own. He switched masks and air from Stuart's cylinder flooded his lungs. Miles sat on the wooden floor for a while, breathing in sweet oxygen.

He looked around.

Tattered, chained bodies were scattered across the floor of the cabin, no longer moving. Miles swam to the window and looked out. He could see no sign of the predator. It had to have gone by now.

"Thanks, Stu. You've given me some much-needed perspective."

Miles still felt lightheaded but was refreshed enough to have a fair chance of reaching the surface. He shook Stuart's good hand, then let it drift away.

"I would have happily stuck to society's conventions, know that? But everybody twists them to suit themselves, so I ended up doing the same. Go big or go home, mate."

He opened the cabin door and cautiously ascended, recalling - just in time - to stop halfway up. It would be beyond ironic to get the bends this close to freedom.

Miles hung in the translucent water, watching the light filtering down from above. He had always loved diving. He was comforted by that sense of being cocooned and shut off from everything, alone in a silent, muffled world.

He was about to begin his journey again when the Great White emerged from the gloom. Must have measured 20 feet from tip to toe.

Miles tried to flee but was gripped by a terror more overpowering than anything he had ever experienced. He thrashed wildly but his arms and legs refused to comply. It felt like he was moving through soup.

"Please. Please, no! Don't hurt me!" he screamed. "I'm sorry! I'll do anything!"

The mask stopped any sound from escaping.

The creature opened its mouth, revealing two rows of vicious jagged teeth. It looked like it might be smiling but the blank, emotionless eyes were devoid of pity. It slowly moved towards him, a killing machine moulded by a million years of evolution. No rules. No compassion. No choices.

Miles continued to beg and plead, though he knew it would do no good.

"Ah," the shark said. "*Now*, you understand."

I Know What You Did Last Trimester

Sara Corris

The worst thing I ever did, I did before I was born.

They call it 'Vanishing Twin Syndrome'. I wish. She hasn't gone anywhere. Four decades later, and she's still bugging me every damn day.

I'll never forget my fifth birthday...

OUR fifth birthday!

"Shut up, Ashlee."

I blew out the candles, mom turned the lights back on, and I saw 'HAPPY BIRTHDAY, TWINSY' scrawled across the wall in placenta blood. I screamed as I watched it drip down onto my presents below...

OUR presents!

"Omigod Ashlee. SHUT. UP."

Mom has never forgiven me. What a bitch. I've tried telling her to educate herself.

"Seriously mom," I pleaded, last time she stopped by. "I was a fetus! You act like it was a conscious choice. Google *reabsorption*."

"Reabsorption?" she smirked. "Is that what you call it?"

"That is what the entire scientific community calls it, mom!"

Mom rolled her eyes.

She brings it up every time we talk.

"I suppose it was a taste of things to come," she told my husband, Dave, over dinner. "Georgie's never been shy at meal times, as you know."

She broke off to watch me take another slice of pie. I refused to look at her. She turned her attention back to Dave.

"She always had a hearty appetite, even back then..."

"You can't say body-shaming shit like that anymore, mom!" I shouted. "It was always fucked-up but now everyone agrees it's unacceptable. Get with the times, you old bag."

Mom rolled her eyes.

She's always liked Ashlee better than me. Which is hilarious because Ashlee never liked her. I remember this one trimester where Ashlee was kicking mom's lower back 24/7, as hard as she could, smiling and gurgling all the while.

Thing is, mom's right. I totally remember doing it.

I made the right call. No regrets. I was hungry and cramped. Ashlee was hogging all the space and nutrients, getting fatter by the day...

YOU'RE body-shaming ME for eating too much? You ate a whole baby!

"Please don't read my thoughts, Ashlee. You know I hate it when you do that."

And now, of course, she wants to eat my fetus.

Somehow, it only dawned on me at my first ultrasound appointment. Until then, I'd been happily blissed-out. Mommy brain, I guess.

"It's definitely a boy," the doctor laughed. She gestured at what I presumed was a minuscule penis. Dave and I beamed and pretended we could see what she was talking about. Dave squeezed my hand. I turned to him and smiled.

My back was still to the monitor when it happened.

"Well!" boomed the doctor. "Who's this little lady?"

My blood turned to ice. I whipped my head around so fast I pulled a neck muscle. It was the doctor's turn to beam.

"Folks, it looks like you're having twins!"

I strained my eyes to discern anything vaguely human. A rounded bulge lifted and turned: a head. A face. I located the mouth when it broke into a grin.

A tiny hand shot up alongside it, giving me the finger.

"Goddammit, Ashlee!" I screamed at the monitor. "I know it's you. Stay away from my baby, you crazy bitch!"

Dave and the doctor stared at me, aghast.

That night I had the most terrible dreams of giving birth to my twin.

"Turns out there was only one in there after all," the doctor announces. "My bad."

I'm flooded with relief, until they hand me the baby and I see it's Ashlee. I know because she looks exactly like me in my newborn photos.

My hands clench around the tiny squalling bundle.

"Fuck you, Ashlee!" I scream, as I shake her. "What have you done with my baby? Give me my baby or I'll bash your brains out!"

By then, security has reached the room. They wrestle my evil fetus-twin away, before dragging me down to the psych ward, where they lock me up for the rest of my days.

I awoke with a shriek. The bedding was sweat-soaked; my heart thumped audibly. I glanced over at Dave but he must have been preparing himself for fatherhood by sleeping through it all.

I drifted into a sleep, plagued by nightmares of presents wrapped in cauls and trimmed with umbilical cord ribbons.

"She'll be fine," my mom reassured Dave on her next visit. "Georgie's just got a bad case of mommy brain. Pregnancy is a disgusting and horrible experience. Never trust anyone who says otherwise."

They looked over at me, seated in a La-Z-Boy on the other side of the room. I ignored them and continued to whisper quietly at my belly:

"C'mon, baby. We can still be a happy family. You've just got to eat her. Mommy did it. So can you."

"Georgie was my most difficult pregnancy by far," mom continued. "I'll never forget that second trimester. Georgie spent it kicking me, so hard, so viciously..."

"That wasn't me!" I screamed at her. "It was Ashlee! I tried to make her stop, but she was so much bigger—"

Dave whisked me back to bed before I could finish.

"How the hell did you even get in there?" I asked Ashlee as I stared up at the ceiling.

I was always in here. You just didn't know before the ultrasound.

"How does that work? If anything, you should be haunting my colon..."

Ever heard of a wandering uterus, dumdum?

"That's not what that is at all!"

How would I know? You robbed me of any halfway decent schooling! I tried following along, but everything's so muffled in here.

"Who are you talking to?" Dave asked from the doorway. He flipped on the lights and looked around the bedroom with a frown.

"Nobody." I sat up hastily and grabbed the book off the nightstand. "Sit down, Dave. We need to talk."

I took a deep breath.

"I've never been completely honest with you about what went down between my twin and I."

"What are you talking about?" Dave tried to laugh. "You didn't do anything. It's a normal occurrence that happens early on in a lot of pregnancies..."

"No." I shook my head. "Not me. I did it in month seven."

"That's not possible."

"I remember locking eyes. We had eyes to lock."

"You can't remember that! No one recalls being a fetus!"

"I've got a freaky good memory. Always have. You know that." I thrust a *Guinness Book of World Records* into his hands. "See for yourself. I'm in the book. Why do you think I've never allowed a copy of it into the house?"

Dave continued staring at me incredulously.

"Look it up," I said impatiently. "Latest reabsorption in Vanishing Twin Syndrome history."

I cleared my throat. "Also, only known case of a baby being born with gout."

Dave swore he didn't think I was a monster but he slept in the spare bedroom that night.

What's the big deal about this baby, anyway?

"Ashlee, please. I'm trying to sleep." I rolled onto my side, sighed, and gave in. "I dunno. Babies and moms are supposed to have this incredible, indescribable bond. I guess I want to experience that."

Please. You know that's a load of hooey, right? Some people experience it that way. But there's nothing inherent. You realize that siblings share the same amount of DNA as a parent and child?

Shit. Is that true? Then why the heck am I even doing this? Siblings aren't special.

You have no idea why you're doing this, do you?

"Goddammit, Ashlee! You know I hate it when you read my thoughts."

Actually, because we're twins, we've got more shared DNA than you'll have with any offspring.

"You better not eat him," I mumbled with far less conviction than before.

She ate him, of course.

Dave took it hard when the next ultrasound showed only one fetus. I was relieved. I know it's terrible but I felt disappointed in the kid.

It's not terrible at all. He was a dud. Trust me. I knew him better than you did.

"Ashlee, for fuck's sake…"

He was weak. He could never have done what you did.

"He was only a fetus…"

No younger than you were, when you stepped up!

"Honestly? That's kind of how I feel." I closed my eyes and sighed. "I guess I've never really apologized, have I?"

There's no need. You did what you had to do.

"No, but…"

Seriously, you need to forgive yourself. If you hadn't done it, I would have. It was only a matter of time. We both knew it.

"Are we even now?"

Yeah. I guess it's only fair. I'm sorry, sis.

"Me too," I said, feeling generous. "Hey. Have you given any thought to what name you'd like? I know I call you Ashlee, but mom had planned on naming you Sarah. Which she mentions every time we talk."

Ewww, no. Soooo boring.

"I agree. It's not a terrible name, but it's just a bit… blah."

Too common. Like, 50% of girls born in the 80s are named Sarah. Why?

"Yeah, I don't get it either. Lose the H, at least. Sex it up a bit."

Totes. Actually, I like the name Ashlee. Especially with the porn-y spelling.

"Cool." I swallowed. "Looking forward to meeting you IRL, then."

Soon, bitch. Soon.

Hell is…

Keith Gray

Hell is not a volcanic pit full of boil-in-the-bag demons wanting to poke you with pitchforks. But neither is it a corporate boardroom with Big Boss CEO Lucifer spit-balling ideas for new Halloween merchandising with his shareholders. Too easy. Too clichéd. If there's a god who created leprosy and childhood cancer, a god who flicks between genocides like TV channels then, rest assured, this god's imagined Hell is going to be a 100% nightmare.

Hell is a cinema. A big cinema - maybe even a two-or-three-thousand-seater. And me, the condemned sinner, I get a front-row seat. Bang up there, only centimetres away from the massive IMAX 4DX Dolby Surround Sound super screen. The rest of the audience are my friends and family. Kids I went to kindergarten with and hardly remember anymore. High School teachers. Work colleagues I liked. Work colleagues I didn't. Facebook Friends I never met in real life. The barman at my favourite pub. In other words, everyone I've ever known. All of them. Everyone. They're all sitting comfortably, waiting to watch the movie of my life.

My mother is especially looking forward to it. She's proud of me and my achievements. She's sitting right next to me and gives my hand a reassuring squeeze - smiles at me. On the other side are my wife and children. My wife and I grin nervously at each other. She kisses me on the cheek. My children are excited to see Daddy on the big screen. My Uncle Jack, the black sheep of the family who was regularly avoided, thanks to always being the first to get drunk at

31

christenings and weddings, slaps me on the shoulder from his seat behind mine

"This is gonna be fun!" he shouts.

I'm not so sure.

All of the seats are plush, comfortable, homely - but on the arm of my chair is a big, red, ominous button. The words *Emergency Descent: Going Down* are written in bright letters next to it. It makes me nervous. I don't know what it means. I'm worried about bumping it with my elbow.

Then the lights dim. The curtains draw aside. The music crescendos. My name is HUGE on the screen. A message scrolls, Star Wars-style, in front of everyone's eyes:

"This is your life. Every single second of it in real-time. If you watch it all the way from beginning to end, you may enter Heaven and enjoy an afterlife of carefree, peaceful harmony. If you decide you don't want to watch any more, you can press the red button on the arm of your chair. The film will stop, and you will rot in Hell for eternity. The movie lasts as long as your life. You are the star. The people around you are the supporting cast. This movie is executively produced by God (or maybe the Devil). But ultimately directed by You."

The screen flickers and brightens and I see myself as a baby.

I'm sooo cute. No, honest, I am. I was blonde. My mother is glowing and happy up there on the screen and she's still smiling, sitting next to me, here in the cinema. She squeezes my hand again. But I look at the big red button on the arm of my chair. *Emergency Descent.*

What's worse? Watching my life in minute, intricate, intimate detail? Or eternity in Hell?

So, obviously, the first thing I feel is embarrassment. All these people watch me poo. It's not so bad when I'm a pooing baby but they get to watch me grow and poo too. It makes me shudder. How much shitting does one person do? So much that, eventually, it becomes boring and, at last, my children stop laughing.

As I get older, up on that screen, embarrassment turns to humilia-tion - because everyone I've ever known gets to watch me drop my pants for another reason. My first sexual awakenings, my awkward fumblings. My first kiss looks sweet. My first fuck is awful. And the girl I lost my virginity to, Emma Fletcher? Well, she's next to Uncle Jack in the row behind me. He's laughing so hard his false teeth pop out.

It's not just sex with other people we get to watch, it's sex with myself. As a teenage boy, the only thing I seemed to do more than shit was wank. We all watch me wank. My mother doesn't want to hold my hand anymore. I daren't look at my children. I stare at the big red button. I can stop this. But, maybe, Hell is worse.

As we all sit and watch this long, slow, plotless movie, I tell my-self I can handle the humiliation. But how about the guilt?

I stole money from my mother's purse when I was 8. She sits next to me in the cinema and watches as I sneak into her bedroom, open her purse and take out the £20 note - up there on the big screen. Then she listens to me lie about it when she confronts me. Says she has no money for her own lunch that day. It's not the first lie I tell and defi-nitely not the last. I never realised how many lies. Was my youth all shitting, wanking and lying?

No: there's worse. I watch the cowardly me too. I'm ten years old and I don't stick up for my friend David when a bully steals his new sneakers. I'm too scared and run away when the yob grabs him. At the age of 11, I do nothing except watch as a gang of older boys corner a stray dog and throw rocks and broken bottles at it. The dog yelps and howls as bad as David did. Still I do nothing.

And I reckon my own children, watching this, must be thinking I'm a hypocrite. All the stuff I've told them that they should be... Well, I'm obviously not any of it.

Because the movie shows me telling horrible-hurtful jokes about the black kids in my class, horrible-hurtful jokes about the gay kids in my class, horrible-hurtful jokes about the kid in the wheelchair. Back then, I reckoned it was OK to do that, because everybody was telling those kinds of jokes, weren't they? But sitting in the cinema, watching with my own children in the audience, I see how very not OK it is. My guilt rises like the mercury in a thermometer. My face is hot and my back sweaty against the cinema seat.

Everybody I've ever known is seeing those parts of me I'd always tried to keep hidden from them.

I'm desperate to point out the nice, genuine, good stuff I've done. There is a lot of that in my life, there really is. We watch me being helpful, friendly, kind. But was it enough? Have I been helpful, friendly and kind enough in my life to outweigh how often I could be cruel, cowardly and dishonest?

I look at the big red button. But I don't want to go to Hell.

Now my mind is racing ahead. This is just me as a kid and I know what happens next. I know how this story goes.

Emergency descent.

I can't concentrate. I can't sit still. The once comfortable seat feels so very, very hot and my head is burning with thoughts of what I know is going to be shown. I'm remembering the hateful thing I did when I was 17. I'm remembering selfishness when I was 22, intolerance when I was 35, deceitfulness when I was 40. I'm thinking of people who I could have helped but didn't. I'm thinking of people I told I loved but didn't. If I turn around, I know I'll see them sitting in the rows behind me. So, I face forward and don't turn. I am on fire with shame.

My mother refuses to look at me. My wife is weeping. My children have walked out. Uncle Jack sure as shit isn't laughing anymore. I look at the big red button.

Would you press the button?

Me? I press the button.

I hit the button, I punch the button. I lean my whole goddamned weight on that button.

But the button is fake. It doesn't work. Of course, it doesn't. There's no descent into Hell.

And, as the movie of my life continues, set for repeat viewings - I come to understand I'm already here.

My Year With The Perfect Family

Mark Nutter

DAY ONE

I gunned down the mother and daughter in their respective beds. When the son came out of his bedroom, I shot him in the hallway. And when the father came home late from work I stabbed him to death at the front door.

DAY TWO

Hmmm. That may have been a mistake.

My name is Davis Barnes and I'm a documentary filmmaker. I'd already been paid half my five thousand dollar fee to make *My Year with the Perfect Family* for the Perfect Family Network. I was excited at the prospect of spending a year with a family so unlike my own.

Now the subjects of my documentary were dead and I had 364 days to go before I got the rest of my money.

I sat down on the living room sofa. I filmed a few seconds of the father, crumpled in a bloody heap at the front door. I didn't need a crew. I was shooting the doc on my phone using DocumentaryPro and, while it was a versatile app, it still couldn't make a dead guy who didn't move look interesting.

I put the phone down and thought about my situation.

DAY THREE

Got a call from Norman Spleen, the Executive Director of the Perfect Family Network. He wondered how things were going with the perfect family.

I said. "I murdered them."

He laughed.

I said. "No, I'm serious. I murdered them."

He laughed again.

I said. "I really, really murdered them."

He said, "Okay, take it easy," and hung up.

I was glad I could brighten his day.

DAY FOUR

Still on the sofa. Still thinking.

As a documentary filmmaker I'd seen my share of ugliness. I reflected on my previous work:

My Year in a War Zone. My first documentary. It was ugly and loud.

My Year Riding to Fires in a Fire Engine. Also ugly, with the burning buildings. Also loud, with the siren.

My Year with Rabid Dogs. Even though the dogs were good-looking, they tried to bite me all the time. Which, to me, made them ugly.

My Year Locked in a Closet with an Ugly Eighty-Nine-Year-Old Woman Suffering from Halitosis. That film won all kinds of awards. People responded to the intimacy. Unfortunately, it didn't make a dime.

It was an impressive body of work but all negative. It was time to make a film that captured the best of humanity and affirmed wholesome family values.

I shot a few more seconds of the father's rotting corpse.

DAY FIVE

Still thinking.

This time, instead of being in my film, I wanted to be a fly on the wall. I wanted my subjects to forget I was there, which I guess they did. That was why it was so easy to kill them.

Why did I do it?

The simple answer is, because they were *too* perfect. And you know what? The simple answer is the right answer. I mean, come on.

They said "good morning" and "good night."

They said "please" and "thank you."

The son and daughter were straight B students. They could have been straight-A students but didn't want to make their classmates feel bad by being too perfect, which was another perfect thing about them, which is why I killed them.

They wiped their feet when they came in the front door. If the father had spent a little less time wiping his feet, he might've seen me coming with the knife.

I approached when I saw them patiently waiting at an intersection for the walk light. They said they'd do the documentary, not so they could be on TV just to be famous, but so they could help people everywhere feel better about themselves.

"Wish I could say I felt better," I said to the dead dad.

DAY SIX

They flossed three times a day.

DAY SEVEN

I thought I should stare at the other dead family members for a while. But I liked the sofa. It was comfortable. So I dragged it upstairs.

DAY TWENTY-TWO

(I'm skipping the days when I left the house and stayed at a hotel because, man, that smell. Made me miss the old lady with halitosis).

So I'm back in the house now, having gotten some nice footage of the breakfast buffet at the Holiday Inn Express.

Norman Spleen left a voice mail message saying that the joke about murdering the family was really good, but now he needed to see some film.

I left him a message saying, would he like to see footage of their bloody bodies, hoping to get a wee bit more mileage out of the gag.

Maybe I have a problem with the concept of perfection. What is perfection anyway? Different people have different ideas. To some people, perfection is a family that's considerate and kind. To others, perfection is dead bodies sprawled around a nice house. I need to develop this thought further, for when they catch me.

DAY TWENTY-FIVE

I've wasted enough time pondering perfection. Time to get busy doing what I've been paid to do.

Where to begin? Air freshener.

DAY TWENTY-SEVEN

Bought about five hundred of those little pine tree air fresheners and hung them around the house like I saw in the movie *Seven*. I need to pose the stiff bodies in domestic scenes and then film them. Shouldn't be too tough.

I need to move their hands and arms around a little. Tricky, but I can handle it. Plus, I have to do all their voices.

This is impossible. I give up.

DAY TWENTY-EIGHT

Got a call from Norman Spleen, demanding to see footage of the family.

I said, "How about footage of dried blood on the carpet?" and he replied. "The time for levity is over."

Spleen told me if I didn't send him something in the next forty-eight hours I would never see the rest of my money.

DAY TWENTY-NINE

"For this food we are about to eat, we are grateful," said Dad with his head bowed and me crouched down behind him, holding his hair. Then I lifted him up, careful not to accidentally snap the head off his body.

I thought saying grace was a nice 'perfect' touch. I'd placed Dad at the head of the table and applied makeup to everyone, which helped a little bit - although I also planned for everyone to say to each other, "You don't look well," because I'm bad at makeup.

In addition to complimenting Mom on her perfect turkey dinner, and Mom blushing (tomato paste), I thought I'd have the kids talk about their day at school, and how they almost got A's until they remembered to get B's to make their classmates happy. I wanted them to sing a song in four-part harmony, about how important it was to make others happy, but I'm also bad at ventriloquism.

These were my plans. All I really managed to shoot was Dad saying grace, then falling face-first into his mashed potatoes.

I sent twenty-two seconds of film to Norman Spleen.

DAY THIRTY-ONE

I'm in a panic. Norman Spleen and several executives from the Perfect Family Network liked the twenty-two seconds I sent and are going to pay me a visit. They want to meet the family in person.

I said, "Don't come, the family is sick."

They said they could see they were sick. But they had to meet a family where the father said grace while the others sat there so quiet and respectful.

What am I going to do?

I know! I will say the family left on a family vacation in the family car to a family destination. A Disney something-or-other park. And they decided to take me with them, once they remembered I was there, since I was doing such a good job being a fly on the wall.

I would put the family in the car and drive it around the corner, out of sight. Then I would fly to some Disney something-or-other park and buy postcards and mail them to Norman Spleen.

Greetings, Norman. Signed (their names).

Note to self: find out their names.

Once I'd formed my plan, I no longer felt panicked. I sat on the sofa and reflected one last time on the nature of perfection before I fell asleep.

DAY THIRTY-TWO

Bang! Bang! Bang!

I jumped three feet in the air when I heard pounding outside the house.

Workmen were boarding up the windows!

I ran to the front door and threw it open.

Norman Spleen was standing there with a bunch of guys in suits I didn't recognize.

"Good morning, Davis."

"Good morning, Mr Spleen."

Norman Spleen gestured to the guys behind him.

"I showed your twenty-two seconds of film to them and they were impressed."

"Are they with the Perfect Family Network?"

"No, they're with the Ghost Family Network."

"Ah," I said, trying to grasp the big picture and failing.

"I've sold your project to them. From now on, it will be called *My Year with the Ghost Family*."

"So I get paid double?"

"No, you don't get paid anything. You violated our contract when you murdered them."

"That must have been in the fine print. And... hey! Who says I murdered them?"

"Come on, Davis. It was obvious from the footage they were dead."

A toothy young executive stepped forward.

"Hi, Davis. Bart Withers, Ghost Family Network. We're looking very much forward to working with you. We're boarding you up in the house with the dead family. You'll shoot footage of their ghosts. At the end of a year, I'm confident we'll have a terrific product. I'm very excited."

The other toothy young executives nodded, indicating that they too were very excited.

"And what if I don't want to do it?" I asked.

"Uh..." The Ghost Family Network executives stood there in confused silence.

"I'm pulling your legs," I said. "Of course I want to do it. I'm very excited too."

The young toothy executives smiled more toothy smiles.

"See you in a little less than a year."

I went back in the house.

DAY TWO HUNDRED SEVENTY-NINE

"For this food we are about to eat, we are grateful," hissed Ghost Dad.

"Amen," hissed Ghost Mom, Ghost Son, and Ghost Daughter, raising their heads.

"That's a keeper," I said as I filmed the family from the far end of the table. Thankfully, their physical bodies lay rotting and stinking in the basement. Only their ghost bodies remained.

"Unfortunately, the light wasn't quite right. Can we do one more?"

"Of course," said Ghost Dad.

"We'd be glad to," added Ghost Son.

"We'll do as many as you want, Davis," said Ghost Daughter.

"We'll do whatever makes you happy," said Ghost Mom.

"Guys," I told them. "All you have to be now are ghosts. You don't need to be perfect anymore."

"Okay," they said.

But they couldn't help it. They couldn't help being perfect.

I would have killed them again if they weren't already dead.

The Night Hank Came Back

Maxwell Price

As 1952 turned to 1953, the greatest of all the honky-tonk singers sat in the back of a second-hand Cadillac. His bloodstream was seasoned with a potent mixture of whiskey, morphine, chloral hydrate, and a pair of vitamin shots that doctors had administered back at the hotel in Knoxville.

The young driver, uneasy since their departure, had made a half-hearted and unsuccessful attempt to rouse his passenger at a greasy spoon earlier in the evening. Having received only a long, low moan in response, he had entered the diner alone, tucking into an over-cooked steak, while keeping a grim stare fixed on the car outside. He only ever took his eyes off it while making a short but necessary trip to unburden himself in the diner's restroom. Soon enough they were back on the road.

He tried to tell himself that it was only the great man's taciturn nature that held the eerie silence in place, as they continued on their way. But, when he stopped to re-fuel, dawn broke over the mountains of West Virginia, and there was no ignoring the obvious. For the last few hours, the driver had been steering a convertible, chrome-and-eggshell-blue-coloured tomb.

Hank Williams had quietly expired on a black-leather deathbed, surrounded by spent beer cans and clutching a piece of paper scarred with fresh lyrics.

At that point in his life, it was the best thing he could have done for his flagging career. In 1951 - only a little under two years ago - Hank

45

Williams had been riding higher in the saddle than he ever thought possible. There had been television appearances, national tours and a song that crossed over to the hit parade. But a bad fall had brought the pain roaring back in his crooked spine and he, once again, turned to painkillers and alcohol to quiet it down.

That had led to a number of incidences. Little hiccups, really, but the missed shows and such resulted in a lifetime ban from the Grand Ole Opry - which had caused several songwriters and sidemen to abandon poor Hank. Likewise, he had rapidly burned through the goodwill of one wife and was dangerously close to losing another, given that his penchant for absent or drunken performances had extended even to his honeymoon.

For the record company men in Nashville, Hank had already started to carry the unmistakable stench of rot and decay, well before his unfortunate ride in the Cadillac.

But, with his worldly death, the world wept for Hiram King Williams. And nobody cried louder and longer than the ones who had turned their backs to him in life. Stars lined up to sing hymns at his funeral and the record men arrived on bended knee. Not one but two black-clad widows were in attendance, grieving and weeping in stereo. Fans swarmed by the thousands, and trucks hauled no less than two tons of flowers to the service. It was a spectacle fit for a prophet or pharaoh of old, only dusted with the cheap glitter of tabloid headlines and sealed beneath a towering monument of broken shellac and unspooled celluloid.

Tributes were recorded by the dozens and most of these spent some time scrabbling up and down the charts. The record company men took note of this and more tributes were waxed and rushed to market. They noticed, too, who sat at the very top of the charts once again, with no small sense of satisfaction. *Your Cheating Heart* had been recorded only months before and there were still more Hank sides waiting on the release schedule. A portion of that star power was all bottled up and set aside - but without the troublesome man who went along with it.

Every one of those hit records was still in heavy rotation that night at WSM, its 50,000 watts beaming out from Nashville to cover nearly every southern state - a balm in such troubled times. It had been only three and a half weeks since Hank had been laid to rest in his hometown of Montgomery, Alabama, in a silver coffin purchased by his mother. From Montgomery to Nashville is about four hours by car, though it is much longer for a lone man on foot.

But there are other ways to travel, silent and unseen.

There are ways, not particularly well-traveled but known to some. Ways that are more akin to the wanderings of mist and moonlight than anything a human being ought to be able to do. And there are ways, just as unlikely, to get past the locked doors of the WSM building and sniff out the small crew working the graveyard shift - like a hound on the trail of small game.

Among the many oversights and missteps, made in the hours following the discovery of Hank's body, was the haste with which he was delivered to a mortician. The mortician, a simple and practical tradesman, had embalmed the corpse almost immediately - to the detriment of ongoing attempts to piece together the exact time and cause of Hank's death. As a result, the half-hearted autopsy of the now-embalmed body found several hemorrhages in the heart and neck of the King of Country Music. But, ultimately, they failed to uncover the small, scalpel-thin punctures that could have told the full story.

Inside the control room, a late-night DJ was busy with his familiar sales pitch. All over the Southeast, people sat by their radios, passively receiving a primer on the virtues of Crawford's Canned Peaches.

"Crawford Peaches, with no need for heavy syrups, because Crawfords picks the sweetest peach!"

He could recite the copy in his sleep and often did, according to his bemused wife. With the left side of his brain on auto-pilot, he was already picking out another hour's worth of music with his right. As long as he had enough coffee and cigarettes for fuel, he could and would be at this all night, every night.

Then, the creak of an opening door broke his rhythm.

"Hey," he said, as the dark figure strode into the room. "You can't just come in... G-g-good Lord!"

He hadn't had a stutter like that since his Ma had whupped it out of him in grammar school. And taking the Lord's name in vain was the nearest thing to profanity he'd ever uttered over the airwaves, in all his years in the business. It was still, as the pious would note, a commandment broken. The DJ's voice dissolved into a blubbering plea, then to a series of wet gasping sounds. Folks all over the south leaned in closer to listen.

Many of them sprang back as the gunshots rang out, fired in quick succession from the pistol the station manager always kept in the top drawer of his desk. Folks used to the ricocheting 'zip' of the weekly western shows furrowed their brows in confusion, but stomachs sank in those who recognized the dry 'pop-pop' of small caliber rounds.

Something hissed loudly, like an angry possum, and another shot was set loose in response. Then two more. Then, for the folks that were counting along at home, the final shot came - punctuated by the clatter of a useless gun sliding across the tiled floor. It was followed by a mercifully short burst of what could have been stalks of celery being torn to pieces.

Things were quiet after that, quieter than seemed natural, as if the pleasant hum of electric tubes and static that usually buzzed away in the back of the radio had vanished, leaving everything feeling naked and uncomfortable. Like too-bright house lights had come on, at what was supposed to be an all-night juke joint.

The few that were brave enough, or maybe just crazy enough, to stick their ear up to the speaker would swear you could hear a sound like a suckling calf. That, and the far-away sobs of the station's sound engineer.

There was the scrape of a chair being dragged across the floor, accompanied by the slow click of boot-heels. The radio static seemed to come alive and start purring again - a sound of pure anticipation. An open guitar chord rang out, tentatively, fingered by unsteady hands. As people pulled ever closer to their radios, they heard the old familiar voice, welcoming them to a special broadcast.

"Howdy, folks."

It was Hank Williams, doing the second-best thing he ever did for his career: come back. He offered an apology, of sorts, for the commotion.

"It's just that, well, laying in that silver coffin for so long, it kind of irritates you to death. Might as well bed a man down in a pile of itching powder and barber's trimmings. Something like that can make you act a little meaner than you ought to. Nearer to a damned wild animal, in fact."

But, now that all that nasty business was over with, old Hank was feeling more like himself again. In fact, he was feeling mighty fine. Why, he felt like singing.

And then he began to strum, singing a song about the blood of Christ, over and over again. His guitar playing was as austere as ever, especially as he was shaking off a stubborn bit of rigor mortis, yet his voice had returned with renewed power. Its cracked and weathered tone was now an immaculate ruin, its tremulous urgency verging on the apocalyptic. Each time he took the listeners further out, lingering on the crying notes a little longer.

There were no more commercial breaks on WSM that night. Those still listening found it impossible to switch the channel or shut their radios off. Whether they were compelled by a supernatural force or just pure morbid curiosity would be a subject of many debates in the coming years. Then and there, however, no one could deny the power of what was coming out of that room. They were the simple torments of a man that was more than a man, yet still doomed to live out a man's folly. More than a man and still nothing but.

He quoted from the Bible, sometimes in tones of booming authority, other times whispered off-mic - a private prayer made public. He began to sing all the old hymns and then all his biggest hits and then, as the morning sun rose but did not penetrate inside of the darkened control booth, he began to sing his new songs.

Hank had always dealt in guilt and sin, remorse and redemption. His new material spoke of a hunger that drove a spike in him, deeper than the booze or the pills or even the morphine that had numbed him in the last years of his life. He wept and pleaded and revealed himself before man and God alike. The crippling pain in his back was now gone, completely gone, for the first time since he could remember. Now he hungered not for drugs and drink, but the very essence of life itself.

The broadcast ended at 6:37 AM, when Hank Williams crept into a utility closet to sleep and the terrified engineer fled the studio for the waiting arms of the police, who had the station surrounded. Half-crazed as he was, the engineer was still able to confirm that this was no hoax.

Hank was back.

People had listened, transfixed, many of them staying up all night. Amongst them were the long-haul truckers and night nurses, police dispatchers and third-shift factory workers. But, also, another special group listened intently, smaller in number yet no less intrigued. The night people. The blood-drinkers and skin-walkers pitched their sensitive ears to a new frequency and the ghouls and bogeys all tuned in.

They listened, and some of them were afraid - for here was the attention they had always shunned. Someone had broken ranks and passed his gift along to one of the mortal men. Worse, in this new electric age, they had chosen foolishly. This was a man who had already possessed a power over others even the night people could envy.

The elders were fretful, and many bayed sorrowfully at the waning moon overhead. They all knew at once that the Great Age of Hiding was over. Some had grim visions of discovery, of vicious mobs winding up lonely roads to meet them.

But others, as the night unfolded, found themselves humming along, in spite of themselves. Scaly heads bobbed approvingly and hairy feet tapped in time with the music, accentuating the beat with the click of black talons.

And so, as the sun set that night, two things happened. First, Hank Williams emerged from his ersatz tomb not to a hail of bullets or a horde of pitchfork-wielding villagers, but to a crowd of Nashville's most prominent record men. They stood in a half-circle around the closet door. Though some of them had strung cloves of garlic around their necks, they were armed - not with fire or holy water - but with a blood bag lifted from a local hospital. That, and a brand-new recording contract.

The second thing that happened was, miles away in the remote and lonely places, a number of the night people began to pack their things. They carefully stuffed webbed toes into ill-fitting cowboy boots and slung homemade guitars over their massive shoulders. They cleared coffin-dust from their parched throats and practiced yodeling with vocal cords that, heretofore, had mostly gibbered or howled. They emerged from mausoleums and root cellars or pulled themselves out of abandoned wells and sinkholes. They straightened their ties, slicked back the hair on any number of heads and, with a skip in their step and a song in their rotted hearts, they lit out for Tennessee.

The tallest of the record men entered the station with neither garlic nor a cross strapped to his person. Instead, he carried a .38 pistol tucked deep inside his cream-colored suit. He spoke with a voice as smooth and cloying as honey.

"Now, I know we've had our little fits and hissies in the past, but in the light of something so, uh, extraordinary..."

"It would be foolish to let the past drag down the future," finished another man, the first nodding along. The second man was short and squat, like a muskrat, and laden with all manner of charms and apotropaics. His wife, always a worry-wart, had outfitted him with most of these - even begging him to stuff his pockets with a clutch of their expensive silverware. It clattered and poked at him as he walked and, inwardly, he hoped it caused the unholy things at least as much discomfort as he was feeling.

The shadow in the closet shifted, as if trying to work out a persistent numbness in his limbs. The sight of the cross caused him no particular pain or, at least, none that he was unaccustomed to. The garlic and silver and such he found no more bothersome than a lingering fart. The sight of another contract, though, had his every last nerve a-twitching warily.

"The future…"

His voice wavered, even as his eyes shone like copper pennies, the way an animal's did in the moonlight. They had come to hate him before, these businessmen, and that was when he was just a wretched sinner being led around by frail human appetites. Despite their new contract and their nervous smiles, what must they think of him now?

"That's right, son," said a third man, who couldn't be bothered to smile. He chewed an unlit cigar and adjusted his enormous silver belt buckle. He was a number of years older than the others and, before he found his way in show business, had toiled away in a coal mine with his brothers and daddy. Deep in the ground, working day and night, he had seen things that neither the Bible nor carbon monoxide poisoning could adequately explain.

One day he had spied something with flashing silver eyes in the dark down there. That was how he came to be the only one who made it to the surface before the cave-in that claimed over half his male relations. After that day, he was a coal miner no more.

The belt buckle he wore was no mere superstitious affectation. It was simply the first worldly thing he had purchased when the royalty checks had started rolling in. He had seen many things, strange in their own way, since he started in country music - but the only thing that scared him was the thought of ever having to climb underneath those mountains again.

"The future," repeated the third man, growing impatient. "It seems like you actually have one again. If you want it, that is."

A pale hand reached out and found paper and pen.

"Reckon I do," said Hank. And he scarcely waited another second to sign.

They were nothing if not pragmatic, these record men. For last night's impromptu broadcast had captured a greater segment of the market than any of them ever dreamed possible. That disembodied voice on the radio had commanded people's attention until dawn; held the audience so rapt, even the papers trying to debunk it as hokum were claiming some kind of mass hypnosis was involved. A performer with that kind of charisma? A performer with that kind of charisma who might never die? That was something that could pay for the record men's great-grandchildren's children to attend the very finest schools. Nobody bearing their family name would need to descend into a coal mine or slaughterhouse ever again.

Already blood donations were pouring in from all over the southeast. Record stores were inundated with calls inquiring into the availability of not just the records Hank Williams had cut during his lifetime - but those containing the otherworldly new songs that were, as yet, uncommitted to disc.

There were arrangements to be made. More contracts to be drawn up. Legal challenges were forthcoming from both widows. And just how stringent would the Opry be about old Hank's 'lifetime' ban? They would all find out soon enough.

As for the station manager and the DJ? Well, there were good odds that they would simply rise from the dead themselves. If they did, they could look forward to cushy promotions and performance royalties from future sales of recordings made from any portion of last night's broadcast.

And if they did not rise from the dead, as the great Hank Williams had done? Then their great-grandchildren's children would still live and die without ever knowing of roughened hands or an aching back. The record men swore it to themselves and to Hank. Whatever they had thought about him, now or then, none of them were ready to anger him anytime soon.

So it was that Hank Williams' career began its second phase.

And, soon after, the monsters came to Nashville in droves.

Composters

Anita Sullivan

TOM SHAW

Tom parks on the hard shoulder behind the abandoned Toyota Yaris. The driver's door is open, headlights hazy in the floating drizzle. His partner pulls up the details. The car is registered to a Sinead Curran. It doesn't take long to find her.

She is face-down near the top of the bank, where the grass turns to brush and gloom. Tom calls her name as he climbs up, not expecting an answer. A faint luminance shows her face turned to one side, smiling. He mutes his chattering radio and crouches beside her. He doesn't need to touch her to know - but looks at her for so long the motorway sounds fade away.

Why did she take off her shoes?

VIDYA

Vidya rests on her spade and watches a robin investigate the soil she's turned over. Hers isn't the tidiest plot but it's the only one on the allotment with sand lizards. She coaxes aubergines and okra through the British seasons, gathers armfuls of coriander and spinach. And unlike the retired men with their ranks of onions and spuds, she harvests every week of the year.

This late in October, it's just apples, leeks and squashes - but sprouts are budding and soon she'll be planting broad beans. The robin grabs a worm, juggles it down, the cycle of life. She breathes the sharp blue-sky air and, for a moment, is utterly content.

Then Vidya's conscience tugs. At home, Matt is doing the inventory. Jars lined up in the basement, guarding against the future. There will be a spreadsheet to update.

ALICE CAIRNS

Alice Cairns eventually finds the café, tucked between a cashpoint and a sex shop. The shopfront is narrow and the building stretches back, impossibly far. She walks straight as a castle across the black-and-white tiles, past mismatched chairs, to a wooden counter with brownies under glass domes.

She had expected Jez to be young and hip but the man facing her is at least sixty and eyeing her suspiciously over half-glasses. Her turquoise hair reflects in his lenses and she glimpses herself as he sees her: young, inexperienced. A tourist.

She holds his eye. Names what she wants and the botanical Latin works like a charm. Jez puts on surgical gloves and reaches under the counter. He places a glass jar before her, his hand resting protectively on the lid.

"Do you know how to let go and still hold on?" he asks.

A riddle. A safety catch. She answers honestly.

"I didn't the first time. But I've learned."

"Good," he says. "Because, if you fight this one, you'll lose your head."

The journey back across the chessboard floor is shorter and she finds herself blinking in the winter sunshine, fruits of the underworld in her pocket.

VIDYA AND MATT.

Vidya makes notes on a clipboard as Matt checks sell-by-dates on bags of dry food and tins of pulses, tuna and soup. She checks condiments and spices: rations don't have to be dull. There are labelled boxes of matches, water-purification kits, wind-up lights, camping gas, bin-bags and loo roll. The medical kit includes three antibiotics, and pills from Mexico they can take, if all else fails. There are also two Christmas puddings. Vidya isn't sure if that's optimistic or pessimistic.

Their inventory is efficient from practice: some of the oats date back to Swine Flu. But, at this point, their values diverge. For Vidya, this is a functional monthly task. Prep for the worst, enjoy the present. Matt, on the other hand, monitors WHO and researches terrifying futures. He assesses risks and makes plans, including a critical stay/go decision-tree. They will not be sheeple, defending a property that cannot keep them safe. They will not run with the herd but in the opposite direction.

Vidya jokes that, one day, Gaia will rise up against humanity and the earth will shake us all off, like a dog shaking away fleas. Matt doesn't find it funny.

It's not a joke. It is the only thing protecting her from despair.

BEATRICE MORROW

Beatrice talks to her subjects as she examines them. The one-way conversation is recorded with her post-mortem notes, a reminder to anyone listening that a case is also a person. Although, in this case, a person with no clear cause of death.

CCTV shows Sinead Curran pulling over calmly, leaving her car and walking steadily up the bank, pausing to take off her shoes before lying down. The time of death is stamped but the state of decomposition is entirely wrong. Under the harsh overhead light, her dark skin blooms coral, ochre and sage, ruptured by fingers of white hyphae. Yet she had been alive just hours before. It makes no sense.

A tattoo of a vine snakes from Sinead's ankle, up her leg and around her thigh. Beatrice finds herself tracing it with a fingertip, to the femoral artery, where a shell-pink mushroom seems to pulse.

Beatrice blinks and realises she is very tired. Not the normal fatigue from the hours she works but a soul-crushing burden she can barely carry.

VIDYA

Vidya has come to collect The Pumpkin. They have nurtured it through the late summer drought, protected it from mice. Now is its moment. She is rolling it carefully into the open mouth of her rucksack when she hears a commotion.

"You said you'd be home an hour ago!"

An elderly woman is shouting at the man with regimented onions. He's sitting on the edge of the bed he's been double-digging, wellingtons off and two feet in his grave. She berates him about Sunday lunch, grandchildren and the phone he didn't answer, while he stares in blank confusion, as if all such things were utterly mysterious. Irrelevant.

Vidya can hear fear rising in the woman's voice.

Then something connects. Understanding comes to him like a patch of light moving across a field. He accepts his wife's hand and lets her help him up. Shamed, he becomes officious and dismissive. His wife is just grateful the man she chose, so long ago, has returned to her. They walk home together.

TOM SHAW

Tom Shaw proceeds to Old Mill Mall at lunchtime on Halloween Saturday. Music blares, people throng. On the floor above, families queue for fast-food tables. As a police officer, he knows humanity too well to relax in a place like this. But, today, he seems drawn to where people are densest.

In the central concourse, parents are applauding while a local radio DJ, Dave Fludd, judges kids' costumes. He is yelling over Ibiza classics, getting people to clap along. Tom walks to the heart of the crowd. The diners above have a ringside view as Tom stops dead, convulses once, twice, a third time. His head jolts with each spasm, as if building to a gigantic sneeze. Then his head explodes.

VIDYA AND MATT

Vidya is making leek soup, while Matt is on his knees, searching the 'everything else' drawer for cocktail sticks. He has carved the words *Fuck Off* into the pumpkin and needs something to hold the centre of the O in place. He's turned their pumpkin into a joke. Vidya is annoyed with him and with herself for minding. She's about to say something nasty when the radio starts screaming.

BEATRICE MORROW

Beatrice can't breathe. The tiled walls are closing in, the lights too bright. She walks briskly out of the room and exits the building, across a small car park and onto the wet grass. There, she lets go of the painful breath she's been holding.

This mortuary is set in the grounds of a crematorium and Victorian cemetery. It's a place of life, old yews alive with birdsong. She kicks off her shoes and starts walking, ducking under low twisting branches, until she finds a clearing of rabbit-nibbled turf hidden from the world. She lets the weariness she carries drop her to both knees, then onto her stomach - and commits her body to the earth.

VIDYA AND MATT

Vidya and Matt can't believe what they've just heard. The DJ turned war-reporter, seizing the moment, describing chaos and panic. A man without a head.

"Still standing. He's still standing," he cries over and over, before the audio silences, like a knife cut. A few seconds later, Vaughan Williams plays. When Vidya speaks, she sounds affronted.

"Who is still standing?"

"The man without the head."

"Was it an explosion? A shooting?"

"I don't know."

"How is he still standing?"

"I don't know, Vidya."

His fear is a bridge she can cross and she goes to him. They wrap up in the other's arms, their place of safety. Lark Ascending.

FABIO

Fabio doesn't like being called 'Cabin-Crew'. It makes him think of greasy overalls. He tolerated 'Steward' as that, at least, carried a notion of care. But, in his heart, he's always been a Hostess. His manners and impeccable grooming pay homage to Pan-Am standards. So, he welcomes the last late-call passenger, Alice Cairns, with grace. Compliments her turquoise hair, efficiently stowing her luggage overhead and her confusion into seat 10C. He's used to this. Outbound from Amsterdam, the younger tourists can be a little red-eyed and disorientated.

He keeps an eye on her through the flight and, when she starts to convulse, he's ready with the sick bag.

Her explosion catches him full in the face.

VIDYA AND MATT

Vidya has slung a shot of whiskey into their lemon-and-ginger teas, while Matt plugs into the laptop. The translation job he should be working on will have to wait.

No one at Mill Mall was harmed in the explosion - but dozens were injured in the stampede that followed. Reports say six hospitalised. A child trampled. Looting and arrests. Then, twelve hospitalised, one critical. Three critical. One dead.

Vidya starts checking on friends.

Matt watches social media. Theories from lightning strike to a dirty bomb to spontaneous human combustion. But he's looking for patterns, not causes. Is it an extraordinary incident? An early warning? Or something already in motion?

Vidya puts her hands on his shoulders. Whatever happens, he's ready. He speaks four languages, has two passports and can make fire from stones.

She is his reason for surviving.

FABIO

Fabio is smoke-spluttering, grabbing blindly, expecting the floor to plummet and masks to drop. Passengers are screaming and pushing into the aisle but the plane remains level, lights on and engine steady. Fabio blinks and his vision clears. The air is full of dust, not smoke. His sky-blue uniform is clouded and the late passenger no longer has a head. The woman next to her is ghosted out. Frozen, apart from two terror-bright eyes. They look at each other speechless, as Lotte's clear, calm voice floats over the speakers.

"Please remain in your seats. There has been an incident…"

Fabio takes off his jacket and lays it gently over the empty shoulders in seat 10C.

The mobile phones are already streaming.

VIDYA AND MATT

Matt has found something. A café in Winterberg, Germany. A headless man. A plume of dust like 'kicking a puffball'. Google translates this as 'football' but Matt knows better. His onward search for *fungi + death* turns up cases of accelerated decomposition in Denmark, Croatia and Switzerland. Some without heads, others entire and lying at peace. All in towns near forests. Are these connected?

Vidya imagines the roots of trees stretching from wood to wood, over roads and bridges. Crossing borders, crossing continents, until her imagination bumps against an ocean. Back to reality. She's got an online meeting with a new legal aid client in ten minutes.

D J FLUDD

Dave Fludd is on leave from his local radio station but he cannot rest. The bloodless explosion plays on a loop in his head. An off-kilter movement in the crowd. A man's face crumpled and then suddenly gone. He hears his own voice screaming from the speakers while the headless body stands rigid. But the thing that haunts him is the dust floating over the crowd, flowing outwards with the currents of panic.

He's always had his followers. He now has thousands more. He posts an image of the face in the crowd.

Who was the exploding man? his caption demands.

FABIO

Fabio is quarantined on the top floor of the airport hotel, along with the passengers from rows eight to 12. It seems an arbitrary number.

His phone has been confiscated and the news channels removed from his TV package. But they forgot about YouTube. He watches the Mill Mall footage and videos of himself, the elegant placing of the jacket. He reads comments about his calm and kindness. And about his gender and sexuality.

Lotte is in the room across the corridor. They chat for long hours on the hotel phone, of places, parties, loves and losses. They order room service and eat together/apart, behind their locked doors.

At night, Fabio hears the hall-guard snoring, cocooned in his PPE. He sometimes dreams of Alice, the passenger in 10C. That he lifts his jacket from her empty shoulders and finds her miraculously intact and unharmed. Smiling.

Each morning the medics arrive dressed like spacemen with swabs and needles.

He puts on powder-blue eyeshadow, matching cufflinks and trims his beard.

If he's going to die, he'll die true to himself.

D J FLUDD

Dave Fludd receives his answer. User judascharlie85 states, on open chat, that the headless man is Tom Shaw - a police traffic officer. Within an hour, the righteous idle have found him on Facebook and identified his bereaved wife. His daughter is sent home from primary school.

"Could Shaw have become infected in his line of duty?" Dave wonders aloud to his 100,000 followers.

The word 'infected' is out there.

VIDYA AND MATT

Matt follows Dave Fludd but his own research is a step ahead. He has been looking for recent deaths associated with Mill Mall. He finds the local mortuary has closed due to the sudden passing of Pathology Technician Beatrice 'Bee' Morrow. Coincidence? Or transmission?

Vidya calls friends, advising them to avoid public places and wear masks. Some will listen. Some may even have stocked the Twenty Survival Essentials from the list she and Matt send out with their Christmas cards. But it's her friends' kids she worries about - in student halls, shared flats and public-facing zero-hour jobs. They can't store 20 things. They can't take a day off. And they won't stop living their lives in order to survive.

FABIO

Fabio is worried about Lotte. She showers again and again because the dust is 'in her pores'. Her skin is raw. She has a headache. She doesn't want to be alone. She is afraid to sleep. He's afraid too, because he needs her. Where is the brave, life-affirming, anything-is-possible woman he knows and loves?

Loves.

He's woken by raised voices across the hall. The low drone of medical experts being reasonable. Lotte getting shriller, rising out of character, as she demands to be set free. It falls quiet. The medics leave.

Fabio tries to phone. Lotte's line is dead. He shouts to her but there is no reply. When he's cried himself hoarse, there's a whisper at his door.

"They gave her something to sleep," the guard says. "She's OK."

Fabio realises the guard is terrified too.

VIDYA AND MATT

Vidya is alarmed to hear Matt laughing. He's watching footage from outside a pharmacy: a trio wrestling over some yellow canister. The canister breaks in the tussle, and all three are covered in white dust.

"Athlete's foot powder," says Matt. "It's anti-fungal, see? Changing hands for fifty, sixty quid now. You can buy doses in baggies. People will believe anything!"

D J FLUDD

Dave Fludd could have urged calm. When the first cases of ongoing infection from Mill Mall are found lying in public parks, the Ibiza-wannabe, turned family DJ, turned influencer, could have spread the love. But something else is driving him now.

"The fungus is spreading," he yells across Waterloo station. "It is deadly. It is dangerous. But the fungus is not the ENEMY. We are."

His portable amp squeals feedback. Heads turn. A couple turn on their cameras.

"WE ARE TOO MANY!" he booms. "We're killing the planet. Killing future generations! The ENLIGHTENED feel it. All that anxiety, that CONSUMING confusion. What phone to get? What benefits/ energy/ tariff/ parking fine? Fight cancer. Fight pollution/ corruption/ extinction/ vaccination/ congestion. Credit ratings/ care homes/ polar bears/ migrants. Save the NHS/ fuck the NHS. Keep holding on; your call is important. But there's no pension/ no mortgage/ no icecaps/ no time. Paralysed, overloaded and putting on so much weight..."

He is echoing to the vaulted ceiling. He is streaming to his legions. He is channelling something immense.

"No wonder the brave few have chosen to end it. To LAY DOWN their lives and give energy back to the earth. They are the MARTYRS and we HONOUR them."

He pauses. Breathes.

"But the CHOSEN," he says. "Must spread the word. The fungus is not our enemy: it is our SAVIOUR!"

He throws out his arms, tips back his chin and opens his mouth unbelievably wide. His face collapses inwards. All the rage he's been holding inside since Mill Mall, and long before, roars out in a pillar of darkness. Spores rain down on astonished faces below, on people fleeing to the tube or into shops. To those further away, unaware of the danger, calmly boarding intercity trains.

FABIO

Fabio can feel it building: Lotte pacing. Lotte moaning and keening. Lotte smashing furniture. Then a stillness, like electricity holding its breath. Minutes pass. An hour. Fabio begs the guard to check on her but orders are orders. When it finally happens, there is no human sound, just wind roaring through trees. A thump. A giant's fist, then silence.

It's over and so is she.

VIDYA AND MATT

Matt pulls Vidya from her work, folds her onto his lap and makes her watch a video.

Rainforest noises. Serious music. An overblown American voiceover describes a 'predatory' fungus that uses 'chemical warfare' to turn ants into 'zombies'. The music becomes ominous.

Vidya watches an ant leave the safety of the nest and climb high into a tree. It locks onto a branch, paralyzed. As the music climaxes, a massive fruiting body bursts from the ant's head. Spores explode over the forest. The video plays it three times in slow-mo, then intones solemnly:

"The ant is dead."

"See! This is the precedent." Matt is excited. "Evolved... or en-hanced, to turn people into bio-bombs."

He wants her to be impressed.

"What about the people who just lie down?" Vidya wonders softly.

BEATRICE MORROW

Beatrice is five days gone. On the green sward, ringed by red-barked trees, she has become a habitat. Her body has been broken open, cell by cell, by its own chemistry. She's become ripe, gaseous, fluid. Marbled skin is ruptured by creatures of soil and leaf litter. She's breached by waves of fungi. Microscopic white hyphae run through her skin and hair, coating her with fur and turning her clothes to mulch. Puffballs sprout like vertebrae. Fleshy boletus mushrooms root with the beetles between her toes and, at her crotch, red amanita fruit. Fallen leaves soften her outline and, by day six, she is food for trees. Chains of dainty pale parasols break in branching lines, leaving her body, flowing from rowan to yew to ash, across the inter-forest network.

FABIO

Fabio has a broad but unappealing view from the top floor. Waste-ground. Railway. The backs of industrial buildings through denuded trees. The distant glitter of a long-stay car park.

Lately, he has noticed changes. Fewer people, all in masks. A man in hi-vis sleep-walked into the trees, dropping his coat. Later, a wom-an left her wheelie luggage standing and climbed the railway embankment, heading the same way. Yesterday, the hotel car park emptied. This morning, no planes. He turns on his TV. Only Netflix is available. No news, no YouTube.

"Hey! Pawel," he calls through the door. "What's going on?"

The guard isn't there.

VIDYA AND MATT

Vidya and Matt watch the news. It's every scenario Matt had ever imagined.

Waterloo on Friday, Murrayfield yesterday. Gatwick South Terminal this morning. Supermarkets, nightclubs, sports events, churches.

Matt screams "Ants!" at the TV.

Depending on crowd density, the first blast infects up to 80% in a five-metre radius. The R rate is exponential and, as spores can live dormant for decades, decontamination is almost impossible.

There's a political need to find patient zero. Fingers point at China, Ecuador, Cameroon, Russia, Canada. But the truth is more frightening than conspiracy. The fungus has emerged simultaneously, globally, wherever people live near trees.

Matt shouts, "Ophiocordyceps Unilateralis!" Like a Harry Potter spell.

There are social agents in play too. Followers of #IamFludd see themselves as 'chosen', called to spread enlightenment through explosive death. They righteously seek infection. Then there are the 'Composters', who calmly accept their fate and lie down in green spaces.

Vidya takes the TV remote and turns off the sound. Footage is a circle of panic. Hoarding, looting, hospitals overwhelmed, doctors fleeing and the dead unburied. In this flickering light, Vidya kisses Matt with an urgency she hasn't felt for years.

FABIO

Fabio longs to feel fresh air. He watches dawn light creep over cement and tarmac.

When he calls to order breakfast, the harried receptionist says she'll try but they're on a skeleton staff. No food comes. Nor do the medics. When he calls reception again, no one answers.

He's not hungry anymore. He doesn't have any clean clothes and that doesn't matter. It doesn't occur to him to phone a friend, call the airline. He wishes he could go outside. But, in this room, he can still fulfil his destiny. He's a first-class host, serving needs greater than his own.

He dampens the duvet in the shower, drags out the dirty towels and makes a nest on the floor. Closing his eyes, he remembers forests he's known in Thailand, Brazil, Switzerland. The wood near the home he had to leave when he was five. He stretches out his fingers and toes. Lets out the breath he's been holding for many years.

VIDYA

Vidya leaves Matt, sleeping with the silent TV, keeping watch. She walks through their quiet suburb in her P3 mask. It feels safe. The lone dogwalker in the park keeps his distance and the allotment is deserted.

She harvests the butternut squashes and apples: they store well. Matt will be pleased. She takes the net off the last raspberries to leave for the birds, turns around and sees him.

The spuds-and-onions man is spreadeagled, face down and naked. Toes and fingers plunged into his well-manured bed. His body teems with life. A reef of coral-like fungi, brackets and fans, delicate mushrooms in purple and yellow, orange centipedes and indigo ground beetles. Everything he tried to poison - snails, slugs, woodlice, rats - are transforming him. He smells earthy and wholesome as home-made compost - and she has been breathing his air for half an hour.

She can't go home.

Realising this makes everything simple and clear. She takes off her boots and socks, walks to the apple tree and lies down. She gazes through the branches into the thin blue wrap of sky, fragile as her skin, with only darkness beyond. So precious. Her fingers push into the earth she has tended and finds the gentle force of a mycelium entity, as huge and ancient as life itself. Not surviving but enabling survival.

"Clever old fungus."

She smiles and closes her eyes.

The Magic Tea Pot

Michael James

The trip to India was sublime. Jane and Cooper collected wonderful memories, an appreciation for different cultures and a magic tea pot that summoned the Devil.

To be fair, they believed they were buying an ordinary tea pot, despite the warnings.

Jane spotted it on a table covered with a cornucopia of items and was quite taken with the way it sparkled in the light.

"The tea pot is magic," the vendor said. Jane was already hooked, though, and didn't need the extra selling point.

Cooper folded his arms.

"Oh yeah? Does it separate tourists from their money?"

He felt very brave, saying such bold things to a stranger in a different country. Before coming to India, he read several blog posts and one of them said to haggle. He had practiced in the mirror.

"Cooper, hush." Jane swatted his arm and considered the item. He recognized that look, one she'd get when she wanted something. He sighed to himself and began doing Rupee-to-American conversion math.

"Good one," said the vendor, whose name was Lillian. He was not trying to rip them off. More than anything, he wanted to sell this stupid magic tea pot which, in addition to being magic, was cursed and summoned the Devil. He did not mention that last part. He was honest, not stupid.

"I will give you 40 Rupees," said Jane, by way of an initial offer. Cooper calculated that worked out to thirty American dollars.

"That is fifty-seven cents," Lillian replied. He was much better at math than Cooper. "Perhaps you can go as high as seven hundred Rupees? That is only ten dollars."

"Deal." Jane was proud of her bargaining prowess, although she had displayed very little. She adored the magic, cursed pot. It was a dull, burnished gold with a rim of mysterious symbols lining the edges. The spout protruded high over the lid and the handle was quite handsome.

There was no practical reason why Satan would bind himself to a magic tea pot but he got bored in Hell and this helped pass the time.

Lillian couldn't believe his luck and struggled to contain his joy. Because he was a good person, he thought it was only fair to tell these stupid tourists about the tea pot, now that he'd made the sale.

"Just remember this tea pot is magic. Like actual, cursed magic. Never rub it."

"What happens if we rub it?" Jane loved this part of the sale and was thrilled to play along.

"The Devil will appear and pretend to be normal but, really, he's a jerk."

"Ooh, like the actual Devil? How thrilling." Jane couldn't wait to put this on Instagram. She'd easily get ten likes. Maybe twenty.

"You already made the sale, pal," Cooper said. "You can skip the patter."

Lillian sighed and counted backwards from ten, or *das* in Hindi.

Jane and Cooper spent the rest of the day exploring, getting into low-stakes arguments with street vendors and sightseeing. They enjoyed themselves immensely and, by the time they returned to the hotel, had forgotten all about the magic tea pot. In fact, it stayed in Jane's suitcase until they returned home a week later, at which point it tumbled out while they were unpacking.

"Oh, this thing," Jane said. "We should make some tea."

"As long as we don't rub it." Cooper gave her a playful swat on the bum. She laughed, and God-damn if she didn't go straight to rubbing the magic, cursed tea pot that would summon the Devil. Even though Lillian, the honest Indian street vendor, specifically told her not to.

Cooper wasn't paying attention and missed all the action. He only heard Jane gasp and then a thud. When he turned around, she had gone sheet-white, as volumes of gray smoke poured from the nozzle.

"Shit, it's on fire." Cooper was, once again, incorrect. It was not fire. It was magic, just like Lillian told them. Seriously, Cooper. Catch up.

"I'll get a wet towel." Jane always had ideas, even if they were dumb, like this one. Who fights fire with a wet towel? What was the plan there, Jane?

Anyway, before she could follow through on her damp firefighting strategies, the smoke cleared. In its place stood the Devil.

Almost everyone is now picturing a red demon with hooved feet and, maybe, a pencil-thin mustache - but that's not what the Devil looks like. In fairness, the Devil can look like whatever he wants. This time, he was fat and unkempt, with coarse, patchy stubble covering his jawline. His big blue belly hung out over his sweatpants. He did not carry a violin but had a harmonica in his back pocket - the harmonica being the most cursed of all musical instruments.

Jane screamed and jumped back, while Cooper struggled to reconcile what he was seeing.

Satan stretched and yawned.

"Ta da."

"Get out of our house," Cooper yelled. "Who are you?"

"I'm the Devil," said the Devil. "That magic tea pot summons me and now here I am."

"Wait, does this mean God exists?" Cooper worried about all the times he'd coveted his neighbor's swimming pool. It was one of those ones where the hot tub was built right into the structure.

"Don't overthink this," Satan said.

"Holy shit, the street vendor was telling the truth?" Jane backed away to stand beside Cooper.

"I don't know anything about that," the Devil replied. "Let me tell you how this works."

"You're a Genie," Cooper jumped in. "This is an Aladdin thing."

"It's not, though."

"You came out of a lamp and you're blue." Cooper was honestly struggling to put the pieces together.

The Devil squinted.

"Okay, you know what? I'm fine to do it your way. Normally I operate a wish-for-soul thing but I'm okay to do a three wishes deal instead. I can work with this."

"I knew it," Cooper grinned. Both Jane and the Devil ignored him.

"I'm going to tell you straight, though. The wishes are cursed."

"Cursed how?" asked Jane.

"Oh, you know." The Devil waved his hands. "Standard stuff. If you asked for million dollars, you'd get it, but it would be because Cooper died, and it's his insurance or something. Pretty standard cursed-wish malarky."

"How do you know our names?" Cooper scratched his head, attempting and failing to understand the core concept behind the word *magic*.

"I know a lot because I'm the Devil, etcetera. Listen, you two seem pretty cool, like you party. Is there any chance at all you've got some cocaine?"

"We have merlot," Jane said. "But don't do any hard drugs."

"Hmm," the Devil considered. "What about a threesome? Neither of you are that good looking but I'll take whatever."

"What in hell kind of genie are you?" Cooper asked.

The Devil sighed and decided it would probably be best to deal with Jane directly.

"Okay!" Jane clapped her hands. "Let's get this wish stuff out of the way. You say all your wishes are cursed, right?"

"You got it." The Devil shot them with gun fingers.

"Even the small ones?" Jane tried to work out the problem. "What if I wished for a new tube of toothpaste?"

She considered herself to be quite smart but was actually a bit of a doofus. Both she and Cooper were. Remember the wet-towel thing from earlier?

"If you wished for toothpaste, I'd fill it with quick-drying cement or something," the Devil said.

"You asshole." Cooper correctly assessed the situation for once. The Devil was, in fact, a huge asshole. None of the wishes needed to be cursed, it's just that the Devil sucked, hated life and himself.

"I know what we'll do." Jane snapped her fingers. "We won't wish for anything. If every wish is haunted.."

"Cursed," interrupted the Devil. "I'm not a mansion in a Shirley Jackson novel."

Neither Jane nor Cooper got the reference, which irritated the Devil, as he felt he absolutely stuck the landing on that one. Jane continued with her plans.

"If we don't make a wish, we can't be hurt. Simple."

She nodded, impressed with how clever she was.

"Suit yourself." The Devil shrugged. "I'm gonna crash on the couch."

The days turned into months and the Devil didn't go anywhere. He sure was a crummy roommate. Every day, Jane and Cooper would come home to find him on the couch, either playing video games or posting conspiracy theories to 4-Chan.

"Look at this," he pointed. "I have them believing squirrels are government drones. I convinced a guy to kill every squirrel he sees. I love the internet so much."

"We need to do something," Cooper said to Jane. "I have a plan."

"I've been researching wishes at the library." Jane held up a copy of *Eat, Pray, Love.* "This book is spectacular."

Jane and Cooper were not on the same page at all.

"What if we wish for The Devil to disappear? It could work. I can't see any way for that to go wrong."

There's about a thousand ways that could go wrong, Jane. Think about it for a second. The Devil has been at this for all of recorded eternity and this is your first time. It's gonna go badly for you.

But Jane did not think about it, and she and Cooper confronted the Devil.

"Are you sure about this?" The Devil said. He brushed crumbs off his belly. The Devil never wore a shirt.

"Completely sure." Cooper folded his arms, feeling even braver than when he confronted honest Lillian. "We wish you would leave."

"Alrighty. Just so you're aware, I'm going to assume you said *livre,* which is French for book. I'm assuming you've wished I would book. Also, your French is horrible."

Jane still hadn't forgiven Cooper for asking that French waiter where the orgy was instead of the bathroom. The words aren't remotely close. *Orgie* versus *salle de bains*. And that was after she'd paid for a Duolingo membership for his birthday. She could have died from embarrassment.

"That's not what I asked for." Cooper was suddenly nervous that, surprise, surprise, the Devil - who one hundred percent told him the wishes would turn out badly - was now devising a way to make wishes turn out badly. Shocker.

"This is good." The Devil cracked his knuckles. "I can work with it."

He pulled out his harmonica and blew discordantly into it. Magic smoke filled the room and, when it cleared, their apartment building was stuffed to the roof with copies of *Eat, Pray, Love.*

It took about two months to get rid of all the books. A bunch of people actually died and the US Congress declared war on Denmark, it being the most bookish of all countries. This made zero sense, but that was the way of war and governments in general.

Jane and Cooper regrouped at a nearby restaurant.

"Look," Cooper said. "We can't get rid of him until we use up the three wishes and, no matter what we wish for, he's going to ruin it. So why don't we just do the smallest wishes possible? Like, wish for a toothpick or something. Or a new hat."

"What if we wished for his wishes not to be cursed?" Jane was three glasses of wine deep and feeling pretty clever. To be fair, it wasn't a bad idea.

"Is there any possible way he could twist that?" Cooper asked.

They pondered the problem and ordered a few more drinks. Then, since they were pretty tipsy, decided to go bowling and had a fairly good time - until the end. Jane shot a one-sixty to Cooper's one-forty, putting in a wedge in their relationship that would never properly heal and would cause Cooper to give up bowling forever.

The next day they confronted the Devil. Again.

"We're ready this time," Jane said. "Our wish is for no more cursed wishes."

"Okay." The Devil burped. Once again, he played a few notes on his harmonica. Cooper could have sworn it was the opening chords to *Wannabe* by the Spice Girls. Jane and Cooper held their breath to see if their medium-clever plan would work.

Once the music faded, The Devil said. "Sadly, the only way to fulfill that wish is to make it so everyone you love dies. It's a super weird subclause in the wish handbook but it's the only way to remove curses on wishes."

The Devil was completely making this up as he went along. He was having a wonderful time.

Jane and Cooper frantically called everyone they loved, only to find that they were all, legitimately, dead. In a twist that upset both of them deeply, their parents were still alive. The implications of that bothered them both more than anything else.

They dried their tears and put their heads together to strategize the next steps. It took a while as they were quite beside themselves. They even tried to explore suing Lillian, the honest and hardworking street vendor - but no lawyer would take their case.

The Devil used the time to play *Tony Hawk's Pro Skater* and, when he didn't get a high score, he fundamentally altered reality so that, yes, he did. The Devil was quite relishing how dense these two nitwits were.

"Okay." Jane put on her no-nonsense voice. Both her and Cooper were convinced this would be the ticket out of this mess. "We're ready. For our last wish, we want to make it so that none of this ever happened."

"Oh." The Devil nodded. "The ole alter-reality gag, huh? Sure, that's no problem at all."

"Seriously?" Cooper said. "You'll do it?"

"You got it." The Devil pulled out his harmonica and then quite ominously said, "See you both in a bit."

If you wanna be my lover went the harmonica and poof... Devil things.

The trip to India was sublime. Jane and Cooper collected wonderful memories, an appreciation for different cultures and a magic tea pot that summoned the Devil. To be fair, they believed they were buying an ordinary tea pot, despite the warnings.

Jane spotted the item amongst the table filled with a cornucopia of items and was quite taken with the way it sparkled in the light.

"The tea pot is magic." The vendor said. Jane was already hooked, though, and didn't need the extra selling point. She bought the tea pot.

For some reason, her eyes filled with tears.

"Something is wrong."

The Brentford Wives

Jen Mierisch

"You're moving *where*?" Amy nearly dropped her latte, stopping midstride and swinging around to face Carrie.

"Brentford," Carrie repeated. "We got a really good deal on a four-bedroom. It's in a great school district and Jack's ecstatic. He'll finally get his three-car garage."

She rolled her eyes, smiling, and zipped her jacket higher against the chilly spring air.

"*The* Brentford?" asked Amy. "Brentford-by-the-Bay?"

"That's the one."

"Home to the most rich-bitches per capita in the entire metropolitan area?" Amy gave Carrie a wry glance above the plastic top of her to-go cup.

"Oh, I'm sure they're not that bad," Carrie blushed. "I know Brentford's got sort of a reputation. But I just learned that an old friend of mine, Tori, lives there. She was president of our high school Key Club. Very socially minded."

Looking skeptical, Amy sipped her coffee.

"Back in college, when I was a server for Cosmo Catering, I used to work a lot of parties in Brentford. The men talked about nothing but their investment portfolios and how big their boats were. There was a certain level of... what's the word? If every little thing didn't go perfectly, they'd pitch a fit."

"Entitlement?"

"Exactly. Like they were so perfect that any tiny problem was a threat to their existence. And you should have seen the females, decked out like they were going to the Oscars. They're the kind of women who buy ridiculous things that nobody needs. Tennis bracelets. They would definitely buy tennis bracelets."

"If they're really that bad, I'll work on them." Carrie downed the last of her mocha. "Give me a few months. I'll organize a Brentford bus to the next Women's March."

Amy chuckled.

"I'm sure they'd wear pussy hats if there was enough bling on them. There you go. Knit them some vajazzled pussy hats."

"Remember that woman in the full-body vagina costume at the march?" Carrie chuckled.

"With the boom box playing *Can't Touch This*? How could I forget?"

"You had the best sign, though. *Damn Straight, We're Snowflakes - Winter Is Coming*!"

"You must have had a hundred people take your photo in that Princess Leia outfit," Amy said. "Long Live the Resistance!"

They laughed and it was just another day on the city's west side, the sun rising over the skyscrapers and bathing them in light.

Amy's smile faded into a sigh.

"What am I going to do without my favorite walking buddy?"

"Rocky will walk with you."

"That old mutt? He's so slow, he doesn't even get me a thousand steps a day!"

Carrie giggled but a twinge of guilt squeezed her gut. Amy had moved to the neighborhood a couple of years ago and didn't have a lot of local friends. One of the first things they'd bonded over was how hard it was to make friends in adulthood. After discovering that they both worked from home, they'd made their morning walks together a habit.

"Hey," said Amy, "I hope you know I'm giving you a hard time because I'm gonna miss you. A lot."

Carrie smiled, relief loosening her shoulders.

"I know. I'll miss you, too."

"When one door closes, another opens, right?"

"That's what they say."

"Promise me you'll come visit."

"Of course."

"And Carrie..."

"Yes?"

"Promise me you won't turn into one of those rich bitches."

Carrie laughed again.

"Who, me?"

The Brentford Women's Club sat on a rise at the edge of town, offering exquisite views of the exurb's rolling hills. Standing next to her car, Carrie pondered which paint colors she would use to capture the misty landscape. Early morning would provide the best light. She squinted, trying to locate her new house.

"Hello there," a voice said.

"Oh, hi." Carrie turned to face a slender woman with pin-straight blonde hair. "I'm Carrie. Tori told me about your meeting today. I'm hoping to meet some new neighbors. We just moved to Brentford."

"Tori? Oh. Victoria. Of course." The woman's teeth were stunningly white. She extended a tanned, jewel-encrusted hand. "Lovely to meet you, Carrie. I'm Kelly Banks."

Carrie shook Kelly's hand and suppressed a giggle. Did people really say *Lovely to meet you* outside of the movies?

"Victoria should be here any minute." Kelly walked towards the building and Carrie followed in her perfume-scented wake.

A silver BMW convertible pulled into the parking lot, sunlight glinting off chrome, as it swung into a spot. Its driver dropped her keys into a leather handbag, pushed sunglasses atop her layered brown mane and stepped out onto stiletto heels, diamonds glittering on the skinny bracelet around her wrist.

"Carrie!" The apparition flung her arms wide.

Carrie quickly closed her open mouth and accepted the hug.

"Tori!" she exclaimed. "Nice to see you. You look amazing."

She gave a silent prayer of thanks that she'd opted for a simple sleeveless dress instead of the jeans and casual top she'd contemplated that morning.

"Oh." Tori waved off the compliment with a manicured hand. "Goodness, it's been ages since I heard that name. I started going by Victoria years ago."

"Right. Sorry." Carrie was still taking in her old friend. Her face was the same, but her hair was different. Shorter. Sharper.

"Don't be sorry! It reminds me of good old West Lawrence High," Tori said. "How is the old neighborhood?"

"Oh, you know Lawrence. It never changes. I'm excited to be here, though."

"We're excited to have you!" Tori smiled. "Come inside and meet everyone."

They walked up the paved path.

"This building is from the 1950s," Tori remarked. "It used to be the town's event hall. But we made them give it to us."

Her laughter was high and carefree.

"Really?"

"Brentford's grown a lot," Tori continued. "People were hardly using the building, and the Women's Club organizes most of the activities in town. For big events, everyone books the yacht club."

Inside, Carrie accepted a glass of Chardonnay from a uniformed bartender and followed Tori into a round, sunny room with a dozen windows overlooking the bay. Seating herself at a table, Carrie struggled to commit names to memory as, one after another, well-dressed women introduced themselves.

"You're in that four-bedroom Cape Cod on Lamson Street, aren't you?" That was Stacy, with the curly blonde updo. "Beautiful place."

"Let us know if there's anything you need as you get settled in." Rebecca's blue eyes met Carrie's.

"You'll need a landscaper right away," Kelly added. "It's spring cleanup time. They're booking up fast!"

"Oh, I don't know." Carrie frowned. "Jack likes to mow the yard himself. I think he'd marry that riding lawnmower if it was legal."

The women laughed and Carrie relaxed a bit. They might be intimidating but how bad could they be if they had a sense of humor?

"Moving is so stressful," sighed Stacy. "Having to find all-new people for everything. I can refer you to our au pair agency if you want."

"And there's a great hairstylist right up the road," Rebecca chimed in.

"I didn't even think about that," Carrie said. "I may drive back to see my old stylist. I've been going to her for years."

The group burst into chirps, loud as if a dog had startled sparrows out of a shrub.

"You're not driving all the way back to the city, are you?"

"Oh, don't do that!"

"Not when Maria is right down the street!"

"She's a magician with highlights," Stacy urged. "She makes my gray hair just... disappear!"

Carrie thought about Gwen, the stylist in Lawrence who had found the perfect cut for Carrie's brown curls and kept them trimmed to perfection. She would miss their chats about their kids and Gwen's off-color jokes. But the ladies were so enthusiastic. Surely it wouldn't hurt to give Maria a try?

"I have the best housekeeper," said Kelly.

"No, I do!" Rebecca laughed. "And you're welcome to her, Carrie. Any time except Friday. That's my day."

"Definitely get a security system for the house, too," added Tori.

"Do I need one?" Carrie asked. "I thought crime was low here."

"Remember Regina and Bob Bellwether, ladies?"

The group murmured assent.

"Bob and Regina didn't have a security system," Tori explained, "They went to Rio for three weeks and, when they got back, they had *squatters*. The house was absolutely wrecked. That gorgeous Karastan carpet. Destroyed."

"Look at Carrie's face." Kelly's crimson lips parted in a smile. "She looks so shocked."

Tori shot Carrie an understanding glance

"I know, right? We're fifteen miles from downtown. How could people like that even end up here?"

They were all looking at Carrie. She had to say something.

"That must have been shocking for them. And how sad that some-one would be homeless. You'd have to be desperate to resort to breaking in like that."

"Surely. But Brentford doesn't have any programs for the home-less," Tori said. "The city has much better resources for those people."

Around the room, stylish heads nodded in agreement.

"You're so sweet to care, though, honey." Rebecca flourished her martini glass. "I'm tapping Carrie for my committee at the next Brent-ford Ball!"

Carrie joined the women's laughter. The conversation moved on, with Kelly asking Stacy about her upcoming run for school board.

"What's the Brentford Ball?" Carrie whispered to Tori.

"It's our annual charity fundraiser," Tori replied. "We have a good life here. It's our duty to give back."

Carrie blinked, watching her children devour the chicken she'd placed on their plates.

"Wow," she murmured to her husband. "They didn't even mention the sauce."

"Guess they're too hungry to be picky," Jack grinned. "I had them at the park all afternoon, while you were attending that women's meeting."

"Best playground ever!" five-year-old Hannah piped up, a glob of mashed potato spilling from her open mouth.

"Hannah," Carrie scolded, "Mouth closed when you chew."

"They really had fun," Jack said. "Met lots of other kids."

"I have a new friend!" Zane, their oldest, broke in. "Logan. He lives right next to the park. Can I play at his house tomorrow, Mom?"

"Slow down, there, Buster. We'll have to meet his parents first."

"Done," Jack said. "I met Logan's dad this morning. He's the one who told me about the park."

"That's right. I haven't talked to you since you left for the yacht club. How was it?"

"Well." Jack looked around the table, "I think we're getting a boat."

"What?" shouted Hannah. "No way!"

"Awesome!" Zane's grin revealed chewed-up chicken. He quickly covered it with a hand, glancing at Carrie.

Carrie turned to Jack.

"We are?"

"They have a system here, apparently." Jack shrugged. "The club has such a big membership that someone's always looking to sell their old boat when they upgrade. They call it the 'boat brothers.' The one who sells you their boat becomes your boat brother and then you become a brother to someone else later. Logan's dad, Stephen, offered to bring me in."

"How... fraternal." Carrie lowered her voice. "Shouldn't we talk about this? Surely it's a huge purchase?"

"Not at all." Jack looked pleased. "My bonus should cover it."

"The Brentford boat brothers." Carrie shook her head. She imagined herself sailing out on that beautiful bay, the sea breeze lifting her hair. She could take photos of the coast and use them to paint land-scapes.

"Imagine us, with our own boat," she said. "If my dad could see this..."

"He'd be happy for us." Jack squeezed her hand. "What father wouldn't love to see his daughter doing so well?"

"I guess we really are." She lifted her wine glass. She only intend-ed to take a sip, but Jack seized his own glass and clinked it against hers.

"To Brentford!"

"Brentford!" echoed Hannah, stretching her short arm across the table to click her plastic juice glass against theirs. "Best place ever!"

Carrie set down the laundry basket and reached for her ringing phone, smiling when she saw the name.

"Amy!" she said. "How are you?"

"Is this a good time?"

"Fine. I just wrapped up my meetings for the day, and I was about to do laundry. Now I don't have to!"

Carrie dropped onto the couch and put her feet up.

"Ugh. Work," Amy complained. "My job is absolutely nuts right now. I've never been so happy to turn that computer off."

Carrie could hear ice cubes clinking in what was surely Amy's dai-ly 5:00 gin and tonic.

"So, how's it going in Brentford?" Amy asked. "Met any rich bitches yet?"

"Well," Carrie laughed. "It's definitely a little... different here. Pretty much everyone has maids and professional landscapers. But it's going fine. I've met several neighbors already."

"None as great as me, of course."

"Definitely not!"

"So, what's it like?"

Carrie told Amy about the kids finding new friends, about planning for summer day camp, and their recent boat acquisition.

"You have a *yacht* now?"

"Not a yacht. It's a smaller boat. A Bowrider boat. I can't believe I know that. Anyway, you need to bring the children up some weekend so we can take you out on it."

"The kids would love that," admitted Amy. "What about your old friend? What was her name, Terry? Did you guys meet up?"

"Tori," Carrie corrected. "Victoria. We did meet up. She's done really well for herself. I think she's a CEO or something. You should see her house. It has eight bedrooms! She's introduced me to a ton of neighbors, which is amazing. But she's..."

"She's what?"

"Well, people here seem a little obsessed with their houses. Tori went on and on about this Brentford couple who took a vacation and some homeless people got in while they were away. Granted, that would be shocking, but it was the way she said it. 'Carrie, they had *squatters*'. Like how you might say 'they had *rats*'."

"Oh."

"Yeah. I mean, this was the kid who once donated all of her Girl Scout cookie sale money to help the homeless." Carrie sighed. "I guess she's got a point, though. About the security system. And she's still a nice person. Just... different."

"Different."

"She's head of the Brentford Women's Club and they hold a charity ball every year and raise thousands of dollars. So, it's not like they have no social conscience. Maybe I just need to get used to things. People with this much money are bound to behave differently from..."

"From who? Us? Oh, wait, you're one of *them* now."

Ice cubes clinked in the silence.

"Carrie, I didn't mean it like..."

"No, it's okay," Carrie said. "I know what you meant. Living here is taking some adjustment, is all."

"Well, if Jack tries to buy you a tennis bracelet, let me know, so I can stage an intervention."

They laughed, and it was like old times again. Almost.

As Carrie started the washing machine, her friend's voice echoed in her ears. Amy's tone had sounded almost concerned. Odd, Carrie thought. Why would Amy be concerned about her?

Maybe she shouldn't have said anything about Tori. If it weren't for Tori, Carrie wouldn't know anybody in town. She ought to be more grateful.

"Excuse me," Tori said, lifting a hand to flag down the waiter.

The man scurried back over, a towel draped across his arm.

"Ma'am?"

"Take this salad back and remake it, please. It was supposed to have salmon, not shrimp, and I asked for the dressing on the side."

"Sure." The waiter, who looked barely eighteen, took the plate and headed for the kitchen. Tori rolled her eyes at Carrie.

"*Sure*," she repeated mockingly. "Not even a 'sorry'. It's a shame they hire servers who can't handle the task. I mean, literally, their entire job description is to serve us what we ordered. I might have to let the manager know."

Carrie shifted uncomfortably. Tori obviously expected a response.

"Good for you, sending it back," she said finally. "I probably would have just eaten it and not said anything."

"I really feel it's the feminist thing to do." Tori sipped her cocktail. "I mean, weren't women expected to be demure for too long? To sit and look pretty and never complain?"

"True," Carrie agreed.

"Being assertive is the way to go. If I hadn't embraced that, I would never be where I'm at in my career, that's for sure."

Carrie thought of her own job, processing payroll, as she'd done for the past eleven years.

"Tell me more about your work," she said. "Mine is pretty boring. Sometimes I feel like I've been there a little too long."

"Have you read *Lean In*?" Tori smiled. "I know it's a little passé nowadays, but it's got a lot of good points about embracing risk and change. Nobody can take charge of your career except you."

The rest of lunch was spent chatting about the politics of promotions and their workspaces. In Tori's case, a corner office. In Carrie's, a corner of her basement. Both agreed the gender pay gap was not shrinking quickly enough. Carrie chewed the last of her BLT thoughtfully. Maybe Tori was right. Maybe Carrie did deserve more.

"Ready to go to the outlets?" Tori handed back the payment book without a glance at the waiter.

"Definitely. I'm dying to see this Andy's Art Store that Rebecca told me about."

The wind ruffled their hair as Tori drove them along Route 18 in her silver convertible. As they passed the exit for North Beach, Carrie thought about her kids, off at the beach with their dad. She hoped Jack had remembered sunscreen.

Carrie felt the car slowing. Tori was pulling over next to a minivan stopped at the side of the road. A man, a woman and three young children were climbing out, all wearing swimsuits and carrying beach gear. Carrie could see smears of white sunscreen across their coffee-brown skin.

"Hello," Tori called, as the family looked at her curiously. "Do you know you're not allowed to park here for the beach?"

"The parking lot is permit only," the man replied.

"Yes, it is," Tori agreed. "And so is this road. So why don't you move along now."

"We're just going to the beach, lady," the man said. His wife looked uncomfortable. The kids glanced back and forth between their parents and Tori. "What's the big deal? It's a public beach."

"And the roadside parking is permit-only for Brentford," Tori replied. "Surely there's another beach you could go to."

She removed her phone from her purse and idly tapped at it.

"It would be a real shame if you came back and your car was towed. Don't you think?"

The man's jaw clenched.

"Kids," he said. "Let's get back in the car."

Tori pulled away. Carrie heard a small child's whine behind them. She sat in the passenger seat, stunned. The word was out of her mouth before she could stop it.

"Wow."

"Wow?" echoed Tori. "What do you mean?"

Carrie stumbled over her words.

"I just… what you said. It…" She frowned. What specifically *had* Tori said that bothered her? "I… I didn't know Brentford regulated parking for the beach."

"Well, of course we do. We all moved to Brentford for a certain type of community. One with a beach that isn't too crowded or too loud, where we can relax with our children. Shouldn't we get what we pay for?"

The kids had ridden gleefully across the bay on Jack and Carrie's boat, then shed their life jackets to build sandcastles and splash at the beach. Now, in the late afternoon, Carrie and Amy walked them down to the park. Amy's husband, Kevin, grilled burgers and hot dogs with Jack back at the house.

It was like old times, watching their kids play together. They'd even gone to Starbucks before boating, just the two of them. Carrie had called out the man who'd cut in front of them in line. She'd felt Amy's eyes on her and felt a twinge of pride. Apparently, her friend had noticed her efforts to be more assertive.

Now, relaxing on a bench, they watched the children run toward the swings.

"How they still have this much energy, on such a hot day, is one of the mysteries of the universe." Amy leaned back and wiped her brow.

"Seriously," Carrie agreed. "If I could bottle that energy and sell it, I'd be set for life."

A movement across the park caught her eye. A young East Indian couple had stepped out of an older-model Chevy. They began strolling around the park's perimeter, looking up at the homes, occasionally glancing at the kids playing. The woman stopped and smiled at Hannah, who was clambering hand over hand across the monkey bars. Carrie's eyes narrowed.

"I'll be right back." She got up and strode toward the couple, who smiled in greeting.

"Can I help you folks?" She rested one hand on her hip.

"We're looking at real estate in the area," the man said. "We thought we'd take a walk and get a feel for the neighborhood."

"Oh," said Carrie. "Where's your agent?"

"Agent?" Their smiles faded.

"Your real estate agent."

The man and woman looked at each other.

"She's not here. We came on our own."

"I see," Carrie nodded. "I'll leave you to it then."

They were frowning when she turned around and walked back to the bench.

"What was that all about?" Amy had a look on her face that Carrie hadn't seen before.

"I asked them…"

"I heard. I wondered why you felt the need to approach them."

"Well, I don't know them and they were looking at the children. I figured I should, you know, tell them this is the kind of neighborhood where people keep an eye out."

"I think they got the message." Amy looked over at the couple, who seemed to have cut their walk short. Their car doors closed and the Chevy pulled away.

"Carrie," Amy said. "You've changed. Can't you see? You wouldn't have done that back home."

"Done what? I like to know who's in my neighborhood, that's all. I think that's a good thing."

Carrie opened her mouth to say more, but Amy was staring at her phone.

"Kevin texted," She stood up. "Kids! Dinner's ready."

Was Amy developing frown lines between her eyes? Carrie had never seen those before.

And then they were busy with their children and husbands, as they saw to the logistics of eating dinner, cleaning up and filling water balloons for the kids to throw at each other. Then the sun was setting, and the youngsters were finally running out of steam. Amy gathered her purse and sunglasses.

"We had a great time," Carrie told her. "Thanks for driving all the way up here. Let's do it again soon."

Amy opened her mouth, glanced at Kevin approaching and closed it again. Instead, she leaned forward to hug Carrie. She smelled of sea spray and cherry soda.

As Amy, Kevin, and the kids piled out the door together, Amy looked back at Carrie one last time. Shook her head, just slightly.

"Goodbye, old friend."

It might have been Carrie's imagination, but her smile seemed a little sad.

Carrie touched the sides of her new, shorter haircut as she gazed into the mirror. Tori – Victoria - had been right, she thought. Maria really was a wizard. She had applied the blonde highlights as skillfully as any painter, and they complimented Carrie's skin tone.

She glanced out the window at her new shrubs. They were all evenly spaced, except for one at the end, which was noticeably askew. She should call Ever Green Landscaping and demand they come back and fix it. She'd hired them to landscape her yard to her specifications, after all. Wasn't that their entire job description?

It felt good to take charge. Carrie sat up straighter, shoulders back, admiring her reflection. Maybe this was what being successful felt like. She smiled.

Perhaps she should update her name, like Victoria had, to go with her newfound confidence. 'Carrie' sounded so childlike. Her full name was much more elegant.

She lifted her chin and gazed boldly into her mirror.

"Lovely to meet you," she said. "My name is Caren."

The Nature of My Game

Mike Deady

The place is perfect for my needs.

It is a fairly large house with an attic and two main floors, the second of which has multiple bedrooms. It's even got a basement, not always the case in this part of the country. The house is old but in good shape. It is separated from its neighbors by thick foliage. Just a typical dwelling in the country.

What raises it to perfection is the family now moving in. A couple around forty with four children. All girls, ranging in age from pre-school to teen. Mother and daughters are very pretty. They have moved from the city to the country because of the man's new job. This will entail working long hours and he will not be home much.

An ideal situation.

I enter the house. I wait for the family to settle down and go to bed. I watch the man and woman christen their new bedroom and I get aroused. I consider paying a visit to the teenage daughter but it is much too soon for that. I will stick to the script I have been following for many a long year.

I start off by making scratching noises in the attic.

I listen to the family at breakfast. They are talking about the noises and wondering if there are mice, or maybe even rats, in the attic. The man says he will take a look and set some traps. After breakfast, I watch him pull down the trap door, move the ladder into position, and climb up into the attic. He putters around with a flashlight for a while.

93

He goes away and comes back later with some old-fashioned spring traps, baiting them with cheese and scattering them in all the corners.

That night I set off all the traps and remove the cheese.

In the morning, I watch the man check the traps. I enjoy his look of confusion. He leaves. He returns later with different traps, the glue pad type. He places them in strategic locations.

That night I move all the glue traps to different locations, putting a couple directly on top of the trap door.

In the morning, I watch the man pull down the trap door. One of the traps lands, glue side down, on his head. He curses. The woman brings him into the bathroom and carefully cuts away the stuck hair. The man comes out and steps on the second glue trap, which has landed sticky side up. He rips it away and curses again. The woman stifles a laugh. I am beginning to like her. The man goes up to the attic. He sees glue traps strewn all over the place, none of which are attached to mice or rats. He curses some more. He leaves to go to work.

Time to kick it up a notch.

During the day, I wander around the house. I make scratching sounds in the basement and in several of the rooms. I knock a picture off the wall that the woman has just hung. I slam a door or two closed. There is no radio - no one seems to have them anymore - so I turn the television on and off at random. I make a cold spot or two. I pile dead flies on the windowsills. All the usual bells and whistles.

At exactly three o'clock in the morning, I knock loudly on the front door three times. After a long while, the man comes grumbling down the stairs and opens the door. He looks around, closes the door and goes back to bed. As soon as he is back in bed, I knock three more times, louder than before. The man does not take as long to come down and open the door. He looks around as before, swears, and goes back to bed. I knock three more times, three booming thuds. The man runs down the stairs, throws open the door and looks around. He has a flashlight and a baseball bat this time. The woman closes and locks the door behind him while he circles the house. He finds no one, of course.

I repeat this for the next two days and nights. On the third night, the man even waits by the front door, yanking it open as soon as he hears the knock, finding nothing.

By now, the family is frazzled. They call the police, who search the house and grounds but find no sign anyone has tried to break in. The entire family is tired and on edge. They know something is wrong but are not yet ready to accept the truth.

It is time to make my presence truly felt.

I think about which female to use as my lure. The youngest is very promising. Preschool age, innocence personified. The next oldest is at that in-between stage, which has little interest for me, unless there are no other alternatives. And I have plenty. The third oldest is just entering puberty, traditionally a favorite choice of mine. The oldest daughter is a fully matured eighteen-year-old senior in high school and, somehow, still a virgin - which is always preferable. I have ruled out the mother at the moment for that very reason.

It is a tough decision. In the end, I decide to go with tradition. If it ain't broke, don't fix it. But I will have a little fun tonight first.

I slip into the youngest girl's bedroom. She shares it with the in-between aged one. The closet is next to the youngest girl's bed. I hide in the back of it, then open the door slowly, making sure it creaks. The girl wakes up and looks into the closet. I let her see me, though not in my true form. She giggles and asks who I am. I lie - that is what I do, after all - and tell her I am a poltergeist. She cannot pronounce the entire word, so she just calls me Paul.

We talk for a while. I teach her a few simple tricks she can play on the sister who shares the room. Eventually, she yawns and goes back to sleep. On the way out, I yank the covers off the in-between aged girl, just for shits and giggles.

I bypass my intended target's bedroom and slip into the oldest girl's room. Carefully pull the covers down. She is wearing only panties and a tank top. I instantly spring to attention at the sight. I would love to deflower this succulent creature but I want to keep her in reserve - just in case my first choice does not work out, for some reason.

I see a crucifix on the wall above her bed, so I turn it upside-down. I cause her smartphone on the nightstand to blink the time. 6:66. I leave a polished red apple next to the phone. She will have a lot to think about when she wakes up.

My next stop is the woman's bedroom. The man is working late. I slip into bed beside her. She is on her side, back to me. She half-wakes up, thinking her husband is home from work, and pushes in closer. I grab her hips, lift her onto her knees and mount her from behind. I ride her until I hear the sound of the man's car coming up the driveway. I reluctantly pull out and ejaculate onto the man's pillow.

The woman hears the sound of her husband's car door closing and the beep of the electronic lock. She looks around dumbly. It is difficult to look otherwise with her ass sticking in the air. She hears his footsteps coming up the stairs. She gets under the covers and pretends to be asleep.

The man enters the room, wearily undresses, and crosses to the bed. He must be exhausted because, somehow, he does not register the pungent aroma of sex tinged with brimstone that permeates the room. I watch with delight as he flops into bed and lays his face directly onto the steaming puddle of my discharge. He yelps and jerks his head up as if he has been shot. The pillow is stuck to the side of his face. He frantically peels it off and hurls it across the room. He gags as he finally gets a whiff of my sulfuric spunk, gobs of which are oozing down his face like molten lava. He runs to the bathroom and vomits. Then he carefully washes his face and rinses it with cold water to soothe the burning.

The man eventually returns and pulls down the covers on his wife's side of the bed. At some point, she has fallen asleep for real.

Or, as my ego prefers to think, has passed out from pleasure. He studies her for a long time. He sees the semicircles of red crescent-shaped marks around her hips where my nails dug in as I rode her. He does not get back into bed. He moves over to a chair in the corner and tries to sleep.

I leave the room, satisfied in every sense of the word with my night's work.

I eagerly watch the family come to breakfast. The woman walks in very gingerly. The man follows. The left half of his face is red, like he has a bad sunburn. They sit down, looking at anything but each other. The oldest girl comes in. She is pale and withdrawn.

The other girls enter. My intended victim, the only one I did not visit during the night, makes a joke that her father looks like Two-Face. No one laughs. The youngest girl chatters away about her new friend, Paul, who lives in her closet. Nobody pays her any attention. My target looks around and wonders what is wrong with everyone.

I will show her tonight.

I wait for everyone to go to sleep. It takes longer than usual. But, finally, the time has come for the main event.

I slip into the girl's bedroom. I whisper in her ear. I coax. I cajole. I take advantage of all the new swirling emotions and insecurities caused by her recent puberty. She puts up a good fight but I have centuries of experience at this. Ultimately, I find a weak spot in her defenses.

I enter her.

In the morning, we walk into the kitchen and urinate on the floor. The rest of the family gapes at us. We walk over to daddy and sit on his lap, grinding our pelvis into his crotch. He sits up quickly and throws us off. We run back up to our bedroom.

Mommy follows us, asks what is wrong. We tell her that daddy has been doing things with us and with our sisters. Mommy's jaw drops, and she leaves the room. We hear yelling downstairs that goes on for a very long time.

Much later, mommy and daddy enter our room. They tell us they know we are lying and want to understand what is really going on. How can they possibly not know yet? Don't these people watch movies? We think mommy suspects the truth but daddy is pretty dense and needs more convincing. We get on our hands and knees and tell him we want it doggy-style, the way mommy likes it. We perfectly mimic mommy's moans and cries of ecstasy that we know so intimately. Mommy's face turns pale. Daddy's face turns red or, at least, the side that is not already red.

They leave the room. More yelling ensues. Mommy insists on bringing in a paranormal expert. Daddy scoffs and refuses. The next time they return to our room, we are floating three feet above the bed.

Daddy changes his mind.

The paranormal investigators arrive. They are new and unfamiliar to us. We realize we miss the married couple from Connecticut who used to investigate so many of our infestations and possessions over the years. The investigators have brought a local priest with them. They need evidence to convince the bishop.

We know the drill. We give them a few of the classic symptoms of demonic possession: we contort our body into unnatural positions, speak in languages we have never learned, tell them things about themselves we could not possibly know. Parlor tricks, really.

The investigators and the priest are convinced. Just one more step remains. Per the bishop's insistence, we undergo a complete medical examination to rule out any mental illness or physical cause, such as a brain tumor. We pass with flying colors.

The big day finally arrives. Two priests enter our room, the exorcist and his assistant, along with a doctor. We know the exorcist, of course. We know them all. We have battled this one many times before. He is older now and looks frail. Has it been that long since our last encounter? The assistant is the local priest we met before.

Without any fanfare, they begin the ancient rituals. They pray incessantly. They sprinkle holy water on us. Just to throw them a bone, we pretend it burns. At one point, we raise blisters that read HELP ME. We give them the customary vomiting, urinating, obscene talk, bed rocking, and levitating. The priests are not fazed. The doctor is.

They keep at it all day and night, rarely taking breaks. We watch to see if there is a pattern to the breaks, if one of the priests is ever alone in the room, at any point. Not so far. They are very careful and disciplined.

We allow the priests to go at this for days, letting them tire out, waiting for a slip. We make ourselves appear to be near death. The priests desperately increase their attempts, taking fewer and fewer breaks. Finally, our patience pays off.

After leaving for a respite, one of the priests comes back in alone. To our surprise, it is the lead exorcist. We were sure it would be the younger priest - it almost always is. He asks us to leave the girl alone. We laugh. He begs. We laugh harder. He pleads. We urinate on the bed. He looks beaten. Then, he says the magic words.

Take me instead.

We are elated. A voluntary surrender from a priest. And not just any priest, a seasoned lead exorcist.

This is huge. Having Z and Q on triple letters while being on a triple word and using all seven letters huge.

I leave the girl and take the priest's soul.

Game over.

I meet with my Opponent to compare scores and determine the winner. I hand Him my report. The front page summarizes the souls I have taken, with the total score at the bottom underlined three times in red. My last one has given me more than enough points to put me over the top. My Opponent is dismayed.

"Looks like you win again," He says dejectedly. He leafs through the rest of my report. "I see you went down to Georgia for your last one. Is there any cliché you won't use?"

"Technically, I went *up* to Georgia."

He sighs and shakes His head.

"It's bad enough you won the game and took My best exorcist. But couldn't you have left the woman alone? You broke at least three of My commandments. I should deduct points for that."

I am indignant.

"I did nothing wrong! She was willing." I give Him a leer. "Very willing."

"She thought you were her husband!"

"All on her. She wriggled up against me. That's entrapment. My only real regret is that I didn't despoil the oldest teenager when I had the chance."

"You are depraved."

"Thank You."

"It wasn't a compliment! Your behavior is appalling. Why must you try to seduce every female you come across?"

"It's more like I try to come across every female I seduce."

"Enough!"

"Hey, blame Yourself. You created everything, which includes me."

He sighs and shakes His head again. He does that a lot when we meet Face to face. He gives up.

"Speaking of Creation, which prize do you want this time?"

A few decades ago, after centuries, millennia, of boredom and status quo, I proposed a game for us to play. The rules are simple. Whoever racks up the most souls during a specified time period is the winner. Certain types of souls earn bonus points, as the exorcist's just did for me. Each time I win, He has to uncreate one of His seven days of Creation that I choose. Each time He wins, He can restore one. Or, if all seven are in place, He can select a punishment for me from a list. This includes a decade of celibacy, a year of listening to non-stop country music and other horrors.

I won the first time we played and chose to eliminate Day Seven. The Sabbath, day of rest. The day itself still exists, of course, but its function is shot to hell, so to speak. Blue laws have been repealed. Liquor stores and malls are open. Attendance at religious services is drastically down. It has worked out very well for me.

I carefully consider. I do not want to select a day that would eliminate the world or its humans, since I am enjoying them so much. Although, if I keep winning, it will eventually come to that.

I choose Day Five, when He created the fish and the birds.

"Tell You what, though," I say to Him, "I'll give You a break. Keep the birds around. Just get rid of the fish. I've always hated fish."

Nunavut Thunderfuck

Dale L. Sproule

I was chillin solo at the club, three hours before opening, when I heard the brap of an iron dog on its last legs. Went out to find Anyu Kigutaq, just sittin there on his retro Ski-Doo, in the middle of an ice storm. So I grabbed him by the hood of his parka and dragged him in the side door.

"What the fuck you doin out there, kid?"

Tell the truth, I knew Anyu was coming and had an idea why. Thanks to my bro, DJ Crispy Kay, we got taps and spy-cams at three separate police detachments. He got access while workin security for Baffin Hydro, when they were runnin the power lines from Jaynes Inlet. He da power bear. Even designed and installed our 'industrial perimeter harpoon rig round the welcome mat at the old lab. Durin the long darkness, if somebody we didn't like came snoopin - presto - they were on an instant fucking ice cube floating into Hudson Straight. Smart motherfucker, my brother.

But still, he's a polar bear, so his employment options are limited.

After he stopped opening and closing his jaws to thaw out his facial muscles, Anyu said, "Nice to see you too, Tulok."

I didn't make a habit of consorting with humans, but Anyu's old man Karpok and I went way back. When I was living with my sister on the fringes of Dorset City, he was yard supervisor on the night shift at the dump. Turned a blind eye when Manny the Fox and I put some heat on a gang of lemmings to honeycomb under the bear fence, so we could run a big culvert, eh? That was some concession we had - movin

103

upward of eighty kilos of meat scraps every day, all summer long. Karpok even gave us the heads up when the Nunavut Sanitation Authority twigged our scam and came to plug the hole.

So, I liked to help out his family when I could. And Anyu was always kinda special. True, half the humans in Cape Dorset who can hold a hammer end up sculpting, but he's one of the truly talented ones. Previous summer, he came out on a mission.

"All the sculpture galleries want dancing bears these days, eh? Walking bears - dime a dozen - but dancing ones are the shit. Problem is, I've never seen a bear dance. I need live models and I heard there were a couple sows out here who could boogaloo like nobody's business."

"Whoa, whoa. Round here, you don't call em sows unless you wanna wear your nanooks as a necklace."

"Wha...?"

"Sedna's an equal partner in the club and she thinks the word 'sow' is misogynist bullshit. 'Bear-assed bigotry', she calls it. And that don't cut no ice with her, eh? As for the dancing? Ask her to boogaloo, she'll tell you to watch the *Jungle Book*. But she'll be happy to freestyle for ya. Maybe throw in a little lockin and poppin."

Turns out my warnings were unnecessary, cause Anyu and Sedna got on like a house on fire. Wood frame house - not an igloo, eh? So, anyway, last I heard, he was makin a killin with his dancin bear sculptures.

"What brings you back here in the middle of winter?" I asked, this time in a considerably less friendly tone than I greeted him in the summer. "Got some heavy-duty ursine kink going on, kid?"

"Lemme lubricate you, Tulok. You drinkin Canadian?"

"Blood," I deadpanned.

He gave me a gap-toothed grin.

"If it were blood, your muzzle would be covered with it, steada just foam."

I grabbed the front of his parka and pulled him real close.

"Polar bear foaming at the mouth ain't no fucking joke, kid. We can smell you from three glaciers away." I licked my teeth for emphasis. "Come evening, there will be twenty starvin bros in here. Think it'll be a cakewalk keeping you off the menu? Winter's no time for polaroids."

"They're not polaroids. I have a digital camera."

"I know. Just a polar bear joke... never mind." Embarrassed at my lameness, I got straight to the point, "Nobody comes out here for a joyride in minus fuckin fifty."

I leaned forward menacingly.

"I know for a fact you're working for the Dorset Metro Police. I was told they caught you and Gilbert Etok with a kilo of sour diesel at the airport. That little cooler is crawlin with po-pos - what were you thinkin?"

"Thought the jar was vacuum sealed. It's Colorado hard goods, medical-grade. One of your bear buddies musta sniffed it out."

I raised my eyebrows skeptically, but he didn't miss a beat.

"My uncle's sitting in the territorial legislature, eh? He's gonna introduce a Medical Marijuana bill. Maybe we can change the law before my conviction comes down."

"Good luck with that," I said.

Anyu held up the palms of his sealskin mittens.

"Hey, you can't lecture me about selling pot while you're running a meth lab. Look, I don't deny that the Mounties busted us. And told me they'd let me off if I helped bust your operation in return. But I'm not here for that. You're my illamar - my buddy. So I actually came to warn ya."

"Spill already!" I growled.

"When I was at the cop shop, there was another guy there, sittin' in the captain's office, eh? An elder with one arm. I asked about him but nobody answered. Just traded these spooky stares, like the guy was freakin them out. When they put me back in lockup, my buddy Gilbert's there, eh? He asks me, 'Did you see him? 'See who?' I says.

And buddy says, 'Torngasuk'. And I say, 'Fuck you. Torngasuk's not real.'"

As Anyu was telling me his story, we heard a voice from somewhere inside the club.

"Oh, but I am."

"Who's there?" I shouted, kickin' my chair outta the way as I stood. How could I have not smelled him?

"It's me, Torngasuk." This feeble old one-armed man steps into the light.

"How'd you get in here?" I demanded.

"Rode on the back of Anyu's iron dog and followed you guys in. But I was invisible, so neither of you could see me. The Mounties didn't know where your base was, but they figured Anyu here would come to warn you. And they were right."

"So *that's* why I ran outta gas!" exclaimed Anyu. "Carrying the extra weight."

"No. You ran outta gas because you forgot to fill the tank, you blubber head," says Torngasuk. "You're always too stoned."

I gave him my steeliest glare.

"Okay, so you're here. What now?"

"I'm supposed to bring you to justice, eh?"

"For what?"

The old shaman shrugged. "Breaking the taboos, of course."

"Whose taboos? The Mounties? Whose side you playin on?"

"A taboo's a taboo! You're cookin crystal meth and selling it to our children."

"I just run a nightclub." I shook my head. "Welcome to Sedna's Dance Emporium. Feel free to look around, eh? You wanna drink?"

"Don't usually imbibe. But I been livin up on Ellesmere Island by myself for so fuckin long...."

"Got Polar Ice Vodka," I said.

He shivered visibly. "I'm thinkin a hot toddy. Or maybe a Mai Tai?"

"Our bartender comes in at two-thirty. But I can get you a coconut rum." I poured him a double and brought the bottle to the table.

Torngasuk sat down and we debated the word taboo and talked about the white man's hypocrisy.

"*If* I *was* cookin meth," I remember saying early in the conversation. "Who could blame me? Seal hunting is all but impossible. They say, in the old days, you could stack bowhead whales eight deep before one of those ice floes would crack. That true?"

Torngasuk shrugged. "I never stacked any bowheads."

I rolled my eyes and carried on with my rant.

"Anyway, ice like that is rarer than auk feathers these days. Try to get close to a breathing hole, guy my size would pop through the ice like a card slidin into a cash machine. Sneak up on a seal, my hairy ass! Might as well go krumpin on plate glass. And nobody can out-swim those fuckers in open water."

Torngasuk pushes his empty glass toward me, so I pour him some more and keep talkin.

"So, there's half our food supply gone, eh? What's a bear supposed to eat these days? They shoot us if we go into the dumps, get all pissy if we compete with em for the caribou. Woulda loved to get in the family business - kill seals and pretty much anything else I can sink my claws into. But it's not viable, eh? So now I run this joint, and I make lotsa cash, so I don't need to do anything *taboo*."

Don't know that I was convincing him of anything but it felt good to get that shit off my chest.

"The Mounties intercepted a package to your cousin," said the old shaman.

"Which cousin?" I asked. With just 13 sub-populations in North America, I have more than a few cousins. So I could believably plead ignorance. It's not like I put a return address on Zed's packages.

Zed used to be a popular attraction at the Chief Saunooke Bear Park in the Carolinas. A little undignified, for sure. He couldn't go for a shit without some little kid pointing and laughing. But, to tell the truth, he loves all those insecure townies marveling at the size of his dick. When they shut the place down, he put in for a transfer to that Danish zoo, figuring he'd be in line next time they decided to feed a giraffe to the predators. Never tasted giraffe, eh? Instead, they shipped him off to some little game farm in Two-Farts, Saskatchewan.

He got depressed and started hibernating with the brown bears - till he began hearing rumors that there was some *Kill Bill* 'Pussy Wagon' action going down. That sticking their dicks into a live polar bear had become something of a coming of age ritual for the locals. He swore never to sleep again. When he asked me if I'd got anything that could keep him alert, I sent him a freebie.

Course, I didn't tell any of this to our friend, Torngasuk. But I did keep refilling his glass. He was still there when the customers started coming in and it was nearly midnight before he passed out.

We sat around the table, looking at the shaman flopped unconscious across the table. Sedna had joined us by that point, and she wasn't impressed.

"Why don't we just eat him?" She suggested.

I gave a skeptical look.

"Hmmmm. He *is* a god. So it could backfire."

"What are you saying? He'd give us gas or diarrhea?"

"At the very least," I nodded. "He might even repeat on us in other ways. Ya know, come back to possess us or smite us, somehow."

"He doesn't look that powerful to me," Sedna said. "Couldn't even grow back that arm."

"And he *has* been marinating in coconut rum," I observed.

"Oh, come on, guys. That's gross," Anyu protested. "And not a good idea. Might even be a trap. That may be exactly what he wants you to do."

"You got a better suggestion?" I asked, stomach rumbling. With all this talk about a late-night snack, Anyu was looking pretty tasty.

"Might be better to just imprison him somehow. Build a tomb out of ice and set him adrift."

"What with global warming, he could be melted by April."

"By which time he'll be a long swim from anywhere."

I gave Sedna a side-eye and saw her nodding.

"Okay fine. Let's get er done before he sobers up, eh?"

The igloo we built was like a bank vault. Took six bears to push it out into open water. We watched until the current picked it up and it started moving faster. We were just about to go back inside when Anyu nudged me.

"What's that? Got any binoculars?"

"No," I said, "But your camera has a zoom lens."

"Oh yeah!" After a minute, he gasped 'Holy shit' and started snapping pictures like crazy.

"What's going on? Let me look," Sedna and were both bugging him.

"Oh man," said Anyu. "He's working some old-time transformation mojo! He just turned into a narwhal and he's using the tusk like a jigsaw. Cutting a hole in the top of the vault."

At which point, Sedna grabbed the camera from him.

"Sonofabitch! Now he's turning into a bird!"

"Press the button," Anyu cried. "Take some pictures!"

She scowled at him but I could hear the click, click, click.

"I think it's a snowy owl," Sedna said. "No, wait. It's w-a-a-ay bigger than that. Some kind of white thunderbird or something."

"Whoa." I was suddenly able to see it with the naked eye, as it flew in our direction. "We could be screwed now."

Then I noticed something else.

"Do you know Gilbert Etok's brother?" I nudged Anyu.

"Christian?"

I nodded.

"Didja hear about the trouble he got in when he was a kid? Animal cruelty. He soaked bread in booze and fed it to the gulls and terns down at the harbor."

"What's so cruel about that?" Sedna asked.

"Well, birds and booze don't go well together, eh?" We watched the big white thunderbird swerve erratically over the water. "They kept flying into the rocks…"

As I explained, Torngusuk swung abruptly toward the ice cliffs. Unable to slow down or stop, he smacked headfirst into a wall of ice, splatting like some blood filled mosquito on a windshield.

"Ewww," said Anyu.

"Told ya we shoulda ate him," Sedna shrugged. "What a waste."

Blood poured down the jagged cliff face, forming an asymmetrical Rorschach blot - an arrow pointing straight at the entrance to our lab.

I shook my head.

"We'd better get that place cleaned out before the Mounties show up, or we could lose the whole batch."

"I can hook you up with my pot dealer, eh?" Anyu suggested. "They got a new strain called 'Nunavut Thunderfuck.' If ya swim down to pick it up, we can avoid the airport altogether."

And that's how Anyu and I became partners. We've been doin pretty good. If ya wanna see his transformation sculpture *Torngasuk Intersecting with the 21st Century*, it's on permanent display in our new ice hotel up at Iqaluit. I'm the one who came up with the inscription on the base.

'The old Gods ain't nothing to be afraid of. It's the new ones you gotta look out for'.

Wamid!

Ken Hueler

Exiting the library, I stop, appalled. Behind a parked car's rear wheels, lying like a dropped rag, is a drunk. Three teen boys are taking turns jumping their bikes over him, as a girl records on her phone. I storm back into the atrium which, dependably, contains at least one security guard. But, by the time we emerge, the teens have evaporated. As the guard rousts the sleeper, I assess: Lot of good meat on that body, and pre-marinated, too. Alas, one must respect the living.

After checking behind my van for nappers, I drive - under the speed limit, of course - to the funeral home.

O'Hare's face slides from unctuous to alarmed. Every time I appear, he reacts as if a ghost has finally thought to haunt him for his crimes. But what modern person still believes in ghosts? A funeral director certainly shouldn't.

"I've come to claim a relative, Mr O'Hare. Do you happen to have any?"

The man nods and ducks through a door. I follow, annoyed as always, by his lack of an invitation. So rude! The Department of Transitional Assistance pays his funeral home one thousand dollars per unclaimed body and, since the bare expense for a burial is triple that, each corpse I accept means pure profit for O'Hare. Some measure of respect ought to be accorded me!

O'Hare stops at the freezers. Inside, society's forgotten leftovers await kin, or me, to claim them.

111

"I have two that might suit your tastes," he purrs.

He'd better please my palate. I am taking a loss off his hands. I select the youngish, plump woman.

The doorbell rings insistently. Panicked, I leave the woman on the basement stairs, compose myself and throw open the front door, like a man who has nothing to hide.

It's the phone girl from the library.

I keep my appearance calm but for a trembling rictus simper. How did she find me?

"Yes?"

She unlocks her phone with a thumb, skips across icons, and turns the screen to me. O'Hare and I are loading the corpse into my van. It auto repeats. Now I am cold and sweating.

"We followed your slow ass. My grandma drives faster'n you. Can we come in?"

I see the other three teens across the street, astride their bikes. I nod.

She waves, and two walk their bikes over.

"This is John and Richard," the girl announces, "We're also leaving a lookout. So, no funny business."

Bikes clatter onto the porch. The girl snaps a picture of my face as she pushes past.

"Taking Elsa's phone won't do anything," the gawky redhead stammers. "It backs up to the cloud."

Then the teens are in my house. My sanctuary.

"What do you have to drink?" the blond boy asks. He's broad, athletic.

All I can offer are water, juice, and, of course, the cordials and liqueurs. The blond removes the stopper from my rosemary liqueur, sniffs, then vomits onto my clean linoleum. No one else requests a drink.

The arrogant blond is sucking down tap water to calm his stomach. The gawky one seems as terrified as I am.

"So," says the girl called Elsa. "What's a law-loving citizen like you doing with a corpse?"

What can I say? I panic, tell them I'm a medical student who can't afford tuition for anatomy classes. But my lie is so bald, so disjointed, so illogical, that I can't even finish it. I take them downstairs, hoping to trap them. Then I remember I have a corpse. I can fix this. I just need to find a way to lure that last teen inside.

"Go ahead," Elsa says.

I stare at her.

"What you normally do." She waves her phone. "You can wear a mask if you want, but we want to see it."

"It'll kick everyone else's ass," the blond adds. "That's for sure,"

"Whose asses?" I ask, confused. I had assumed they intended blackmail.

The girl smirks.

"John parkour jumps on buildings with a GoPro and we do things like knockouts and bike leaping over drunks and crap. But whatever you're into will slam the competition. So, go nuts, perv. Unless you want to explain your deal to the police."

I carry the corpse to the table. The trio are watching, waiting, filming.

"Pretend we're not here," Elsa laughs.

I nod, trapped. I take a deep breath, lift an arm, sniff for preservatives in case O'Hare got forgetful again, and bite hard. My shame deepens upon hearing the celery-crunch of ice crystals. An unthawed body! I am a disgrace. What would my peers think?

The two males avert their faces and back away but not Elsa. As I take the second bite, she cries out.

"Holy shit! No one's gonna believe this."

Blond John vomits up the water.

Alone again, I sit in my study, refreshing the computer screen. Finally, it appears. Me, my meal, my shame. Most of my fellow ghouls have adapted to the modern world, so how long until one stumbles across this?

Is that Wamid eating a corpse on YouTube? A frozen *corpse?*

A ghoul's existence must be private and unobserved. We are not loved. That is why so many of us have emigrated across the globe, to lands that do not expect us.

Wamid's folly risks exposing us all. He must be killed, they will say.

None of those scattered loners know where I live, but with this motivation, will they search? Maybe I can escape. Maybe.

I drink to make the world seem a better place, knowing it will not be. Rewatching the clip, I decide that, despite my unhappy expression and slightly disheveled hair, I don't look so bad after all.

Morning. I examine myself in the mirror: My features have softened, my hair lightened to blonde. I can leave now and not be recognized.

"Thank you," I say through to floor to the body downstairs. After breakfast, I've started gathering my essential belongings when the doorbell rings. The police? Neighbors with torches?

No, it's the jittery geek, who Elsa introduced yesterday as Richard. On being greeted with the dead woman's face and body, he flees. Five minutes later, he returns with Elsa. She's got more nerve, this one.

"Ghouls," I explain. "Take on the form of the most recently eaten."

She studies my face.

"You've still got the weird eyebrows and that little birthmark on your chin."

"Every ghoul retains unique features throughout the changes. Those are two of mine."

"Well, you're a hit, freak. Biggest thing we've posted. We doubled our views before we got taken down but Richard scored a spot on the dark web."

"Can you come back later? I'm rather busy..."

Elsa spies the suitcases and shoves past.

"John - the blond guy - took a pic of your license plate, so don't even. We need content, so be ready or be busted."

Elsa and Richard make me help carry their equipment into my basement. As usual, the lookout loiters outside. Later, John arrives, twitchy and suspicious - and filming commences.

Fresh corpses are not bad: they taste like pork. I know because I do eat human food whenever my grave-robbing has been discovered, or when I have just moved to a new location and have yet to learn the lay. But nothing compares to the honeyed warmth of decomposing flesh. Otherwise, why live this life? I've tried. Let beef sit on the counter for days. Gobbled down old roadkill. But flesh that's marinated in soul is what I crave. Nothing compares. Absolutely nothing.

It's not enough that, because of my transformation, the woman appears to be eating herself: The teens suggest I also chew open-mouthed and, though the crassness offends me, I oblige.

I am debased. A wretch.

At least the corpse has defrosted.

"The eyeball," Elsa mouths from behind her camera.

Richard works on his laptop, editing Monday's shoot and adding graphics. John helped set up the lighting but left before filming. The previous week he kept throwing up, which Elsa liked as background ambience. Now he refuses to stay. She confided that he no longer bounces around buildings anymore. He's terrified, finally, by mortality and worried I'll treat him like 'street pizza', as he calls it. I love that term and often work it into conversations.

I hook an eye out with a finger and stare back at it, displeased. Elsa forced me to get a new corpse when the old one started stinking.

"Go! Go!" she whispers.

It pops between my teeth like a cherry tomato, which is fine, I suppose. Yet eyes taste better aged, when they can be slurped from their sockets like oysters.

I lack enthusiasm but they cheer nonetheless.

"We're *so* bad," Elsa gloats afterwards. "Can you get a new corpse for next week?"

Humiliation boils over.

"I loathe fresh meat! Corpses must ripen, like cheese or wine."

Richard looks queasy.

I rush to the corner, jerk off the concealing blankets. A moment's work unseals the coffin's metal lid, and the escaping air rustles through my hair. The scent, to me, is like opening an oven door and getting hit with the promise of a meal worth eating. The humans clear the room in seconds. Later, I clean their vomit.

Why can't they clean their own vomit?

I looked better this week. Not so cowed, except when I first tried to avoid eating the eye. The comments are positive.

psycho some attic: 2 hours ago
First! You outdid yourself, man. I almost hurled.

destinys childs 2: hours ago
Your sick in all senses of the word.

I look up the definitions of 'sick' and am oddly pleased. I start using that term around the teens.

Several weeks later, my corpse has matured. In the edited footage, I appear happy and relaxed. If I must be humiliated, I should enjoy it. That's fair, right?

slap happy: 10 minutes ago
First!

Elsa leans over my shoulder.

"We need some fresh twist. Hey, I'd love to see you chew balls. Or a new corpse, maybe?"

I do have a new corpse. I just haven't told her because she'd make me eat him too soon. Instead, a few days later, she interviews me. Richard reluctantly mans the camera. He no longer speaks to me.

"How do you find your victims?" She's wearing a masquerade eye mask and a smirk.

"I don't have victims. I only eat the dead, who are beyond victimizing."

"I'm not sure their relatives would agree."

She's needling me, hoping for a reaction. I've been surfing the internet more and more and I'll admit, to my shame, I'm drawn to the trolling and hysteria as much as anyone. No, Elsa. I will, instead, be engaging and interesting - not a spectacle.

"Ghouls believe in souls and we are sworn to harm nothing that has one. Yet, once dead, a human's soul has either left the body or, if you are a cynic, never existed."

She nods, considering.

"Isn't that rather convenient, your belief? I mean, not killing means you fly under the legal radar, am I right?"

I bob my head agreeably, although I'm experiencing physical discomfort.

"True, true. We specialize in eating corpses and looting their graves. Unlike, say, vampires or werewolves - who kill the living and lose interest afterwards. But I think you'll agree ghouls are nobler. Corpses are insensate; they do not suffer pain or succumb to terror. And, as I said, once souls depart their mortal coil, they leave a wonderf... *sick*... aftertaste."

I smile.

"You should try some. Wouldn't joining me for a slice of street pizza make a good video? You could offer a human's opinion."

"If you taste soul - and what does soul taste like? - doesn't that mean it's still in there? Do you absolutely know it's gone, or is it just a con?"

She's burying me under questions, keeping me too busy to circle back to my offer. Very well, but I keep it in reserve.

"Remove a tea bag from a mug. Can you say the bag remains because you taste the leaves? I think not. A soul tastes…" I pause, thinking, "You have no spice or herb to compare - like sunshine filtered through honey, is the best I can do. And like honey can ripen into mead…"

She opens her mouth to interrupt.

"…Again, you can join me. I'll even get a fresh corpse, if you like."

I am becoming more uncomfortable, an unfortunate side effect of my meals.

"You've changed genders several times since I met you. What are you? I mean, originally?"

I pause, stumped. I've been on Earth so long, eaten so many corpses, I actually don't recall.

"I have a man's name, so I must have been a man."

"Which gender do you prefer?"

I detect a challenge. I'm ancient, and modern nuances can perplex me, especially gender roles.

"I enjoy both. As a man, I get more respect and fewer challenges. But, as a woman, I find people are more solicitous and friendly."

"Really? As a woman…"

Finally, I cannot suppress it any longer.

Even to me, the stench of digested corpse farts offends. Elsa ends the interview, fleeing off-camera, though Richard has the presence of mind to pan and film the careless splatter of vomit bouncing off her legs and coating my stairs.

And, just yesterday, she bragged her stomach was getting stronger

;)

"A cooking segment?" Elsa sips her Coke, taps a fingernail on the can.

"Yes," I blurt, with what I hope is infectious enthusiasm. "Me in the kitchen sharing my favorite recipes. I don't always eat off the skeleton. I think we should vary our content. People found the interview - abrupt as it was - most illuminating."

"Can you use a new corpse? I think that dude's about done and a fresh face couldn't hurt."

"I already..."

Wait, did she mean *my* temporary face? Is she hinting I should be choosing more telegenic corpses?

"I got one two weeks ago. He's buried between the herb garden and the shed."

She's annoyed I haven't told her until now, I can tell. I don't take orders as well as her boys.

Blue bedsheets duct-taped over the window dye my kitchen aquamarine. Elsa, wearing her mask, stands beside me at the prep island. She insisted.

"We're back," she announces. "And our ghoulish gourmet wants to share some of - his? - favorite recipes. What have you got for us today, Wamid?"

I almost scream. She used my name! I'll force Richard to bleep it.

"I have many fine dishes to share, but today I'm starting simple, with a cordial."

"I didn't realize you could make alcohol out of a body."

"Humans have fermented meat for thousands of years. Do you enjoy salami and sausage?"

"Who doesn't?"

I decide I don't care about my name. My fellow ghouls, if they are aware of my show, will have identified my permanent features. That is why we have them, I suppose. To recognize one another.

"First, you need some fresh flesh. I picked this up yesterday."

"Really? When?"

I open the fridge and pull out the large Tupperware container.

"Now, there are various methods, but I find a pressure cooker works best."

I slide the lidless device into view.

"Why a pressure cooker? Are we going to heat it?"

"No. The meat releases gas and other containers tend to burst or even explode. Alternately, you can also seal a whole corpse in a metal coffin and, later, tap in a spigot - like collecting syrup from a maple tree. Next, place a cross-wire canning rack inside."

"Why?"

Why does she keep interrupting me? No one clicks to hear *her*.

"It allows juice to collect on the bottom. Now we rub in a little salt. Salt releases water from the meat and binds it, so water is present but inhospitable to most bacteria. That leaves the way clear for lactic acid-producing bacteria, which we *do* want. And that acid kills any harmful bacteria which does get a foothold. I'm adding less salt than a human would recommend,"

I start sprinkling.

"And less powdered lactic acid, as well. I don't want an easy bio-logical victory because the residue is best after a really good war."

I drop the meat onto the rack and crank the lid tight.

"Into my bedroom this will go, like a scented candle, to encourage pleasant dreams." I lift the other pressure cooker into view. "Now, a few weeks ago, I started this batch."

"Wait. You said to use fresh meat. Which means yet another corpse. When did you get that one?"

Elsa is gloriously outraged, as I had hoped. I smile as I unseal the lid. She covers her nose.

"The meat will make a good stew later." I transfer it with tongs in-to the Tupperware container and set an empty vodka bottle on the counter.

"Could you hold the funnel?"

She doesn't flinch as I pour the clear liquid.

"Very good. Now, a flavoring. Fruit is always nice, but let's do a savory one. Bay leaf is classic."

I stuff leaves inside until the liquid rises to the lip.

"Infuse too long and the taste spoils, so I'll decant in a day, two at maximum." I swap the bottle with one waiting on the windowsill behind the sheet. "This make-ahead has steeped two days."

I set a bowl on the counter and pour, using a sieve to collect the bay leaves, and then repeat through a thin cotton cloth. I transfer the liquid to a smaller bottle.

"Care for a sniff, Elsa?" There. I've used *her* name.

She wrinkles her nose but does.

"Not so bad. Guess my stomach is getting stronger."

I set two sherry glasses on the counter. Fill both.

"Not so bad at all. This may be an acquired taste..."

I extend a glass. She doesn't take it.

"One sip. A tiny degustation so you can offer a human's evaluation."

Reluctantly, she accepts. We clink, and as I down my drink, she takes the daintiest of sips.

What a reaction! (: O= = =X

"Absolutely not!"

Elsa frowns. "Why? I can even help you load."

I wave the suggestion away.

"I'm inhumanly strong. Corpses are just ungainly, that's all. Listen, O'Hare must not know of our broadcast, otherwise he would never allow me back. And should his face be recognized?..."

My normally cautious temperament roars into terror.

"What if someone recognizes one of our corpses? Officials trace the path to O'Hare. O'Hare betrays me. Vengeful ghouls catch the news."

"Okay, calm down." She sags. "Would have been nice to film you selecting a vic... eh... body."

She crosses her arms, bonier than when we first met.

"So, if not that, what? If you give people same-same, they just re-watch favorites."

I ponder. The cooking show went down well but Elsa is dragging on approving a second episode. She knows she'd be expected to try whatever I make and doesn't seem game. What can I do that does not entail untenable risk? I like this feeling of celebrity and want to nurture it. Yet, it's also a trap: I can no longer go outside without first transforming into a still-anonymous corpse-body. And I can only enjoy fame from afar. No pressing flesh with fans, no magazine covers beaming from supermarket kiosks, no bacchanalian parties, no libidinous devotees. But... perhaps I can experience some of that adulation with people who know me.

"Elsa, I'm making us famous."

She nods. "Yeah?"

"Would you consent to sex?"

She backs up three steps.

"What the hell is wrong with you? No! Ew!"

"I can switch genders if you like."

She is running up the steps.

"Okay, do you think Richard might?... no, I'm not that desperate."

And I'm not, I tell myself as I pour a drink and sit to brainstorm.

"I am loved," I tell the empty basement. "By many."

I only see Richard briefly now. After he sets up the equipment, he disappears upstairs to watch whatever movies I've checked out (he's begun to appreciate my taste in the classics). His editing has become minimal - perfunctory, I would say - and bare of graphics, noticeably so to the commenters. John, I'm told, has descended into debilitating paranoia, fearing I will display his naked, desecrated corpse to the world as I eat him. I confess I have been jotting down ideas for a piz-za-themed cooking segment starring John. Penis pepperoni, anyone?

But Elsa? She clings grimly on. What are she and I striving for? We cannot flaunt our fame. We'd be incarcerated immediately. Worse, my fellow ghouls are no doubt, by now, wise and eager to erase those who are exposing them. Any day, they might throng down my basement stairs and end us. Me, they will not eat. Ghouls have no souls; we taste foul. I will just die, cease to exist.

Not harming a being housing a soul is our tenet but how much can Elsa and Richard trust my kind not to make an exception? The teens will carry memories of their interesting demise to the afterlife, if such there be.

So, where are our efforts leading? I want to ask Elsa the endgame. But I'm afraid, if I do and she cannot answer, everything will deflate. We've come so far.

I think, like me, Elsa knows this could destroy her. But we're do-ing something, aren't we? Most people will never be remembered. Who will forget me? Books will be written. Maybe films made. If not, features based on our crimes, then documentaries. And each time a video's view count springs upward and the comment crowd cheers, does that thrill Elsa as much as me? I can't tell. But I know neither of us has the upper hand right now. We still need one another.

I shake my head and smile at Elsa. Why am I gloomy? The free-dom! Only my fellow ghouls know who I really am and none my location. I float above the law, above the norms. I, who have spent my centuries blending and hiding, am free!

"I would love to eat someone famous, even once, to say I did it. Yet the famous are different. You can't sneak around Forest Lawn and not expect to get caught. Do you two have ideas on how we might pull off something like that? Not a beloved celebrity, but someone people have heard of and don't think about until they learn they are dead - after which they go back to forgetting them."

"You're off the rails," Richard says. "This isn't cool anymore."

"Yes, it is, Richard," Elsa snaps, "And we're going to keep it that way. But Wamid's right. Too risky. Keep brainstorming."

My dear Elsa, you are our rock.

In the library, I run my finger across spines, hoping a title will spark inspiration. Yesterday I had suggested we do another interview but, despite no risk to herself, Elsa dismissed that. Our quarrel ended with me storming out of my own basement and slamming my bedroom door. After later reflection, gently assisted by cordials, I decided to insist I be permitted to vary my repertoire, enrich it. But I also realized that Elsa has valid points: Viewers do need a reason to click and, by offering only slight changes on what I'm already doing, I'd test their attention. By going bigger I'd, at some point, exhaust the limit or fall into self-parody.

I had another revelation before passing out. Elsa seeks to dictate and make the decisions because I am the star. And, like the talentless partner she is, she must create the illusion of irreplaceability.

How can I reinvent myself? I need something new, novel...

A book! I should write one. I couldn't profit, of course, but it might increase my fame. I have not lived as vivid a life as some of my kind. I'm as lackluster as basement-dwelling Richard, compared to most ghouls. Ah, the sick stories my compatriots shared back in the old country, before we were so far-flung... those were the days. Adventures, near-captures, rampant excesses. Too bad that wasn't me. I was never invited to a brain-eating contest, but oh, the stories!

Then I realize I can make those tales mine. Describe them as my own. What could the other ghouls do? Take me to court? Admit the atrocities and crimes are theirs? I, not they, will get credit if I get there first! I imagine coming to this library, seeing my book and books about me, lining the shelves.

Giddy, I drift outside to a bench, watching bodies pass. What do these people want? How can I give it to them? When they start to blur into an undifferentiated mass, I blink to clear my head and drive home.

"You can't have the password," Elsa repeats.

"I have all kinds of ideas. I want to make posts, reply to comments."

The teens wear joyless faces, like aging strippers financing an addiction. I should run things. I have enthusiasm. I am alive with possibility.

"You've got some interesting ideas," Elsa admits, "But some of the… who's going to compete against you in a brain-eating championship? Or a body parts blind taste test? Not me. So no, you don't get the password."

Richard and the absent John won't give it to me, either. She runs those boys.

She runs me, too, but must realize how easy I would be to lose. And there she would be, the woman who supported an artist to stardom, only to be unceremoniously dumped for someone fresh. A new start. Yes, that's what I need. A fresh start. A new place. Control my own content. My narrative.

That would be… hella sick.

Elsa returns from upstairs to find Richard duct-taped to a chair. She's so scatterbrained lately, she doesn't register his rag-muffled cries until I'm at her.

"I have a new idea," I gush, waving the knife. "Part of it involves Richard."

"We have a lookout," she whispers. "If he… we… don't come out…"

She has no follow up. She's smart, realizes I must have thought it through. I gently remove her eye mask.

"Time for you to be famous," I coo. I place a flashlight and a charged GoPro cam beside her in the coffin.

"You can broadcast your experience. Talk to our fans. Go out on top. Don't waste oxygen telling viewers where to find you. I'll not be posting your segment until next week. Anyway, the landlord will find you once I stop paying rent. So focus on giving the performance of your life."

She is still beating on the lid as I tighten the last screw. Wasn't she listening? Such a waste. Her screams and struggles only make her breathe harder, which will shorten her time. I worry she hasn't even turned on the camera.

I unlock the phone with her thumb and change the passcode. I hear Elsa mumbling, so perhaps she's appreciated the big picture after all.

"Okay, Richard," I say, pulling out his gag, "no more being the invisible geek in the basement. Now is your moment."

"You can't harm the living!"

"Those who censure me for that would kill me anyway, given my previous crimes." I hold up the phone. "I promise to gift you fifteen famous minutes."

"I have a soul!"

I smile.

"If you want to honor my beloved fans, put on a good show." I smooth a stray wisp of his hair. "Ready?"

I shower, pack and load the van. I text their lookout.

It's OK. Wamid getting new 'friend'.

I press the garage door opener and cruise past the lad. How long before he realizes? A few blocks later, I text John.

Where r u? Wanna hook up ==>(/)

He's home alone, it turns out. The geek was lucky. Too scrawny. But John is muscled and big and young and available. And, because he's feared me so and looked down on me, I take great satisfaction in his expression when I, not Elsa, arrive.

"Ready to jump back on the fame train?"

He's stronger than the other two, but I am a ghoul. Soon he is enveloped in tarp, peacefully dozing eternity away in the back of my van. I have a day, maybe two, to find a new residence before he becomes noticeable to passers-by.

I zip out of the suburban labyrinth of pokey cars, to a highway on-ramp. Life is good: Unclaimed bodies tend to be middle-aged at best, and John will give me time as young and handsome. I should do a self-interview while thus bodied. As I begin composing questions, I pull over to let the screaming police car pass.

It stops behind my van. Why? I've given no reason for the police to notice me. My tag is current. My lights work. I lower the window, clutch the wheel. Was I driving too fast? I did feel euphoric. Might that have translated to carelessness?

One of the two policemen exits the car and approaches.

"Know how fast you were going?"

"No. I mean, I was keeping pace with the other cars…"

His expression changes.

"You don't keep pace with people by passing them. Where you headed?"

"Home," I blurt. No, I can do this. I can be charming. I need to get him on my side.

"Someone almost sideswiped me changing lanes. I guess I'm a little unnerved. I'm sure you've seen that. People all jittery. I guess I should have stopped."

I'm babbling. I wait for his assessment. He's examining my face. I become warmly aware of my eyebrows, my birthmark.

The officer's curious expression remains. He glances at his patrol car and then leans closer.

"I just want you to know, Mr Wamid, I'm a big fan of what you do… but my partner's watching and there's a dashcam. So, could you step out of the car and keep your hands in view?"

Manny

Anthea Middleton

I pointed at a shadowy outline in the flat across the street.

"What is that?"

Emma gave me a cursory 'hmmmm?' - not even pretending to re-direct her attention from the TV.

"In the window across the street. Come and look!"

She finally turned her head.

"The only thing I see is a creepy woman spying on her neighbours."

"I don't spy on our neighbours. I see our neighbours sometimes and this is weird and worth your attention."

With what I considered a largely unnecessary sigh, she dragged herself up and over to the window. I pointed again at the flat in question. Directly opposite, first floor, classic Edinburgh tenement bay window, mirroring our own.

"The hell is that?"

"I told you."

The room was almost entirely bare, save for one solitary manne-quin, right in the centre.

"Did they move and we didn't notice?" Emma asked. "Pretty sure there was furniture there before."

"The furniture is your concern? What about the creepy lifeless tor-so?"

"Does he have a face?" Emma jammed her own face against our window to get a closer look. "It's too dark. Let's go over and see."

129

I hesitated.

"It's very late. And cold."

Emma was already throwing on her puffy jacket.

"You're afraid of a mannequin?"

"I'm... comfy. We could look in daylight."

She took my own jacket off the hook in the hall and thrust it into my hands. "Let's go."

Out on the street, I hugged my coat tight against the bitter wind. The window to number 10, normally a clear view from our flat, was blocked by a tree at ground level.

Inconclusive on the face-front.

We admitted defeat and reluctantly went back inside. Emma worked with a keen bird watcher and said she'd borrow his binoculars. A fairly rich statement, coming from someone accusing me of taking an excessive interest in our neighbours. But I didn't argue. I, too, wanted to know if our new stationary friend had a face.

The following evening, I got home from work to find her with our shutters almost closed and the lights off, staring through a tiny gap with her binoculars.

"Emma," I said. "You're creepier than the mannequin."

"I've called him Manny. He *doesn't* have a face. Just a kind of... facial indent."

She beckoned me over and passed the binoculars. She was right. Up close, he was a beige-coloured naked torso with a bald head. There were slopes and creases where features should be. His hollows stared back at me. Empty, just like the room where he stood. It had the same ornate white cornicing as ours, old panelled doors and a bare Edinburgh press. I could see a shadow where their fireplace probably was.

"Did he just move?" Emma's voice rose an octave. "He moved. I saw him."

"He did not move."

I knew he hadn't. So why did I shiver when she said it?

That night, every time I closed my eyes, he appeared. This was ridiculous. He was a lifeless mannequin. *It* was a lifeless mannequin. When I finally fell asleep, I dreamt about him. It. I dreamt about *it*.

Over the next few days, we kept a keen eye on number 10. The light was always on, the shutters open. But no one, apart from Manny, ever appeared.

"Wasteful on electricity," Emma tutted one evening. "They have that light on when I get up for work too. They're not even using the room."

"I'm going to go over there," I said suddenly.

Emma's eyes widened. "You can't!"

"Why?"

"It's dangerous!"

"It's an empty house with a limbless doll. I'm pretty sure that's a fight I'd win."

I said it with more bravado than I felt. But I needed to resolve this, once and for all.

"What if it's not empty? What are you going to say?"

I shrugged.

"Something like *what's with the mannequin?* Want to come?"

She shook her head.

"No. You can't go over to someone's house and ask what's with their mannequin. Suppose they think you're crazy?"

"I think they're crazy."

There was no persuading her, so I ventured across the street alone.

The huge red door had eight doorbells on the side, like ours. I scanned it for number 10. There was no name. Not that unusual. We had no name either, being a rental. I could feel my heart start to beat faster in my chest, so I pressed the buzzer before I could talk myself out of it.

Crackle. A pause.

"Hello?" said a female voice.

"Er, hi," I began. I suddenly realised I had, in no way, thought things through. "This is a bit weird but… I'm your neighbour from across the street and I just wanted to uh… to talk to you about something."

Silence, as she no doubt contemplated whether she was going to get murdered today.

"Okay, I guess… Want to come up?"

"Yes, please."

BUZZ.

I pushed the heavy door open, into the usual decrepit crack-den looking hallway that every single Edinburgh tenement seemed to have. The dark blue paint was peeling off the walls and there were various chunks missing from the plasterwork.

I was about to meet Manny.

I climbed the concrete stairs up to number 10, my breathing getting shallower and faster with each step. I tried to tell myself that the mystery was about to be solved. That I was disappointed this adventure would soon be over.

A woman in her thirties stood in the open doorway on the first floor, a warm yellowy light spilling into the hall behind her. She looked distinctly normal, with a ponytail, jeans and a cautious smile. Not like someone who'd have an empty room with a haunted mannequin.

"I'm Jane," she said. "Which flat are you living in?"

She stood aside to let me into her hallway, which was messy in a cosy way. Kind of like ours.

"Rachael. Number 41, directly across from you. I think we mirror each other. Which kind of brings me onto my question…"

Jane remained silent, letting me continue, a look of mild curiosity on her face.

"Well, it's a bit odd… But, basically, we can see into your sitting room and… It's been driving us crazy - me and my flatmate."

There was no good way to put it.

"What's with the mannequin?"

Jane squinted, confusion written all over her face.

"What mannequin?"

"Okay, I know it sounds like we're stalking you but I promise we aren't." I embellished the truth a little. "We can always see your sitting room because your shutters are open and it seems weird to have such a beautiful living space only being used for a mannequin. We've called him Manny."

"Um... I don't have a mannequin." Jane looked thoroughly bewildered.

"Yes you do! We've been looking at it every day. Sorry, that sounds crazy. We see it every day. From our sitting room."

"I really don't. You're welcome to look for yourself."

She walked over to a white panelled door, in the opposite spot to where ours would be. Opened it into her sitting room, switching on the light.

There was a couch, an armchair and an Edinburgh press overflowing with books and photos. Some house plants, three rugs, a flatscreen TV and a fancy stereo system. Her shutters were half-closed. Absolutely no Manny.

"What?" I stared at the room, completely baffled. "No, this is impossible..."

"Maybe you have the wrong flat?" she suggested. Are you sure it was number 10?"

"No, this is right. It's definitely right. Because look, you'll be able to see into *my* sitting room."

I pulled back her shutter to show her and my insides turned to ice.

The lights were on and my own shutters were open. But there was no furniture.

No Emma.

The only thing in the room was a beige mannequin.

Staring back at me with hollows for eyes.

In Our Own Realm We Are Lords

Cliff McNish

To be of the Shadow people is to be of the dark. It is to be obscure. To be faithfully oblique. To perspire in the willful gloom.

Even so, proudly shadowy as I am, it is embarrassing to have delayed so long before braving the light. We are all expected to do so at least once in our lifetime. Mother having to extract me from the damp wall and the grubs I was eating to forcibly shove me Upworld was... well, humiliating.

All the way up the byzantine curves of our family tunnels, my sister harried and poked me. And thus here I am, sliding out belly-first onto Forest's dreaded surface, mewling like a baby.

Strange, for should I not welcome this moment? Do our legends not state that the Original Darkness contained not just every shade and shadow of the dark, but its opposite - LIGHT - which thereupon spilled forth, cast jaggedly out like a child's nightmare? Therefore, surely, the creatures we see disturbingly transfixed up there, tethered to the light, belong in our loving embrace too. Why must we treat them with such disdain? Why, especially, must we hunt them so voraciously?

"Just fetch something back," my sister muttered, when I argued this again as she harried me to the surface. "Grow up! Do your three!" She bit my lips. "Bring back a plant and an animal. And something belonging to Other. Even a child can do their trio!"

135

Not quite dawn, but already I'm panting uncontrollably. Trying not to weep, I hug in the last embers of night's moiling murk. The predawn air is cold, mercifully, though not nearly cold enough. Even winter-blown night up here is never bitter enough for us. As solace against the warmth to come, I carry with me a dead rat's frozen corpse. From time to time, I bring its iced fur to my cheeks.

"Too much comfort," my sister rebukes, reaching up from our tunnel below to snatch even that small consolation away.

I do not fight her over the rat. I understand her sharpness. After preaching so much theoretical love of the Others, I have much to prove.

Even so, the first thing I do after my sister slips back Underneath is search for an animal that may have died in the night. Finding none, I decide I will not kill a living thing just to have something to hold. Instead, I cling to the dewy wetness of a nearby fern and lick its damp roots.

Birds! Those are what I see first in the pre-dawn! Finches taking anticipatory wing. Not yet light, but how they prepare for it! Clustering companionably, astir and a-twitter! *Remember this*, I tell myself. *Your first memory of Upworld.*

Silent as I am, I could easily snatch one of the finches from the branch above me and stuff it into my thigh folds. From thence bring it home: my animal proof. But no: every child brings back a bird the first time, and I am no longer a child. Unless a creature is strong and dogged enough to fight me, I will leave it in peace. Even then I will probably let it go unharmed. My mother is forever gurgling at me not to be so soft-hearted. I am her shame. I am my whole family's shame, my tribe's, my people's. I speak profanely, heretically many would argue, of respect for Others. It is always odd to me that I have not been strangled in my sleep.

"Love of everything, is that all you can ever talk about?" my mother rebuked me recently. To which my sincere reply was, *"When all is said and done, what else matters but the heart's affections?"*

My sister's laughter, overhearing the exchange, chugged our family tunnels for hours.

Despite which, she and the rest of my clan in the broad Underneath are wrong. Without love, what do we have? Surely nothing! Nothing but enmity, cynicism and conceit. Someone must try to breach our divide with those in the Upworld.

Dawn! Here it comes, sluicegate of LIGHT IN ENTIRETY and I try not to scream. *Hello, incorrigible sun!* I whimper, telling myself I'm ready. But, of course, no Shadow ever is ready, not the first time. And, as my face is struck, I contract like a slug.

Then I brace. Spread my tail. Stabilize. The slant-wise rays are tepid this early, I remind myself. The burn will be minor. My skin, when I raise my mottles, can endure it. I am not a child. I refuse to bury my head.

Then - how pathetic! - I do. I grub in the forest undergrowth, covering myself in mulched leaves, hiding like the littlest of our children. The only thing that prevents me burying myself entirely is the arrival of a worm.

Thank you, Darkness! I murmur, as it pops out its wriggling head. A lucky charm!

The worm nods its segments, greeting me, and I drop it gratefully inside the dark pinch of my mouth. Before swallowing, I make the standard prayer of respect, but the worm seems uneasy on my tongue. In our own realm we Shadows are lords - any worm would treasure being consumed by me - but up here, in these harsh dry soils abutting the light, it seems the worms are their own masters. This one writhes in panic.

I lower it from my lips onto the moist grass. Let it go.

Adieu, small one. We never eat anything that does not consent.

It is full dawn now and warming. Rays tilt provocatively. They test me. Light. Heat. Powdery soil. Naught I have been taught prepares me for such terrifying extravagances, and I cower. I splurt. My eyes are only slits, white and shy, purblind in Upworld. In any other situation, I would shut them altogether. But no. I want to see this world. I want to behold it, to fall in love with its mystery and, somehow, my curiosity wins out. As I am slowly rotating my nostrils from side to side in Upworld's contrary breezes, tasting the fruity air, that I smell my first... Other.

Oh. That's unexpected. I had not anticipated chancing across one so soon.

The Other is female. From the startling aroma and flex of her hips she is young but full-formed. A woman, then, not a child. Good. I would hide from a child. We do not frighten children unless they ask us to.

She wears darker material on her lower half, lighter material above. I have no words for these garments, as we wear none. Nor for their colours. How sad, I realise, that we of the Underneath have no vocabulary for such bold, lavish insignia.

She picks her way amid the lit up areas between trees with staggering ease. Her footsteps mesmerize me. A giant's raucous crunch. How can something so small be so unintentionally loud? She whistles to herself as she walks, an unnervingly high-pitched sound at odds with all of nature. She is delightfully inept!

Why is she out so early? Perhaps she is not inept. Perhaps she is a hunter come to track me. The Others hunt our kind when they get the chance. Our meat is unbearably sweet to them. As is theirs, of course, to us. I refuse always. Another reason I am despised.

Am I being baited to show myself? Seeking only heartfelt dialogue with Others, will I find myself instead on their meal-plates?

No, I decide. Or perhaps yes. But the risk is worthwhile. I must not forget why I am here. *Love, love, love.* To bring that to the Others! Which means I must first trust them. Trust that pockets of goodness prevail in Upworld, as they do in the Underneath. I must give imperiled love a chance. All of which sounds honorable, but right now - with the woman's daunting colours shrieking at me from the nearby river bank - any such idea seems ridiculous.

What is she doing here? Has she come for water? Perhaps, I fancifully imagine, she is a poet like me. She has arrived on a whim. An impulse merely to wander at break of morn. To begin her day with a dalliance. To meet, perchance, one such as I.

Is it possible? Is this fate?

I clack a greeting. She does not notice. Her ears are whimsically small. She does not register my presence at all until I rise before her. I deliberately face the oncoming dawn so she can witness me clearly, since this is the way of seeing. I wish to be gallant. The last thing I want is for her to be afraid.

But she is, nevertheless.

Will she dance with me? When we Shadows greet strangers in the Underneath we always taste one another, roll and dance. I have heard that those in the Light only do so at special times, but perhaps I can persuade her?

I spread my claws, offer my full girth, but still she does not truly see me. She sees only a vast object, my umbra rising. This woman is no hunter! She is as wondrously feckless as I am!

Eventually her mouth screams - a proper animal's scream, I am relieved to hear. And that profoundly calms me, is something I can finally understand.

She staggers off. Rushes to a clear patch, still screaming. Waving her arms. Retreats whence she came. It is all wonderfully vivid, her cries exotic, her jangly hues flashing, but I see I have frightened her badly.

No. We will not dance today.

But wait! What is this? She has left an item behind. A floppy thing that was wound about her neck: a scarf I will discover it is called.

"Left by accident, or deliberately?" That is the question my sister would ask. *"Trust not the Others."*

Could this be a trap? Perhaps. I am literally incompetent to decide, I realise happily. I know nothing of hunting. I know nothing of *preda-*

tor assessment and my ignorance frees me. In the absence of expertise, I let charitable instinct and a pure heart guide me.

I whip my tail high. *Let love decide!*

And it decides…

SHE WANTS ME TO GO AFTER HER!

So I do, thrusting my forelimbs, shaving clods from the ground as I
scamper. But then… no. What am I thinking?

Delay, generous febrile heart, I tell myself. If I go after her now, in
this exuberant state, I will smear my messy scent all over the daytime
grasses and be hunted down for sure.

No: love must wait for night-time!

Delighted with everything I have experienced so far, I pack the
woman's scarf in soil and bring it back Underneath with me, along
with a vole and the fern. Not much, but enough to avoid the worst of
my sister's scorn.

I do not show my sister or mother the scarf, however. I do not
show anyone. And, later that night, tucked up in my rooms, love calls
to me.

Ah! I had a feeling it would! And I know it is the woman's very
own love seeking me out, for why else would I be yearning for her so?

I tell no-one what I am about to do next. I daren't. We are not
meant to bring Others to the Underneath. Not unless they are trussed
up or dead. We must never lead them to us.

Unless, I decide, love tells us to!

Feeling for once in my life like a wanton thieving adventurer, I
sneak from my rooms. I mount our serpentine tunnels. Clamber Upworld. Once above ground the scarf's reek leads me across cool
expanses of sky to the woman. I break into her home in the small
hours. She is alone. When she shrieks I subdue her. Carry her away.
Bring her Underneath.

Into my rooms we vanish. My private quarters. My poet's quarters,
which no-one else bothers with. I crinkle my papers to show her what

I am. She does not understand. Only shrieks. I have to subdue her again.

When she next wakes, I place soil in her mouth to keep her from alerting anyone she is here, and am gentle with her. I dance upon her as I would one of our own when they are frightened. She does not, however, reciprocate. She fights me. Uncertain about what to do, I pin her scratching hands and smother her in welts of toad-skin and my best, most calming body odors - but stop when I realise she dislikes this as well. Not a single moment of the dark is she enjoying as I roll with her.

So, I let her go. Of course I do!

She must not be here against her will!

As she scrambles back to the surface, I help her choose the right path at each tunnel intersection and twist, biting her rump from behind to show her how friendly I am.

When she finally emerges Upworld - gasping, spitting out soil - all I want to do is leap on her. To squash her against me, smooth out her ungainly, thin legs! But she is in such a hurry, I decide on a smaller tribute: a simple loam-dunking, squitted from my cheek pouches at her in a final farewell. She waves her arms wildly as she runs off. I have heard that this arm gesture is the Other's way of saying goodbye, and do the same.

Fascinated by her uncoordinated motion, I watch her for as long as I can. Spitting out a clod of earth, still screaming, she finally wipes the last of the loam I caked in friendliness over her eyes and prizes them open. Opens them wide. I see her desperately drinking in Upworld's risen sun, choosing light over dark. Astonishing me with that choice! I have so much to learn from these Others!

I can't stop watching her. Her spine jerks as she flees. She is still running, but more slowly now. She keeps falling over. Is she injured? Or... is she just pretending to be? Giving me a last chance to look at her? Teasing me? Teasing my love?

I want it to be love. It is my nature to react that way. I can't help myself and a familiar warmth suffuses me. Sunlight - incandescently bright! - flares off her bobbing light hair. I could fall in love with that hair. We Shadows have only naked, pock-marked flesh. How impoverished we are!

For two days and nights after that I do nothing. Though I inform Mother about most things that stir me, I do not tell her about the woman. I know she will only seek her out and kill her. No Other must ever know where our tunnels entrances are.

But I think about the woman constantly. Oh, why is my heart so romantic? Why does it attach so clamorously to everything that breathes? I know not, but it has always been so!

On the third night of missing the woman, I decide her stumbling gait and lavishly waving arms were sending me a clear signal. A signal to pursue her, to woo her like a true lover.

And understanding that, I go to her. How can I not? With poetry in my breast, with feet clammy and adamant and unctuous, I sally forth. From my rooms through the rising tunnels I ascend.

This time, from the exit, I call her using love's voice. My sister explained once that the odor I emit is nothing to do with love.

"It is a unique chemical lure for foraging, drawing meat towards us," she told me. "Nothing more, you versifying fool!"

Perhaps. But I am not using my allure to forage this time, am I? I am after love, only love, and I let my scent seep from me... until... until...

...Mussed from sleep, she comes!

She is bleary-eyed. In a thick gown, still half-asleep, she runs breathlessly towards me. She is barefoot. Is she already so much in love that she has not thought to even fasten on footwear? How wondrous! How glorious! Forestward, sniffing the air, sniffing the ground, she seeks me out, and I know what my pragmatic sister would say.

"You gave her a taste of true darkness, you idiot. What did you expect? Now what will you do with her? Recite your poems? Make of her meat instead! *Give her to me.*"

No, unkind sister, I will not.

I delay dancing with the woman this time, however. I must be milder. Parting the leaf-fall at the surface, I serenade her with my foraging love scent. And the woman shivers. From the rain that is falling, yes. From the cold, too, she shivers but mainly it's me. It's me, me, me causing her to tremble so and twist.

Naturally, I make her wait. She teased me, so I pay her the same respect. Bubbling out more scent, I tighten our love-bond until she is literally shaking with longing. Night after night, I keep her waiting outside. Until finally she is wailing. Until she is pounding the ground for me!

And then I do go to her. Of course I do! I am a creature of passions, of exclamations! Besides, only a monster could resist the outrageous desire with which she glows!

I carry her back Underneath to my cave-dwelling rooms, which every year are simpler and simpler, nothing but shade upon shade, and wholesome dark. The woman falls still. She collapses on the floor as if she needs nothing.

Nothing except me.

Which is untrue. She must eat. She has not done so for days. She refuses the beetles I offer her. Initially.

I keep her presence a secret. I would like nothing more than to proudly show her to my family, let them marvel at her, touch her, taste her feet. But I dare not. I have broken every rule and taboo in bringing the woman here. If anyone finds out I have done so, my entire family will be executed.

I do not hold the woman against her will, however. Anytime she wishes to leave, she may do so. Yet... she stays. My sister would say the reason is the stifling dark and that the woman has no idea where to go. But I prefer to think she stays out of love, or at least love's first shades. I continue to crouch over her and vent my scent discreetly into her nostrils to help with that. Eventually, she is so addicted that she crawls across to me. Dips a finger in my flesh. Brings the liquid to her lips and sighs. Later she drinks the oil directly from my glands.

Soon after that first deep sup, she becomes more serene. Until now, starving, she has held out from eating solid food. But in her newly tranquil state her fumbling fingers chance upon a beetle. And she silently eats it. Even now, though, despite being in the dark, she shamefully hides her face as she does so.

Later, she does not hide it.

And - increasingly willingly on her part, I like to think - we dance. We dance, we slide, we play hide and seek with my scent. From time to time she laughs or screams - it is hard for my ears, untutored in the ways of Others, to hear the difference - and we dance again.

But I dance formally with her now: raise myself like a spider, forelimbs arched. She, unable to match that, or see what I am doing, can only guess at my movements, and swings her complicated pelvis to meet me poorly. I make allowances. I am in love, after all. We both are now, I think.

"I'm useless at this," she says, many weeks later, having calmed down further. I'm delighted she's finally talking to me, not just making animal noises. In truth, however, I have no idea what she means by such words. Useless *at this?* Down here, she is wondrously useless at everything!

For a long period she tries to escape via other linked tunnels.

"No, not from you, of course not from you," she reassures me when I catch and loom over her. But I am nervous. Is he already falling out of love with me?

"Is there anything you want?" I ask.

"...Can I leave?"

I adore the way she teases me!

Eventually, she begins to relax entirely into the life of the Underneath. She asks me what it is like to live amongst so much darkness.

She marvels that, beyond the territories of visibility, we Shadow people are at one with ourselves.

"To be dark is to be impenetrable," I tell her. "It is to be unwise at times, to dwell inside deep, approved fear."

She nods avidly but does not understand yet. I promise I will keep her here until she grasps the full meaning and I think she smiles. Others have such expressive faces! Even when I dig my thumbs deeply into her cheeks I cannot always fathom the meaning.

"I want to know more about your family," she says to me one day. "Your sister. Your mother. Why haven't I met them?"

"They would kill you."

That gives her pause.

"Then, instead, tell me all about your world," she says. "I want to know about your customs, your ways. Explain the tunnel systems. Where do they lead? I want to know everything, to feel as close to you as possible."

And, after I tell her about the tunnels, she suggests we dance again. We do so. But I don't tell her about *all* the tunnels. Not the ones containing our deepest secrets.

Even so, she learns fast. She begins to feel her way with more confidence through our scalloped chambers and domes. Until, what her toes had previously felt only as smooth whorls, she finds nicks and edges. And then my joy, when the day comes that she enters a serpentine tunnel she is sure she cannot crawl through, but holds herself still a moment, empties her lungs... and is suddenly slithering through a space that seemed impossible.

Her sense of time and place gradually loosen. She begins describing a feeling, as of the darkness pouring over her. Which, in her innocence, she does not realize is our greatest joy.

"Show me your poetry," she says, and my heart leaps with pride - the first time she has shown an interest.

But I prevaricate. What if she does not like it? I decide to start with something light. A few verses about seeping pools inscribed upon the flesh of our dead children. The woman's fingers have learned a semblance of touch now and she feels the raised scars, the puckered words of tribute beneath.

"I see how isolated you have felt down here," she says uncertainly. "You, personally, I mean. Unappreciated."

"Do you?'"

"Yes, certainly."

My sister would say she is lying. Anything to gain my trust. Anything to get out of here.

Later, hesitantly, the woman says,

"I want to become one of you. I know I can't physically do that. But... um... as close as possible." And her face tilts up to mine. I can see that face clearly now. I have vouched her a candle, one pinched from our ceremonial stores. Initially, I offered it to help her adjust. But she liked the flame so very much we kept it, and I have grown used to it, in a way.

"You can remove the candle if you want," she said to me recently. But, when I went to do so, she stayed my hand.

"Don't you want to see me?" she murmured. We were dancing at the time, and as we danced, she showed me more of herself, more of her body than she had ever done previously. Showed me, indeed, everything. And suddenly I understood: that touch, smell, sound and weight have always seemed enough to our kind. But the Others were blessed with a dimension that *looks for affection,* that sees it *USING LIGHT.*

So: I too can learn. The candle stays. And I indulge her further. I sneak into our most worshipful tunnels. Steal further candles.

Soon after that, we marry in secret and together make our nuptial bed. I gather tree-fungus and roots as a base while, for extra comfort, my wife crawls to the surface. Feeling her way blindly, insisting her eyes be covered, she uses touch alone to delve between bracken stems for soft willow and flower petals at the tunnel edge. These she returns with and lays on our floor and we sleep together in the breath of the dark. And, for a time, we make a life together and are happy.

"I hate secrets," she says one day. "Our life is perfect, but I just can't bear secrets, my love." She has started calling me that. "I know there is much about the cave networks down here you have not told me," she mutters with a sigh. "You hide them from me, even during our close crawls."

"You would have to be truly one of us for me to reveal those mysteries to you," I explain, and she turns silent.

"My eyes are useless to me now," she says shortly after. "I might just as well be blind down here."

There is a suggestion in her voice my heart has been waiting an eternity to hear, but it must be her choice.

"Do you... do you want me to blind you?" I am so excited now that I can barely speak.

"If I am blind," she murmurs. "Would that be sacrifice enough?"

"Enough for what?"

"For you to finally trust me. With everything."

I nod. And raise a cutting nail querulously to her face. Her own hand stills mine.

"Not yet."

In the end, she does not ask me to remove her eyes. She has more grace. She simply does so herself one day, without fuss, whimpering prettily. I help her heal the wounds with soil-balms and crushed beetle carapaces.

She is slow to recover, so I place further medication beside her inside a mechanical rat. My idea is to make her run for it, like we would one of our own if they are sick - but this does not excite her as it would us. I still have so much to learn about Others! I ask and ask, and she tells me, and everything is a wonder.

"You have never shown any interest in my name," she says shortly after this.

"We do not have names here," I tell her.

'I know that," she replies curtly. "But amongst Others I have a name. You have never even thought to ask me it."

I swallow. "I'm sorry. What is your name?"

"I'm not telling you," she mutters, then bursts out in tears. "My name is Feetha."

I am so much in love with her.

I take both Feetha's removed eyes and place them lengthways and reverently next to our bed, one on either side. They rot humidly.

She finally understands that, in doing so, I am venerating her.

My dear Feetha spends many more months growing familiar with our Shadow ways. Somehow I continue hiding her away from my family. Love makes me cunning.

"Tell me everything about the Shadow people," she whispers in my ear. "Everything, everything."

And I do. I do. I tell it all now. I explain where we congregate. Our customs and rituals. Our darkest prayers. Her lips slide over mine.

"I am bound to you now," she says, and I realise she must have forgotten or misunderstood that, amongst us, to say so signifies the opposite. It means to bind your partner, master them utterly to your will. Only under dire circumstances do we ever make such statements in the Underneath.

She wishes me to take her to our most clandestine places and, because I am leashed root and trunk to her now by the binding, I do so. We have carved out valleys down here. Steep mountains, rich in majesty, populate the Underneath. Feetha kneels upon a precipice, asking me to describe what is below. I tell her about our warrior armies and she is afraid.

"Do you miss the light?" I ask her one day.

It is the one question I have resisted asking, but love demands I do so. I have to be absolutely sure she is happy. Feetha's skin is white now. Almost translucent like ours. I kiss her and there is a long pause. Then Feetha's breath is moving over mine.

"Yes, I miss it," she says, and my glands sag.

She sits up.

"Really? Did you think I had forgotten the light?" She takes my claws, presses them to her breast. "Oh, it is not the light I miss so much," she murmurs. "It is family. My mother especially. She has no idea I am here. Our own people will have detected your smell after you abducted me that first night. She will assume you killed me. I would like... just to leave her a note. Let her know I am safe in your loving embrace."

"Then what?"

"Then return to you forever, my love."

"When?' I ask breathlessly. "When do you wish to leave this note?"

"Tonight?" She looks anxious, ready to suggest a later date. But I smear her with cool murk.

"Yes! Tonight! Why not? Why wait!"

Her hands find my long mouth.

"Will you accompany me?" she asks softly. "I do not wish to do anything or go anywhere without you."

Feetha speaks as we in the Underneath do now. In fateful whispers. Meltingly. I cannot resist her. I don't want to.

I empty my mind, bring my claws together, and trace a great womb of love for my Feetha, fill it with darkness. She squirms when I rub my besmirched fingers over her, giggles.

"We live always in the dark, imagining the light," I tell her. "What else can I offer you?"

She lifts a brittle neck I now find lovely.

"Nothing. I have everything I want, dearest. I just wish to visit my mother one last time."

Night, and up the tunnels we creep. Feetha leads the way. She knows them as well as I do now.

We emerge into heady moonshine. I smile, watching her turn her cheeks in the breeze. She utters a gasp of relief.

"Oh thank god, thank god..."

She disentangles herself from my grip.

"Wait here," she commands me. "I need a moment alone."

I stay at the lip of the tunnel. Feetha walks some distance away, bashing into trees, swearing mightily.

"Fuck shit... fucking hell!" Then she calls out loudly. "WHERE ARE YOU?"

And... oh, my surprise... as Others appear. Many Others. Hundreds. All camouflaged. But with spotlights and guns. They train them on her - and me.

A big Other, male, in bulky armor, glances in my direction, says to her.

"What shall we do with it? Kill it?"

I prepare to grasp my wife, leap with her back into the tunnel.

"Don't be stupid," she grunts at the man, then turns to me.

"Come here," she says and, bound to her, I must. I scamper across.

"Sit like a dog," she orders. "Stay silent."

I do so, tucking my tail beneath my flank.

The Others around us stare at me in disgust, then peer into the tunnel. They are clearly all hunters.

"How much have you learned?" the big man asks Feetha and, astonishingly, he kisses her. "Jesus, look at you!"

"Fuck off!" she yells at him, then slumps on his shoulder a moment.

"Everything," she whispers after a time. "The entire layout. Or what I do not know, he'll tell us."

She shakes her head grimly, says to the big man. "Give me a knife.'

He hands her a serrated blade.

"Do not cry out," Feetha warns me as she sticks me with it. "Fucking hell, I've waited a long time to do this."

She hacks at me. Takes her time. I gaze down. One of my ears lies severed on the ground. Also my dancing tube. My tail clenches in agony.

"You're blind," the big man says to Feetha.

"No shit, dumbhead!" She shakes her head, spits on me.

"Yeah, OK," the big man growls at her. "But how can you show us the cave layout if you can't see anything?"

"Pen and paper," she demands.

"What's the point?"

"Oh ye of little fucking faith." She is fetched writing materials and, from memory, draws the entire layout of our clan's cave network. Not just the main tunnels but the tributaries, including those leading to the crèches where we keep our new-born.

"Bomb those first," she says. "Light them up. It's a whole generation."

I wish I could turn off my love for her in this moment, but I cannot. Even though I have been betrayed, I simply can't. It is not in my nature to deny love.

The soldiers awkwardly begin descending the tunnel. Feetha calls them back. Makes them remove their boots. Tells them how to imitate the crawling of large burrowing animals. They practice.

"This is the time the majority of them are asleep," she says. "Make the most of it."

Finally, Feetha and I are alone again. Or almost. The big man has stayed behind with us. She suddenly weeps into his chest.

"Oh, I'm sorry." He lifts her chin. "Look at you! But look at what you've achieved! We've never had information like this before."

I see how happy she is to be in his embrace and not mine. She tilts her head towards me.

"Prop your forearms like this, like a proper dog," she says coolly, and I do. "From now on, only bark. Oh. Wait. Eat your own shit."

I am attempting to do so when I see my sister. She erupts in that special winsome way she has, from a tunnel I did not know we had.

Of course, being only a poet, I know very little of such matters. Ten or more of us, including my mother, surround the big man and sever his head. Feetha is not so lucky. She is trussed, and her mouth sealed with vomit, her nose cut off. Her mouth and throat are left pristine. She will sing tonight.

Meantime, embarrassingly, I am stuck as a begging dog. Because Feetha cannot release me from her instruction, I am left with my arms up and dangling, while my head roots around my anus. My sister leaves me like this for longer than is necessary.

"You told her everything, didn't you?" she says and, with shit in my mouth, I bark yes.

"Knew you would." She winks at me. "Wait till they find out what's waiting for them in the crèches."

Her slits brighten, and I bark again, because… what else can I do?

"Good boy," she says, patting my head. "Good boy."

Burden to Bear

John Mahoney

Phil Novak balanced the insulated bag on an upturned palm as he
kneed the Volkswagen's door shut.

"Because she's my dog," he shouted into his earpiece. He adjusted
the device with his free hand, the stupid black Domino's visor-hat
knocked it askew whenever two thoughts occupied his mind.

"Discipline yourself! You don't hit Mycroft for you being an idiot!" Phil glanced around. "Call you back."

Tapping the earpiece's button might have been a formality. The
first step he ventured in the sun-obscuring woods could be nothing
less than a total sacrifice of reception. A log cabin moldered in a vale,
half a football field from where the road tapered to a treacherous mud
trail.

Best to hoof it. Phil didn't relish being docked for any tragedy be-
falling one-third of Neshoba County Domino's delivery fleet. Dozens
of tracks marred the mire. Mostly deer but larger prints traipsed
among them, left by some predator whose reign Phil meant to leave
unchallenged.

Perched in a rocking chair, close to fulfilling its destiny as fire-
wood, was an old man. Phil commenced his slog through the muck,
blessedly firmer than it seemed.

"Got me walking all this way and you don't even order toppings,"
he grumbled.

153

Birds above the autumn foliage cheeped, not quite in harmony with the trickling purr of the Pearl River, somewhere off to his right and hidden by trees.

Maskless, the geezer lifted a withered claw in greeting as Phil entered the clearing presided over by his shack. Phil wondered which gust of wind had the cabin's name on it. Even so, he couldn't guess whether home or owner had witnessed more decades, and he'd be unsurprised to find this guy's signature on the Declaration of Independence. Phil considered snapping a photo of his customer, then contacting the *Guinness World Records* people. His discovery of a six-foot, liver-spotted baby had to be worth something.

Hairless, toothless, and nearly fleshless, the ancient infant lacked only a jug with three X's and a corncob pipe to complete his hillbilly haute couture. The flannel beneath his blue overalls, heavy boots and John Deere hat were accounted for, though the last lay in his lap. Propped against the building's wooden wall, within easy reach, rested a metal cane and a pump-action shotgun. Above them dangled the heftiest wind chimes Phil had ever seen. Copper in color and unlikely to herald weather less insistent than a tornado.

Wading through an archipelago of rusting hubcaps, engines and the occasional disembodied door strewn about the untended, wilting grass, Phil noticed a wrinkled hand grab the cane. It rose to strike the chimes, which boomed rather pleasant, sonorous clangs.

"Dan!" the wizened hick called in a strong voice, incongruous with his frail features. "Get over here, boy!"

Covid-19 was, Phil decided, finally doing him a favor. His mask shielded the uncharitable smile on his lips from a pair of dim brown eyes. No sign of whoever Dan was, though.

A dinner bell? One shade redder, and grandpa's neck would be a crime scene. Phil stumbled on a cracked carburetor, concealed by the unmown wilderness. He cursed to himself. So many car parts but not an intact vehicle in sight. The county must have confiscated this man's truck and license due to advanced age and bumpkinity. Perhaps he was attempting to Igor a new conveyance from this hoarder wet dream.

A grin boasting more gum than the underside of the world's least sanitized school desk welcomed Phil.

"How are you, young fella?"

"Fat, going bald and underpaid," Phil shot back his automatic answer as he creaked up the porch's stairs. "Aside from those three things, life's perfect."

Wheezing guffaws pummeled his eardrums.

"I s'pose that's how you make sure you get a nice tip."

Apparently not. Frowning, Phil hefted the heavy bag.

"Got two medium cheeses. Comes to eleven-forty, with your delivery app discount."

Homo Sapiens Hillbillius nodded sagely.

"Tell me, son. You an animal lover?"

Lacking a mirror, Phil couldn't see his own expression, but it surely sufficed to convey his confusion.

"Heard you yellin at somebody about hittin your dog."

A wad of cash bulged the breast pocket of those overalls. The green paper made a profound case in favor of indulging the old coot.

"Good ear," Phil shrugged. "My brother lives with me, since his old lady left him. He leaves food on the bottom shelf in the fridge. I warned him Mycroft pulls the door open. She doesn't deserve to get kicked for something I taught her to do."

"Must be a bright girl," the talking fossil declared. "You named her for Sherlock Holmes' smarter brother."

Impressed, Phil nodded. He doubted few other patrons of English classics looked and spoke like this man.

"Yes, sir. She's a Belgian Malinois. My best buddy."

"I've got a buddy, too," the hick smiled. "Goin' on twenty years now."

Eyeing the money, Phil asked, "What kind of dog lives that long?"

"Danny ain't no dog, son." The elderly raised a twig of a finger to point.

Phil turned and the pizza boxes clattered at his feet.

Half a ton of bear ambled, with expert precision, through the automotive cemetery that was the yard. Dark sludge matted the brown fur around its muzzle. Drool oozed past teeth larger than nails. Phil felt cemented by the pressure of its stare. No doubt remained concerning the author of those enormous clawed tracks.

"Dan here's been visiting ever since I started feeding him." A soft cackle rasped behind Phil. "You wanted a tip? Don't run. Danny'll walk you right down. Fastest man ever hit twenty-seven miles an hour for a few seconds. Grizzly can hold twenty-eight for two miles."

An anticipatory growl rumbled from the approaching beast's throat, as if agreeing.

Trembling, Phil backed up. The shotgun cocking behind him was the sweetest sound he'd ever heard.

"What... what do you feed him?" he managed to ask.

Metal pressed between Phil's shoulder blades and he froze as the old man answered.

"Delivery."

Murder Mommy

The boy punches a code into the garage keypad. The garage door rises like a squeaky metal curtain, revealing the murder room. The murder room is made of white cardboard panels. A floor, a ceiling, and three walls. They need to be white so the blood can be properly photographed. The opening is facing away from the garage door. He lets out a heavy sigh, hikes up his bookbag, which is slung over one shoulder, and trudges inside.

The boy is sixteen and lives with his mom, who is some indeterminate age. She is neither old nor young. She is a forensic scientist who specializes in blood spatter analysis. She knows about things like back spatter, drip patterns, expirated mist and arterial spurting. She studied fluid dynamics in college. After graduation, she joined the state crime lab, where the dynamic fluid was blood. Mostly. There are lots of people killing each other, so she receives plenty of practice.

Most of the killings are uninspired. Stabbing. Bashing. Strangling. Stomping. Shooting. Etc. A few are more interesting. The interesting ones require experiments. The experiments require a murder room.

There is no *mister forensic scientist.* There had been, once, but he left when the boy was eight. It was not a pleasant separation but, at least, there hadn't been any murders. He rarely spent time with the boy. When he did, it was on neutral ground. The park. The mall. The movies. The boy did not stay with him on weekends or holidays.

After the separation, the mom started a blog. The blog is called 'Murder Mommy'. The posts are pictures and videos of her forensic experiments with her 'favorite little lab assistant'.

The photos show a smiling mother and son. They show she is an involved parent. They show *mister forensic scientist* what he is missing. The blog is a moderate success. Working moms, STEM-enthusiasts and CSI-devotees like the posts, write encouragements in the comments section and buy 'Murder Mommy' coffee mugs, t-shirts, and stickers.

She was featured on several local news stations. Asked to speak at the Rotary Club and after-school science programs. She was interviewed by SciGirlz for PBS but her segment never aired. The producers said it would have been disturbing to their viewers.

During the early years of the blog, the boy had also enjoyed minor celebrity status. The neighborhood moms doted over him. They called him things like cutie-patootie. His friends thought he was cool. They thought he was destined to catch murderers, like his mom. The boy thought murder was the only way one could die. He did not want to be murdered. He would lay awake at night imagining the crimes he re-enacted in the murder room.

Most of the murders were among family members. Maybe, one day, his mom would drive their car into a lake and swim to safety, leaving him trapped inside. Or, perhaps, she would come into his room for their goodnight tuck-in and plunge a long kitchen knife through the comforter and into his stomach. She would smile, but not with her eyes, while she held him down, waiting for him to bleed out. He had a recurring dream in which she playfully buried him in the sand at the lake until just his nose poked out. Then she poured water over his face so he couldn't breathe. He tried to flail but the sand held him firm.

He wasn't afraid of his mom. Not really. He could imagine but not *believe* she would do such horrible things. It was the likes of Ed Gein, William Suff and whoever it was that took Jacob Wetterling that really scared him. They were the ones you didn't see coming. You didn't know who they were until they were caught. They could be your neighbor, Mr Steensland. The boy told his friends this. He didn't have any playdates for a while.

As the boy grew, he took a more active role in the experiments.

Sometimes, he is the murder victim, putting on dead people's clothes and miming the various stages of their brutalization, while his mom snaps photographs. Sometimes he is the murderer. The comments about the cute little assistant disappear. It is not cute when a teenager lies in a pool of blood, swings a bloody baseball bat or drags a blood-soaked wig across a stark white piece of cardboard. In the comments section, they call him Dexter-in-waiting. They say someone should call child services. They say someone should keep an eye on the neighborhood pets. His mom hires a moderator for the blog.

Today, the boy walks slowly to the murder room that his mom constructed. He wonders if he'll be murderer or murderee. His mom says the term 'murderee' is distasteful.

There is a white Tyvek suit, two purple nitrile gloves and a pair of ski goggles laid out for him on a card table. When he spots the goggles, he knows that he will be the murderer. He knows it will be messy. He shucks his shoes and puts on the onesie made of papery fabric. He zips the suit. He hauls the hood over his head. He pulls on the gloves with a snap. He holds the goggles in his hand. The lens is clean but the elastic band is crusted with brown stains. He rolls the band between his fingers, breaking up the hard crusty parts. A dandruff of blood flakes gathers on the garage floor.

The boy's mom emerges through a door that leads from the kitchen to the garage. Her arms encircle a half-dozen bags of blood. One hand holds an empty pitcher. The boy wonders if the pitcher has ever held anything as mundane as lemonade. He helps his mom place the bags of blood on the card table. He is happy to see them. Often, they use their own blood for the experiments. His mom is a terrible nurse. She rolls his veins. When he's older, he wonders what people will think of the track marks on his arms.

The blood is from the blood bank. A civilian isn't allowed to make a withdrawal from the blood bank, not even if the blood is expired. But the crime lab is allowed to use it for their experiments. His mom prefers using their own blood when they can. It's safer.

His mom cuts the corner off one of the bags of blood and empties it into the pitcher. She repeats this with bag after bag. She asks him how school was. The boy tells her he probably failed his AP literature quiz. She tells him that anything other than science and math is for mimosas and kids with trust funds. The boy doesn't feel any better about the quiz.

She asks him if he's met the wooden whore yet. She says 'whore' with a bad cockney accent and it comes out 'ore.' The boy gives her a puzzled look. He is used to her crass language. In courtrooms and official reports, she uses language that is cold and clinical. At crime scenes and in the lab (the boy has been to these places when she could not find a sitter and he was too young to stay home alone) his mom and her colleagues make ribald jokes. They dehumanize. They cope. He still doesn't understand her comment about the wooden whore. She nods to the murder room.

The boy looks inside. There is a crude wooden person standing in the middle of the cardboard room. The legs and triangle-shaped body are made from two wooden canoe paddles that have been placed in an X. The shoulders are two-by-four planks and the arms are halves of another canoe paddle. The arm with the blade part of the paddle looks like a flipper. In the center of the two-by-four is a mannequin head. Lipstick and eyeshadow have been generously applied to the mannequin's face. The boy finally understands the cockney accent. It's a 'whore' made of oars. His mom looks at him for approval. He gives her a weak smile.

Together they wrap the limbs and body of the wooden person in yellow speckled carpet foam. It is kept in place by bands of duct tape at the wrists, armpits, waist, thighs and ankles. When they are done, she pours blood from the pitcher onto the carpet foam. She pours slowly and evenly. Very little ends up on the floor. He watches the red diffuse through the yellow foam to create a sickish orange. He thinks of blood flowing through veins.

She hands him a machete. She explains that he needs to focus on the head and neck. He should take big back swings, she says. The man he's to be imitating murdered a dozen prostitutes in Anchorage and Vancouver. He beat most of them to death with a tire iron but, at least once, used a machete. His mom finds this last bit interesting. She tells him that machete blood spatter has been understudied in the literature.

He tries to put himself into the mindset of a serial murderer. He knows more about them than most. His hand squeezes the handle of the machete rhythmically like he's revving an engine. He stares at the painted face of the mannequin. In his mind, he paraphrases Ted Bundy and tells himself that she's given herself to everyone. Now she'll be only his.

There's a beep. The official crime lab video camera is recording. The boy remains still except for the pulsating squeeze of his hand. His heart rate increases. His breaths become deeper and more frequent. He waits for the second beep, the one from his mom's personal camera, which she uses for the blog. He feels like a sprinter in the starting blocks.

Beep.

He launches himself at the wooden figure. The first blow takes a chunk from the side of the mannequin's face. There is a patch of white Styrofoam where her brains, ear canal, and sinuses should be. With his second blow he tries to decapitate her but the neck is made of hard plastic and he knocks the entire wooden person sideways. He drops the machete and catches his teetering victim. He sets her upright. His hands are soaked with blood. He's thankful for the nitrile gloves.

He picks up the machete again. His mom tells him to swing up and down. Like he's chopping wood, not using a tennis racket. His face becomes hot with embarrassment. This will all be on the blog. He knows he'll look clumsy and foolish. He holds the blade over his head and brings it down hard on the mannequin's shoulder. It sticks into the two-by-four. He wrestles it free. More blood on his hand and wrists.

His mom tells him he needs to bring it back faster. They need spatter from the wind-up. He gives her a petulant "I know."

Then he whips the blade back as fast as he can. He plans to take the mannequin's arm clean-off with this one. But, when the blade reaches a fully-cocked position and his arm starts its forward motion, the handle, coated in blood, slips from his hand. The blade shoots backwards while his arm goes forward. There are several small sounds. Tearing fabric. A grunt. A thud.

Then the screaming starts. Wild, animal screaming. His mom is clutching her chest. Blood is pouring through her fingers. There is no tender goodbye. No comforting words of forgiveness.

The boy runs inside the house and calls 911. The screaming stops long before the ambulances and squad cars arrive. The first responders don't ask him questions. They issue commands. Some have guns drawn. The boy, still in his bloody Tyvek suit, gloves, and ski goggles, doesn't blame them.

At the station, they take his clothes, his prints and his statement. The videos confirm his story. They give him a coke. They are sorry for his loss.

They call his dad.

Live Chat

C M B a r n e s

In my first shoot, I played a prom queen with dark impulses.

"Your name is Tina the Temptress," the Director explained. "Your motivation is a desire to seduce all your classmates via the black magic of your pussy."

I fingered my costume. A sash with fuzzy red tassels, a tiara with lizard green rhinestones stuck to the rim and not much else.

"I was a real prom queen once," I said. "A couple of years ago. In Idaho."

"Isn't that cool?" the Director replied. "That's really cool."

He had *discovered* me - that was the word he used - eating at a Taco Tuesdays. I was eating at a Taco Tuesdays because Taco Tuesdays sells off the remainder of its breakfast menu for half price at 11.00 am. I'd spent the entirety of my daily food budget on tacos. Seven tacos for seven dollars.

"I'm just fascinated by you," the Director had said as he slid into the booth across from me.

"I'm not," I replied.

The Director's smile was not predatory. It was also not a smile. He contemplated the crunched-up bits of shell smeared across the neon wrappers spread out on the table.

"I could watch you eat tacos all day."

"I could probably eat tacos all day."

"That's funny," he said. "You're funny."

And then... "Want to make some money?"

I did.

My co-star was a man named Lord Taylor. Like everyone in the city, he claimed to be a native - but he also had a big tattoo of the state of Arkansas on his inner thigh. The Director suggested that I familiarize myself with it before we began shooting.

"Just introduce yourself now," he said. "So it doesn't throw you in the moment."

Lord Taylor obligingly took down his jeans.

"It's become my thing." He outlined the jagged state with a large thumb. "I'm putting the Razorbacks on the map."

Little Rock was marked by a small, hairless mole.

When I asked about a script, the Director chuckled and patted my butt. He had soft, smooth hands. He also had a soft, smooth face, like all the bones had been gradually ground down to nothingness over the course of eons.

"Darling," he said. "If there was a script, it would only look like a couple of cavemen sat down and typed out their inner monologue. *Ug. Ug. Ug. Oog. Oog. Oog.*"

"I can do the *ug*s," Lord Taylor grinned. "Can you handle the *oog*s?"

Afterwards, I had to fill out a surprisingly large amount of paperwork. My full name. My phone number. A photocopy of my license - everything necessary to appease the powers that be. Then Lord Taylor and I shook hands.

"You're a natural," he said. "I mean that as a compliment. Find me on another call list. It's Lord with a U, like the city in France."

I took the bus home, stuck a $500 check inside my freezer (high crime area), and looked out over the backyard of shriveled cacti I shared with a gray cul-de-sac of other renters. $500 was good. It was even great (five-hundred breakfast tacos!) but I needed something steadier if I was going to continue down this path. It would also be nice to have more control over the process - not just the when, but also the where, the what, the who and, most importantly, the *how*.

I called the Director at 3.00 am to ask for advice. He picked up immediately.

"You have regrets?" he said instead of hello.

"Not really," I replied. "What I have is $500 and a desire to make more, but preferably not in a way that involves physical contact."

The line went silent for a few seconds.

"Any interest in pleasuring yourself with an iPhone?" he said finally. "I've got a great, pleasuring-oneself-with-an-iPhone shoot coming up. Five hundred more dollars, and nothing more invasive than the vibrate setting."

"Still sounds a little physical to me."

"Hey. Your body, your rules, right?"

That's when he suggested the possibility of *live chat*. Live chat, as I may or may not know, used to mean phone work. Like 1-800-SEX-CLOWN type stuff. But now that I was officially a visual talent, I could probably get a live camera gig. The chief virtue of this, the Director explained, was the power of choice.

"So, when a creep types something weird at you - *Want to gaze into the darkness of the deep with me?* etc. you can be like *No thanks!* And, if he keeps it up, you can block him. *Bam!* End of discussion. Plus, you make fifty an hour."

I was not convinced - what was *the darkness of the deep?* But I agreed to take the number of a woman who ran such an operation. The woman's name was Cynthia and her phone number was preceded by a real, honest-to-God, local area code.

"You don't want to be famous, do you?" Cynthia said instead of hello. "Because this is not the line of work *for getting your face out there* or whatever. This is not *Gateway to the* fucking *Stars*. You sit in front of a camera, inside a box, and weirdoes type demeaning requests at you. In return, you smile and promptly comply."

"It doesn't sound amazing," I allowed.

"Believe me. It isn't."

"What's *Gateway to the Fucking Stars?*"

"How old are you?"

"I look young."

"How young?"

"Young, but not, you know, *too*."

"Looking young is good. Looking too young is even better. Actually being too young is a problem."

"I was a prom queen in Idaho a couple of years ago."

"Weren't we all?"

"I was a senior."

"You blonde?"

"Can be."

"Cup size?"

"Big gulps."

"Be at the corner of Glendale and 7th at 9:30 tomorrow morning. Chester - who is a large man, don't be alarmed - will let you in."

"What should I wear?"

"If you're truly a barely legal, blonde, big-gulped, ex-prom queen, it really doesn't matter."

Chester *was* a large man - larger, if possible, than even Lourde Taylor. As if reading my mind, he smiled down at me from a great height and held up his fan-like palms. He had the hirsute forearms of a Siberian mammal.

"Don't worry," he said. "I don't perform - at least not for the mooks."

"The mooks?"

"Wow. Cynth said we'd only have to fill you in on *Gateway to the Stars*."

Inside, there were rows of gray cubicles, under the blank gaze of a vast, white, windowless ceiling. Inside each cubicle was a keyboard and a computer monitor mounted with a camera. Before each camera there was a bed and a variety of tools. I picked up something that looked like a cross between a whisk and a jackhammer and held it out to Chester.

"I don't know what this is," I said. "But I don't want it anywhere near me."

Chester took hold of the device and set it down out in the cubicle hallway.

"Not a problem," he said. "This is all about you being comfortable."

I picked out a few more troubling looking instruments - anything with too many nobs, wires, and points.

"None of these either. Nothing that looks like you need a license to operate."

As for training, there wasn't any. We could do a *dry run* if I wanted (titter) but it would be Chester typing the requests and, if he could be honest (which I told him he could), it was usually better for first-timers to jump right in.

"Not that I would judge you," he added. "But it's hard to see certain things and still be cool around the water cooler - not that we have a water cooler, just some weird flavor Snapples in the mini-fridge."

I sat down on the bed in what was to be my cubicle. The mattress was coated in a rubbery white sheet. A dog chewed teal robe hung by the door. The door itself was bounded by a scrunched-up yellow shower curtain covered in tiny, smiling red pandas.

"Makes sense to me," I said.

Through the cubicle wall, I could hear the rhythmic depression of box springs and a woman with a squeaky, baby hooker voice chanting *sugarpuss, sugarpuss, sugarpuss.* The wall smelled like the inside of an old washing machine.

"What am I supposed to say to the mooks?" I asked. "How should I respond to their requests? I've learned not to ask about scripts."

Chester paused in the doorway. He filled it.

"Improvise," he said. "Try to surprise yourself. It'll help keep things interesting for you."

"So, I'm working here then?"

He leaned into the cubicle, pressed a button on the camera, and slipped back out the door.

"It would appear so," he said as he receded.

He pulled the panda curtain shut behind him.

Over my first week of thrice-daily, one-hour live chat shifts, I learned two important things. The first was that the mooks who pay for live chat don't really care what you look like. What they really care about is your willingness to follow instructions. This meant it was more important to be a good doggy than to, say, shower in the morning. The second was that people who work in live chat usually have a good reason for doing so - but they also usually have at least one totally weird reason too. Like the woman with the baby hooker voice in the cubicle next to mine, Cheyenne.

Cheyenne drove a BMW SUV and had two teenage boys at a prep school in the valley - but she also had a lawyer husband *with testicles like baby mushrooms* (her words). He thought she was going to intimacy therapy three times a week. Actually, she was motoring up to Cynthia's and manning a cubicle.

"Don't question it too much," Cheyenne said on our way out after the last Friday shift. "If you question it too much, then you'll start thinking about it too much. And if you start thinking about it too much, you'll find yourself in a world of confusion."

"Is there any other?" I said, trying to be friendly.

Cheyenne grinned and pulled her strangled red hair up into a neat ponytail. She had just applied careful eyeliner to her wet brow and sprayed deodorant up under her skirt. Necessary rituals before heading home to the valley.

"Haha. No. But seriously," she replied. "That way monsters lie."

But I could not help but think about it. I am a thinking person by nature. This has always been my problem and it's probably why I responded to D.E.M.'s first message at such length. It came midway through my second Monday shift (about 1.00 am in the midnight-to-two prime-time slot). By that point, I was starved for any attention that required only thinking and typing.

D.E.M.: *hey*

AMOROUS ANNIE: *hi there!*

D.E.M.: *mind if I ask you a strange question?*

AMOROUS ANNIE: *that bar is set pretty high for me*

D.E.M.: *what is the nature of your reality?*

AMOROUS ANNIE: *cum again* ☺

D.E.M.: *do you have a sense of what your reality really is? do you have a grasp on the nature of your existence?*

AMOROUS ANNIE: *see me doing this with my finger?*

D.E.M.: *yes*

AMOROUS ANNIE: *real enough for you?*

D.E.M.: *not what im talking about*

AMOROUS ANNIE: *how about now? see? whole hand!*

D.E.M.: ☹ *youre not answering my question*

AMOROUS ANNIE: *im not answering cause i dont know what you want me to say*

D.E.M.: *i just want to know what it means to be real to you*

AMOROUS ANNIE: *taking a poll or something?*

D.E.M.: *no*

AMOROUS ANNIE: *you one of those jesus people?*

D.E.M.: *god no*

AMOROUS ANNIE: *how about one of those cult people? are you typing me from a compound? do you want me to be your slave?*

D.E.M.: *ill just ask you again tomorrow. should give you some time to think*

AMOROUS ANNIE: *because i will be if you ask nicely...*

D.E.M.: *just give the nature of your reality some thought. thanks*

AMOROUS ANNIE: *?? will do buckaroo*

And then D.E.M. was gone from my screen. In his digital absence, he left only the usual list of obscene noms requesting that I *touch this* and *smack that.* What type of man (it had to be a man) logs onto a pay-by-the-minute cam site to ask about someone's reality? And not just *anyone's* reality. *My* reality: a girl making fifty an hour to touch random objects to personal places. It was puzzling, even a little disturbing, a real mind twister.

I called the Director after my shift. It was 3.00 am. Maybe he'd done some kind of orgy-at-the-lyceum-type shoot?

"He asked you *what*?" The Director said.

"I know. Weird, right?"

"*Weird* doesn't even begin to cover it, Darling. That's just...that's just...*dirty*."

I felt a cold tide of excitement crest through my body. It *had* felt dirty. *So* dirty, like the dirtiest thing anyone had ever asked me to do: to reveal *the nature of my reality*. Random objects touching personal places was one thing but *reality* was entirely another. It was so *personal*.

"If he types in tomorrow, I'm going to block him."

"He's certainly earned it."

"I'm going to block him so hard that his reality will crumble down all over his sticky little keyboard."

"Drop the hammer, Sister."

"Although, you have to wonder. What if I *had* tried to answer him?"

On the other end of the line, there was a whirring and grinding in the background. Maybe the Director used these late hours to further smooth his face? I was picturing power tools and sandpaper - the kind of rough implements I never allowed in my cubicle.

"Not that you ever would," he cautioned. "You would never stoop so low."

"Don't know. I'm a real stooper."

"I'm just so fascinated by you," the Director said. "I'm just enthralled."

I laughed, hung up, and began to consider the nature of my reality. There was Idaho, of course. Then there was all of the nothingness that was pre-Idaho (all of the nothingness that was my pre-existence). Then there was now and here. Presumably, there would be a whole lot more nothingness to follow, plus or minus a few paltry decades of life. In between, it seemed unlikely anyone would ask me about the nature of my reality again. D.E.M might represent the best opportunity I would ever have to explore this question in deeply qualified anonymity. Maybe it would even be enlightening. It could shed some light on the big whatever of my existence.

I was still contemplating at 5.00 am. I was also staring out my lone window over pale and ghostly cacti. They sprouted up spermicidically in the milky half-light trickling over some famous hills. I *wanted* D.E.M. to contact me again. I *wanted* to talk about the nature of my reality - if only to confirm I actually had one.

Thankfully, he kept his word.

D.E.M.: *hello again*

AMOROUS ANNIE: w*ell hey there!*

D.E.M.: *think any more about my question?*

AMOROUS ANNIE: *you wernt kidding yesterday?*

D.E.M.: *nope. been waiting for your shift all night*

AMOROUS ANNIE: *is that creepy? i think that might be creepy*

D.E.M: *i doubt im the only one*

AMOROUS ANNIE: *guess ill take that as a compliment*

D.E.M.: *it is. besides you choose to do what you do right?*

AMOROUS ANNIE: *dont we all?*

D.E.M.: *some of us have more choice than others*

AMOROUS ANNIE: *sounds tragic*

D.E.M.: *maybe yes, maybe no...but we were typing about your reality...*

AMOROUS ANNIE: *right. well i was thinking my reality might have a lot to do with time...as in what is time really? and how am i existing in it?*

D.E.M.: *is that so?*

AMOROUS ANNIE: *yes! times really important! like we only have so much of it but we always think we have more. but the 'reality' of the situation is*

D.E.M.: *stop*

AMOROUS ANNIE: *what?*

D.E.M.: *1. stop putting quotes around 'reality' and 2. time probably has very little to do with yours*

AMOROUS ANNIE: *how would you know?*

D.EM.: *because its just one of those things people say. time is how you spend your life and so forth. your truth, your 'reality', so to speak, is different than time. it exists both within and outside of it*

AMOROUS ANNIE: *o-k. dont know what to tell you buster*

D.E.M.: *start with the truth*

AMOROUS ANNIE: *sorry. thats my reality and im sticking to it*

D.E.M.: *sigh. im going to give you some more time to think...just in case*

AMOROUS ANNIE: *just in case what?*

D.E.M.: *in case you decide you want to be honest with yourself*

AMOROUS ANNIE: *whoa. simmer down. ive been warned about bad boys like you*

D.E.M.: *o yeah?*

AMOROUS ANNIE: *yeah. bad boys who want you to 'gaze into the darkness of the deep' or whatever*

D.E.M.: *the 'darkness of the deep'?*

AMOROUS ANNIE: *sounds scary doesnt it?*

D.E.M.: *it does scrunch up the mouth a bit*

I ended the conversation there - always good to keep them guessing!

D.E.M. didn't type so much as a *hey* during my next shift. This left me distracted and agitated in my cubicle, so much so, I began to perform poorly. I hadn't thought this was possible. The job wasn't complicated. *Insert Tab A into Slot B. Repeat.* But now, I was finding it harder to smile into the camera, to react to its obscene requests, to make the appreciative cooing noises required by its dark insectoid eye. D.E.M. was right. My reality had nothing to do with time. I was timeless. My shifts were timeless. Even the world was timeless. It might wink in and out of existence, every so often, but was always fundamentally *there*.

Finally, Chester pulled back my curtain near the end of my second Wednesday shift (11:30 pm in the ten-to-midnight early bird slot). He was there to issue a summons.

"Throw on a robe, Girl. Cynth wants to see you."

I shuffled down the cubicled hall after him, in aggressively fuzzy slippers, passing other gray walls and colorful curtains. I felt tiny and ashamed. Had I failed some kind of secret performance review? Behind Cheyenne's curtain, I thought I heard a moan of concern, but it might only have been fortuitous coincidence.

More troubling was Chester's lack of a smile. I'd never seen him not smiling. I'd also never actually *met* Cynthia. Cynthia was just a voice on the line, a presence in the air. She was the invisible wizard of a digital sex hive and I didn't want to look behind the curtain.

In fact, she turned out to be *minuscule*. That is, she nearly disappeared into the black leather love seat I found her reclined upon. This love seat was located in a windowless, electro-lit chamber, behind a small door that read only *MGMT*. In the staticky twilight of this space, she appeared to have sky white hair, blood pink lips and a fragile elfin jaw. She looked me up and down, her nymphet face back-lit by an iridescent wall of television screens. Each one encapsulated a tiny, naked human contorting on a bed.

"I thought we said big gulps," she said finally.

"I might have exaggerated there."

Why did it feel so weird to have eyes on my body *now*? I had eyes on my body *all the time*.

"And the blondness I was promised?"

"Working on it. I bought the bottle and everything."

"Hmm."

She moved as if to rise from the couch, to flutter up, perhaps. Then she reclined even deeper into its gimp suit cushions.

"Welcome to the control room." She waved around an anemic grub of an arm. "Or, as I like to call it, Peep Central."

What to say to this?

"It's nice."

"No. It's not. It's disgusting."

"Okay. It's disgusting."

Cynthia's star prick eyes stabbed up at me from the love seat.

"But it pays *your* bills, Miss Idaho."

This time, I waited in silence and my silence seemed to satisfy Cynthia in a way my words had not. She rubbed a space on the love seat next to her denim-clad thigh and I sat down obediently. I could have, if I'd wanted to, pulled Cynthia entirely within the confines of my robe and still tied it comfortably.

"Prom queen from Idaho," she said, as if to herself. "Another blessing fallen to us straight off the heartland-to-the-coast pussy train. How long you been in town?"

I pulled my knees up under my robe. Girlish cuddle mode seemed like the most defensible position.

"A little less than a year," I said. "It'll be a year next…"

Cynthia raised a wispy white finger.

"Stop," she said. "Never tell anyone who hires talent - even a talented filth monger like myself - that you've been in town for longer than six months. Anything past six months is spoiled goods. Anything past a year has passed through the system and trickled out the other end."

I nodded and huddled.

"Anyway. Prom queen comes to the city of angels, brightest pearl in the vast tiara of light orbiting the darkness of the Potato State, and she starts doing dirty work to make ends meet. Perhaps she's told her loved ones back home. Perhaps she has not. In any case, she's tits-deep in it now and, maybe, she's beginning to feel like it'll never wash away? Stop me if I've wandered off the path."

"This feels like a movie to me," I said. "It feels like you're reading me lines but I don't even have the script."

Cynthia's index finger began drawing tight circles on the exposed bare flesh of my knee. The touch was ethereal, what molecules must feel like, dancing around each other at impossibly close quarters.

"Very perceptive," she said. "But, unfortunately, there is no script, and there is definitely no happy ending - except for maybe the kind that requires a shower."

"Now *that* is disgusting."

Cynthia waved this comment off with her other tiny hand.

"However, there *is* a screen, or, in this case." She swirled the same hand to gather in the opal light surrounding the love seat. "Many screens. But, as you might have noticed, they all show only one thing. Do you know what that one thing is, Miss Idaho?"

I stared at the finger outlining my knee. It looked as pale and snappable as the tremulous icicles that used to grow on the windowsill of my childhood bedroom. But that was another place, another season, another time. This finger was here. It was now and it was much colder than any icicle. I thought about all those tiny people trapped in their screens and shivered.

"Reality?" I whispered.

"*Exactly*," Cynthia said. "Or, at least, our little peep show perception of it. And it *is* a peep show. Make no mistake. The extent of what we cannot see is vast and the darkness of what we can is endless. It's like we barely even exist."

I was still thinking about icicles. About being stabbed by icicles.

"Do you want to fuck me or what?"

Cynthia's elfin paw squeezed my knee, then retracted

"Of course I do. But not, you know, in the *traditional* sense. I just want to exploit your image to its very best potential and I'm worried that something is getting in the way of that. You were doing so good in your box but now you look *pained* or something. Like the doll has a pin in its brain it just can't get out."

"A *pin*?"

"No one wants to see that. Not the mooks. Not me. Not anyone. We've all got enough pins as it is."

"So you don't want to see reality after all?"

But Cynthia no longer seemed to be registering my presence. She was looking past me into the depths of the MGMT room. Contorted shadows danced on the blue-lit wall. Frantic moanings dribbled out of invisible speakers.

"But what even *is* reality?" she said. "What makes it so *real* in the first place? All you have to do is stop thinking about that itsy-bitsy little pin and then it just falls right out."

I grabbed Cynthia's wrist. It was thinner than Lourde Taylor's business.

"Fire me," I said.

"No."

"If you don't, I don't know what I'll do in front of my camera."

"That's the point. Go crazy. Surprise yourself."

"I'll shit on it. I'll eat it."

"Neither a bad idea, actually."

"*Please.*"

She peeled my fingers off her arm, one by one.

"Go back to your box, Miss Idaho," she said. "Go back to your box, turn on your screen and *smile*."

I fled to my cubicle and found a new message waiting from D.E.M.

D.E.M.: *any further thoughts on the reality question?*

AMOROUS ANNIE: …

D.E.M.: *come on. youve had enough time to think*

AMOROUS ANNIE: *i think im going to block you*

D.E.M.: *what? why?*

AMOROUS ANNIE: *because youre a freak*

D.E.M.: *am i?*

AMOROUS ANNIE: *yes. a philosophical freak*

D.E.M.: *is this a bad time?*

AMOROUS ANNIE: *dont patronize me*

D.E.M.: *then take yourself more seriously. answer my question*

AMOROUS ANNIE: *why would i even trust you with the answer? for all i know you just want to convince me that i dont exist*

D.E.M.: *maybe you dont...*

AMOROUS ANNIE: *you can see me right now*

D.E.M.: *i see what appears to be somebody...but it could just be a ghost*

AMOROUS ANNIE: *a ghost??*

D.E.M.: *a very tired looking ghost trapped in a you-know-what*

AMOROUS ANNIE: *I AM NOT A GHOST!*

D.E.M.: *then prove it. describe the nature of your reality*

AMOROUS ANNIE: *i dont know what it is obviously! why dont you leave me alone?*

D.E.M.: *you really want me to?*

AMOROUS ANNIE: *YES!*

D.E.M.: *i dont think thats in your best interest*

AMOROUS ANNIE: *im blocking you now*

D.E.M.; *please dont*

AMOROUS ANNIE: *sayonara D.E.M.... whatever the fuck that means*

I blocked him. Just the click of a key and his mysterious acronym was gone. And gone with it were all those questions about my reality. It seemed as if it shouldn't have been that easy. You can't just block your inner monologue, even if it's just a bunch of *ugs* and *oogs*. But now there was no more D.E.M. on the board. In his place remained only the usual blinking accumulation of suggestions on how to demean myself - if I even *had* a self. I was no longer certain.

I called the Director on my ride home. (Live chat money had upgraded me to Über.)

"You did *what*?" he said.

"I quit." We were FaceCalling now. I enjoyed FaceCalling with the Director. I liked the way his smooth face filled the screen on my phone. It was a calming image, like an oily egg trapped in a jar of black ink.

"I walked out the door without saying anything to anybody."

The Director's face became taut.

"Darling, I really put myself out there to get you *in* that door."

"Well, now I'm out again. That's how doors work. You go in them and then you go back out."

The Director didn't think this was as clever as I did. The driver, a skinny white boy with little lips, was also sneaking disapproving looks into the backseat.

"Then at least tell me we're back on for the iPhone shoot?" the Director pleaded. "I have to confess, I tried someone else but all she did was damage the merchandise. It's got to be you, Darling. My camera needs you. My camera wants you. My camera is *obsessed* with you."

"Please stop."

"Whatever you say, My Love."

"I said I'll think about it."

You're a goddess. You're a queen. You're eternal. You're…"

"And please never talk to me about your camera that way again."

Back at my apartment, I glared out over the cacti. This morning - for it was somehow morning again - they looked unusually lush, as if they had been swelled and greened by some bounteous rain I had neither seen nor heard.

"I do exist," I shouted at them through the window. "I really *do!*"

My phone buzzed out an incoming text. The screen revealed the terror of an unknown number.

hey this is D.E.M.

I stared at the digits (another honest-to-God local area code) then at the message. My thumbs whack-a-moled the screen.

howd u get this #?

my powers are vast

but my # is specific

lets focus on the question at hand

which is?

the nature of your reality (as usual)

already told you. idk

then whats your best guess?

cogito ergo dumb? i think ur obsessed with me

maybe thats what makes you real?

no

maybe youre just a figment of my imagination?

eew

my imagination is a very fertile place...

eww! maybe ur just a figment of MY imagination. ever think of that?

clever

damn straight. i can block ur texts 2

dont you want to better understand your existence (or lack thereof)?

blocking u now...

dont you want to know why you left idaho (if you ever really did)?

dont you dare bring idaho into this!

dont you want to know why you've chosen to sexually interface with lonely individuals via camera and keyboard? Lonely individuals who may or may not exist (just like yourself)?

stop!

dont you want to know what it is that draws these individuals to your digital flame?

its called a vagina asshole

a 'vagina asshole'?

a vagina, asshole!

why do you even do it in the first place?

what can i say? im a flame 4 odd moths

but the choice, annette! you made a choice! this implies agency...

omg, who said anything about making a choice? i needed money!
there are other ways to make money
not if ur a barely legal blonde big-gulped ex-prom queen
but ones reality is always a choice isn't it?
umm...
...or at least continuing to exist is
☹ thats so weird! ur so weird!
reality, some folks say, is also just perception...

I blocked D.E.M.'s phone number and called the Director.

"I'm going home," I said. "I haven't been back in, well... I've *never* been back. But I'm going home *right now*."

"Tell me we're not talking about Idaho."

"The Potato State it is."

"Tell me we're not talking about a place that phonetically self-identifies as a slut."

"I'm afraid so."

The Director moaned.

The road to Idaho (as I remembered it) traversed a vast wasteland that began right outside the City of Angels and continued, unabated, for millions of desolate miles. With the sun bleeding out into the sea behind me, I departed into it that evening. When I'd crossed it a year ago, I'd been heading towards the sun. Now I was moving away - two equally pointless trajectories for someone unsure of their very existence.

Earlier that day, I'd turned all my live chat freezer money into an old convertible and watched the skull-like front of my apartment recede down the skin-colored pavement of my street. A few stunted and lifeless palms, no higher than my bent antenna, listed off towards the Pacific, in a current of smoggy breeze. Supposedly pollution made these sunsets better. In Idaho, there was only sky.

Many hours later, on the far side of a brilliant hallucination of Vegas, I veered to avoid a spectral creature in the highway. It might have been a possum. It might have been from another planet.

"I exist!" I screamed at it. Then I screamed some additional meaninglessness into the darkness.

Soon, the night began to come into focus as I accelerated. More speed brought out colors in a spectrum invisible to those unwilling to put their existence at such risk. A flash in the atmosphere above might have been a satellite or maybe a missile. A flash in the dark could be anything. I did a hundred for a while, then ripped the convertible over to the shoulder and stopped. In the surrounding black, my headlights seemed to carry as far as an ocean. They were green and spectral, as brilliant as one of those ghostly fish at the bottom no one ever sees.

My phone rang - an incoming FaceCall. I put it to my ear without looking at the screen.

"I told you," a familiar voice said. "My powers are vast."

"You still want to see my reality?"

"Oh, yes. Very much."

"You're sure?"

"Show it to me, Darling. Oh, please. *Show it to me!*"

I threw my phone out into the night.

Ars Amatoria

Katie McIvor

A few weeks before my son was born, Uncle Reginald woke me up in the middle of the night. His craggy face loomed over me, crevassed by torchlight. He put a finger to his lips, *sssh*, and motioned for me to get up. In the other bed, my brother Michael rolled over with a breathy groan.

I was awake instantly - the flick-of-a-switch awakening we're all capable of at the age of ten. And I was, of course, deeply curious. Michael and I often stayed with Uncle Reginald during the summer, when our mother needed a break from us. For the most part, he ignored us, content to let us run wild around the attics and ancient gardens of his home. He had certainly never woken us up in the middle of the night before. I guess I felt special, too, because he had selected me and not Michael for this mysterious mission.

I followed Uncle Reginald through the creaking dark of the old house to the library. The lamps were lit and two candles burned in glass holders on the windowsill. In the flickering glow, the shadow of the rolling ladder flared and diminished up against the ranks of books.

Uncle Reginald led me to the long rosewood desk. He normally had a selection of books laid out, some of them partitioned off from the others in neat little wooden boxes. Tonight he had cleared a space.

In the middle of the desk lay one book, a large, leatherbound volume with *Encyclopaedia Iranica* written in golden lettering down the spine. Uncle Reginald leaned over and stared. I stared, too.

Nothing happened for a long moment. And then, the book moved. It wriggled, leaning halfway up on one of its covers, and shuddered slightly, as though in pain. Then it flopped down again.

I hissed at Uncle Reginald. "What's happ..."

"Quiet!"

The book moved again. It groaned, a very soft sound, perhaps just the leather edges pressing against the desk. Perhaps not.

Behind me, in the doorway, Michael said groggily, "What's going on?"

"Hush!" whispered Uncle Reginald. "She's nearly ready."

Michael crept over to join us. He looked at me pointedly, as if to say, *why are you indulging this madman*? Then he saw the book moving and his shoulders contracted in fright.

"Easy, easy," said Uncle Reginald. "Here she comes, now."

He gently stroked the book, rubbing its deep, heavy spine. The volume shuddered, lurched, drummed its covers on the desk. Something was emerging from beneath it.

"There we are," said Uncle Reginald. "Beautiful, beautiful."

He reached underneath the book and pulled, very slowly. It gave a final tremble, an agonized groan, and flopped down against the desk. Uncle Reginald pulled out, from beneath it, a second book which had not been there before. The new book was a slim volume, paperback with a blue cover. It was entitled *A Brief History of Zoroastrianism*.

Michael said, "What in the..." then stopped.

Uncle Reginald held the baby book up to the light of a lamp. He blew on it gently, and fine white sawdust flew from its sides. He stroked it softly, lovingly, as if it were a newborn lamb.

"And that, boys," he said, "is how books are made."

We spent the rest of that summer in the library. The gardens were forgotten, the hide-and-seek attics, the games of spooking each other down in the cellar. We didn't need those anymore. In the library, we shuffled like entranced pigeons around the desk, as Uncle Reginald demonstrated his methods.

"Hardbacks go well with other hardbacks," he would say. "Hardback with a paperback, then you've got a mess, see? Torn covers at the very least. And you've got to consider the gestation period, which broadly correlates with word count. You have to think about content, too. Can't put pulp with classic, or history with sci-fi. Who knows what you'd get?"

We wanted to know. We waited till he'd gone to bed and crept back into the library on our own, communicating in voiceless giggles, skimming up and down the ladder to select our mating pairs.

We put Nietzsche with Nigella Lawson, Ovid with Mark Twain, Stephen King with Milton. The hybrids that emerged we smuggled back to our bedroom and stored in a shoebox, reading them in torchlit huddles under our duvets. The results were sometimes nonsense, sometimes spectacular. My favourite was the chapter where the Gunslinger breaks into the Garden of Eden and shoots Adam through the neck.

Towards the end of our stay, I was reading in bed one night, while Michael was asleep. I had got to the bit in my new-born book where Eve and the Gunslinger have passionate sex in the Garden before being cast out by the Dark Man. I found myself lingering over the passionate sex verses. I had only recently started masturbating, or trying to, after Michael unkindly informed me he had already been capable of ejaculation by the time he was my age. I was only a year and a half younger than him but, in matters of sex, he seemed increasingly of a different generation and I was eager to catch up.

Deliberately pawing myself in my torchlit duvet den, I lingered on the descriptions of Eve's anatomy. The language was difficult in places. I didn't know what 'the bloated sausage of connubial love' really meant. But 'he breasted the mounds of her inmost bowre' sounded sexy - as did the numerous depictions of Eve's 'curvèd abundance'.

When the Gunslinger shouted, 'Haile wedded love!' at his moment of climax, I found myself unexpectedly spurting a clear, viscous substance into my clenched hand. Startled, I dropped the book. Some of the substance got onto its pages.

I scrubbed it off with the hem of my pyjama top. Hoping that Michael was too deeply asleep to have heard anything, I pushed the book back into the shoebox and turned off the torch.

The next day we were busy with an enormous first edition of *Les Hommes de Bonnes Volonté* which, after a lengthy gestation period, was ready to be delivered of - not one but, as it turned out - three young volumes of French literary criticism. Uncle Reginald was beyond chuffed with them. He couldn't speak a word of French but nestled the young books into a bed of wood shavings and dusted their pages with loving attention. The mother tome was cleaned off and put in a darkened room to rest.

I got into bed that night feeling exhausted but elated. Michael quickly fell asleep. I was just drifting off, too, when I heard a sort of scratching noise. My eyes flicked open. I lay listening hard in the dark. The noise seemed to be coming from underneath my bed.

I rolled to the side and stuck my head over the edge of the mattress. The shoebox lay long and angular in the dark. As I watched, the lid jolted slightly and, again, that faint scratching noise came from within.

Cold horror flooded my belly. Was it a rat, or a cockroach, chewing through my beloved newborn book? Moving quietly, so as not to wake Michael, who would mock me for being afraid, I slithered out of bed and picked up the shoebox.

I held it with one hand on top and one underneath, in case the rat, or whatever it was, managed to force the lid up and jump out at me. Then I scurried to the bathroom.

Uncle Reginald's bathroom was monstrously avocado. I dropped the box into the bathtub and snatched up the sickly-green toilet brush. The shoebox emitted a soft yelping sound. Holding my breath, I reached in with the brush and knocked the lid off.

Curled up on top of *Dark Paradise: The Gunslinger* was a tiny creature, humanesque, with long, frail limbs and the shrivelled face of a baby. All the breath whooshed out of my belly in disbelief. The creature was crying, dribbling ugly tears onto the surface of my book. Its skin was papery. Half-formed black lettering stained the white ribs here and there. As I moved closer, the creature raised its head and our eyes met over the rim of the bathtub.

My first thought was to drown it. Poke it down the plughole and let the hideous thing flush out to sea. But it looked at me with eyes which were the exact colour of Michael's. I understood then what I had done. What I had made.

"Hello," I whispered to the tiny infant. "I guess I'm your dada."

I smuggled him home in the shoebox. He cried constantly for food in those early days, mewling like a kitten - and it was a job and a half to keep my mother from discovering him. But, as he grew, his needs diminished. Eventually, he learned to form words, although his speech was always slurred and strangely archaic. I named him Milton. When my mother and Michael were out, I would take him into the garden, wrapped in a blanket to protect his translucent skin from the sun. I would point out to him the blackbirds and the different flowers and the shapes of clouds. He was fascinated by the world. He wanted to go to school and learn to read but I couldn't take the chance of letting him near a book.

Uncle Reginald died when I was nineteen. For reasons which no one could fathom, he left me the house. My family pressured me to sell it, but I refused. Once I am done with university, I intend for us to return to the house, Milton and I. There are endless rooms there where he will be safe from prying eyes. And I want to show him round the library.

So we stumble on together, my literary son and I, through the difficulties of student housing, the lack of privacy, and Milton's endless awareness that he is not like other boys. He has now reached twenty inches in height. My dream is that he will, one day, grow tall enough to walk among humans - passing for an ordinary boy. I forsake the company of others for him. At night I sleep to the sound of his gentle crooning. Curled beside me, he intones half-rhymes, nonsense blank verse, about angels and demons and the Library of Paradise.

His dreams mingle with my own.

Yapo's Magic Pintle

Shelly Lyons

1. Provocation.

See the bloated cloud with lightning in its belly drift across the valley and hover like a sentient thing over the business park and its dozen identical six-story building. See the immaculate pathways winding around the buildings, corporate art installations, stone benches, a volleyball court, a 3-hole golf course and life-size chess pieces.

2. Now.

The sixth floor of the sixth building in Yapoply is an open floor plan of low-wall worker cubicles. Without humans for context, it could be a dollhouse office with 1:12 scale pen cups, computer workstations and miniature office furniture - everything ready for when the dolls come to work.

Look closer. Workers cower under their desks. An HR lady and a sales extrovert slap light switches. One by one, the plastic panels of fluorescent ceiling lights go out, leaving the office in a pearlescent grayness, courtesy of all the windows and the storm above.

See short Gary toss all the files out of a long-drawer cabinet and roll himself closed. See Big Amy curse fate for not possessing Gary's smallness, before flopping into an ergo chair and hiding under her office blanket.

A horrible bass-toned hissing fills the place, getting louder, closer.

"It's coming up the side of the building," Maureen the temp whispers into Amber's ear.

189

A seismic ripple rolls across Amber's ass. She scoots further under the conference table, just before a tectonic thump and explosion comes from the floor below them.

Outside the conference room, the big windows on the open floor plan break at once. Several people go insane and it's up to their co-workers to either calm them or stuff their mouths with copy paper.

If pressed to describe the sound of the oozing mass, Amber might describe it as the sticky glissade of the world's largest snail.

3. Amber. Ten Minutes Ago.

It was the Friday before a three-day weekend. Yay. But Amber still faced a morning of meetings, all of which promised to be filled with platitudinous jack-offery. The rain made her late, which she knew they'd hold against her when it came time for end-of-year reviews. 'Amber doesn't account for freeway closures and acts of God, especially on Fridays,' they'd say - and another year would pass without a raise.

She sprinted from the garage to the building without an umbrella, eyes swimming in the torrential rain and the shades of green denoting Yapoply's color palette. Green used to be her favorite color until she started here, eight years ago, and heard hundreds of the company's most grotesque sycophants exclaim they 'bleed green!'

Entering the lobby, en route to a latte with three extra shots of espresso to get her through a meeting, she passed the CEO without recognizing him. She assumed he was a job seeker awaiting the call upstairs for an interview.

"Good luck," she scoffed under her breath.

Her rage was so prevalent yet undirected, she didn't know if she meant it like, 'Good luck getting the job, you sad-boy fuckturd with zero social skills,' or, 'Good luck because if you get the job, you'll gain 40 pounds from stress eating'.

She opened the door to the Coffee Dispensary, with a last glance back at the sad boy. Then realized he was Yapoply's CEO and founder, Yapo McFlannery, the still youngish genius himself. He was wearing distressed jeans and a t-shirt, ripped in a zig-zag down the center, like a lightsaber had cleaved it. Folks who recognized him chirped their 'good mornings' and 'happy Fridays.' But Yapo's eyes remained distant, as if studying a pointillist painting only he could see.

Minutes later, Amber emerged with a quadruple-shot latte, noting that Yapo still hadn't moved, except for his hand, which trembled as it lowered the zipper on his jeans.

Christ, was he...?

Crazy Marybeth, the receptionist with the three-inch nails, was going, "Nuh-Uh, sir, no, no, no, sir, don't do it, don't do it!"

Other folks bolted towards the elevators. The lady who watered the office plants did an about-face and left the building altogether.

Marvin Peters, the vaunted Chief Operating Officer, passed her on his way in. He shook off his umbrella and noticed his boss.

"Give us one, Yapo!" He came in for a fist-bump but Yapo was still busy slow-motion unzipping.

Marvin was the guy who wrote a memo comparing the company to a jar of mayonnaise being sullied by a bunch of chickenshits too afraid to step out of the box. He warned: if we didn't give an extra thirty percent I want across the board, we deserved to get crushed by the competition. He belabored the metaphor, stating that the mayo's road to Salmonella might be averted if we all worked more strategically and took decisive chances. Instead of being fired, Marvin was deemed 'Boy Wunderkind' and 'Yapo's Tough-Love Conscience'. His memo became the famous 'Mayonnaise Initiative'.

Not a bit of his anointed brilliance helped him stop Yapo from pulling the zipper to the end of its journey. Out flopped a great wadge of curly blonde pubes like a magician's bouquet, followed by Yapo's gentile prepuce.

"Oh, damn, Yapo," Marvin gasped. "I respect ya, bro, but..."

Marvin got no further. Yapo's erection sprang from its foreskin, elongated in seconds to the length of a full-grown man. It slapped

Marvin across the face, the way Mike Hammer PI did to weaker men. On the third whomping, it dispatched Marvin to the floor like a dollop of mayonnaise.

4. Yapo.

Although Yapo's mouth lay slack and motionless, inside his head dueled the sad cousins, Reminiscence and Longing. Yapo was worth more than many countries of the world but he'd give it all to, once again, mesmerize Maureen with a flick of the eye across a conference room. Yes, their courtship was short but oh so sweet. Valentine's Day ignited a longing for the days when the mere cock of the brow would say, 'meet me in my supply closet.'

When he found her today, he would tell her:

Maurie, remember when we made love in my cabin, in front of the Franklin Stove on the Flokati rug? Remember how we got so sweaty from the fire? Remember when Yapo put his weenus through the big pretzel? Remember how we laughed as you dipped it in mustard? Then we made love again and again, until we were so greasy and sticky with Flokati strands that we looked like irradiated Yetis?

Yes, he would say that. Oh, the sweet memories.

"You asked me why I want to stay a temp?" Dear Maureen asked while they cuddled in a pool of their sweat. "It's because I'm trying to become a playwright or a TV writer, and I'm working on a second draft of my first play. So, it's nice to keep myself free from long-term job entanglements."

"You are endlessly interesting," Yapo responded, ignoring the insinuation about her keeping clear of entanglements and, instead, wiping a mustard blop off the corner of her lush mouth. "I could finance you to write full time, if you so desired."

Her frown nettled him. Why should she frown? Women would kill for his attention and cash.

"Um, anyway, I workshop pages? With other company writers? In the lunchroom at three on Thursdays? We have essayists, writer-writers and screenwriters - but no playwrights, except for me. Oh, see, we take our lunches late..."

"You can take breaks any time, my darling. Or forever."

"Thanks, but I follow the protocols. Whatever, it's dumb I know, and I shouldn't be talking about the story until I'm a hundred percent finished, which I am. But my first draft was very first drafty, if you know what I mean?"

Yapo held her cupcake tits in his hands, wanting to eat the cherries off their tops, feel them slide down his throat and push out past his prostate. It made him drool just thinking about it.

"What's the story?"

"Oh, I shouldn't until it's in better..."

"At least tell me the title!"

She pursed her succulent lips.

"It's called *Flowers in the Dung Heap*. And, oh, what the hell! It's about a group of beatniks in 1956 who accidentally ran over a drifter and then buried him in the woods? So they hit the road, where through a series of adventures, they come to terms with their moral barometers. But one of them is a sociopath who knows if any of the others are nabbed by the police, they'll name names for a reduced sentence, so decides to kill them off. But, from all this comes justice and true empathy. Pablo knows how it feels to walk in Lauren's kitten-heel pumps. Lauren learns to forgive. Guinevere comes to terms with sexual addiction. Jeremiah is the sociopath. Or is he a straight-up demon?"

"Ooh, a twist?" Yapo gushed, delighted to see her face beaming at him. Little Partner emerged from his hot pocket and poked her leg. Maureen then mounted and rode Yapo, her wild orgasm bolstered by him calling her Jackie Kerouac and telling her he'd score some pristine cocaine so she could write the book frenetically, the way Jack wrote *On the Road*.

Thinking about their most glorious weekend made Yapo's body taut and shivery.

5. Amber. Five Minutes Ago.

Paralyzed at the door of the Coffee Dispensary, Amber watched Marvin stagger to standing. In this time, Yapo's penis grew to the size of a manatee and pummeled Marvin until his head cracked open. Gelatinous goo wrapped around his legs, and the last she saw of Marvin was his bifurcated face, frozen in a perpetual scream, as the pink mucosa pulled him into its interior.

Yapo's member diverged. Part of him snaked towards Marybeth, who clung to her chair futilely, while the enlarging globule absorbed it. The last Amber saw of her were those nails clawing at the air. The other part slithered towards Amber, rising some ten feet high, threatening to crash down on her head.

"Holy cannoli!" Amber backed into the commissary, just as the Yapo creature banged against its glass doors like a giant gummy fist. Each womp made more fissures in the glass.

By the time the door shattered, Amber was halfway up the stairs thinking, *No way is it getting through the steel doors of the stairwell.*

A thunderous pounding behind her suggested otherwise.

Is this thing after me? Or am I just in the way? Amber wondered. She got her answer when the urethra, which had grown to the size of a gopher hole, bellowed: "Maureen!" An expulsion of sour droplets sprayed Amber.

Of course my goddamned boss almost blew me off my feet with his penis flatulence. Of course he did!

"Maureeen!"

"Stop that!" She flung her coffee and laptop at it and ran up the stairs.

Jerzy, a newer temp, paced by the third-floor entrance, holding the fire ax he'd pulled out of the fire alarm box. She'd almost made out with him at the Christmas party but her inability to work around his cold sore - both physically and mentally - kept it from happening.

"The alarm didn't even go off when I took the ax," Jerzy screamed at her as she passed. "Nothing is working!"

"Your ax won't do jack!" Amber rounded up the next flight of stairs. "Follow me!"

"I'm sure you remember me telling you that I have combat training with both ax and sword," were Jerzy's last words as the gargantuan sucked him up mid-swing. In seconds, Jerzy the temp was no more.

"Fuck this job!" Amber took two steps at a time.

6. Dumbshow.

As it expanded and consumed upstairs, Yapo occasionally slapped it from his place in the lobby, staying on his feet, even as his member sought to fill the entire building. The trick was to anchor himself firmly within his memories of Her.

Using office workers and his imagination as props, Yapo summoned representations of Maureen's play from the depths of his amorphous hard-on, bringing them bubbling to the surface like paper dolls putting on a show.

In the first swell, a woman in a beret representing Lauren bobbed up.

"You should have driven! I mean yes, if I could go back in time, or sell my soul, I'd do it! But I can't, so y'all need to crawl out."

The next swell brought up Guinevere, the cute Japanese beatnik.

"What's happening to the world around us? Is it...shimmering?"

A skinny Latinx dude, aka Pablo, replied, "Reality is bending, people!"

Then a shifty rough, who could only be Jeremiah the sociopath, appeared.

"Careful what you wish for, gorgeous. Mephistopheles has huge ears, all the better to hear you with."

He ended on a maniacal laugh.

As a coda, each character held up a pastel portrait of Maureen, and all her painted images said, "It's called *Flowers in the Dung Heap* and I workshop it every Thursday at three."

7. Amber & Maureen.

Amber pushed open the stairwell door and dashed out onto the sixth floor. Met by darkness and quiet, except for the occasional sob of someone who'd snapped, she took a moment to adjust. Nowhere left to go, except the roof. Building Six was close enough to building Seven that a fire hose and a good running start might get herself and others across to safety.

Which way to roof access?

The second she saw Maureen, she realized what a profound mistake it was to come all the way upstairs. Because here - looking petrified and, of course, beautiful - was Yapo's raison d'être.

"Amber...Amber!" Maureen hissed, waving for her to come into the conference room. Amber sprinted past a half-dozen cubicles and Maureen ushered her inside.

"I was just on the 5th floor but I ran up the stairs," Maureen said.

Somewhere below them, desks smashing together sounded like bowling pins.

Glad to see a couple of work allies huddled under the table, Amber told everyone, "I've seen it, it's horrible. We have to get up to the roof..."

Her last words were muted by a wail of Yapo's rolling thunder.

"Maureeeeeeeeeeeeeeeen!" It crashed through every window. It broke down the steel doors. It burst from the elevator.

"Jeez, this is so embarrassing," Maureen grunted.

Everyone who was crowded under the conference table began to wonder if their lives were worth risking, instead of letting the thing have Maureen. Shouldn't they take the Platonic course of action and sacrifice one for the greater good?

Well, that's what Amber, the philosophical essayist - slash - project manager was thinking. She concluded with a terrible afterthought: At least nobody will ever have to sit through a performance of *Flowers in the Dung Heap.*

8. Writers Break!

3.00 pm yesterday, Amber, Maureen, Debi, Charles, Foton, Chris, Gil, Reiko and Savannah pulled two tables together in the furthest corner of the cafeteria. Everyone set up their laptops and Foton pounded a Dwight Shrute Funko Pop to bring the club to order.

"Today we go over Act Five of *Flowers in the Dung Heap*...uh..." he squinted at his phone... "Then, Gil's 'Black Mirror' episode, entitled *SinguLarry*. Love the title, dude."

Gil doffed an invisible hat to him.

"...And Amber's essay about Marcus Aurelius at the laundromat, bravo, my friend. The part about sock-folding and virtue ethics..."

He chef-kissed his fingers and Amber felt herself blush.

"Shut up, Foton, I cannot be self-satisfied or I'll rot, you dummy."

Everyone laughed because Amber was so incorrigibly caustic.

Then everyone's mirth evaporated for, standing a few feet away from them was Yapo McFlannery, the still youngish genius himself - clutching papers in his hand.

"I wrote a haiku," he said in a voice so soft and vulnerable one harsh word might turn him to dandelion fuzz in the wind.

Amber shot a glance at Maureen, whose face froze in a rictus of mortification.

Yapo cleared his throat.

"I was going to pass out the pages, but it's so short, I guess I'll..." he stared around until everyone nodded, all, 'Oh, please, please share your haiku with us, Yapo.'

During his recitation, he kept his eyes planted on Maureen...

"Delicate Nipples... Erect Incendiaries... Mouth-fruit from the Gods."

Maureen fled the cafeteria. Amber assumed she was headed for HR. Yapo shrieked and ran in the opposite direction.

Everyone worried about the value of their stock options should Yapo kill himself.

9. Up on the Sixth Floor. Now.

Those in the conference room crawl out from beneath the table to peek through the slim windows on either side of the door. Outside, printer stations, cubicles and people get bulldozed. Screamed prayers for mercy are snuffed, seconds after they begin.

"Well, no way we're getting to the roof now," says Amber to Maureen. "You can stop this, you know."

"How?"

"Tell it you love it. Say you changed your mind."

"Say you liked its stupid haiku," Reiko adds.

"That's going to stop it from eating me?" Everyone stands up, encircling Maureen. "What are you gonna do? Why are you all staring at me?"

"Wait," says Amber. "Wait. How can we stop a penis? How?"

A bunch of torpid faces gape at her.

"Guys? Guys." She claps to rouse their attention. "How do we injure it?"

Tom Jasper snaps his fingers. "Kick it."

"Punch it," Reiko says.

"Tear it apart with my teeth," Maureen suggests.

"Let's do it." Amber uses her best project manager voice. "Grab something. If you only have your hands and feet, use them and your teeth. If it doesn't work, we'll toss Maureen."

"It'll work," Maureen assures the group as they scatter away from the door. In seconds, the Yapo creature smashes through the wall, veins thick and protruding, urethra as big as a man-hole. But before it can gobble anyone, Maureen moves to the front.

"You're an ugly bully who's lost perspective of what it means to be a human being, and especially a man!" she screams, before tossing her ergo chair at it. "You could feed the poor with your money but, instead, you try to buy affection! You're getting sued, you privileged, inappropriate little prick!"

Amber and the rest kick and punch it until fetid gas wheezes out the urethra and the pink gob softens. Maureen stomps it with one of her stiletto heels. The skin retracts, like a reel of aluminum measuring tape snapping back into its protective pocket.

10. The Lobby. Now.

The pintle's forceful egress pulls the office back from the dead, spits out bodies, furniture and office supplies; destabilizes the architecture, resulting in crumpled walls and doorways. Marybeth is gooey and lacerated, but still clinging to her chair. Marvin folds his face back together.

Up above, the storm abates, transforming into a white cotton cirrus - scattering feathery pieces across a clear blue sky.

Yapo finally blinks.

Tom, another company bro, has entered the building, with a nearly identical bro, each sporting blinking earbuds. He slaps Yapo on the back.

"You're using the dream magic again, Yapo. That's why you make more money in thirty seconds than we do all year, including bonuses. But you have to be careful which dreams we see, okay, buddy?"

"I have no control over my dreams," Yapo mumbles. "The storm cloud... she came... she made me..."

A tiny sob escapes him.

"It's okay, Yapo. I've got your back. Justin has your back."

"I definitely have your back," Justin says.

"Yapo wants to explode you all from the inside!" The remnants of his blown penis rally back for a last metamorphosis into a screeching dragon before folding into a sad, wilted flower.

People in the lobby wince or avert their eyes. Several of them pull out their phones and begin filming.

Yapo looks down at what's in his hand. Within the space of two seconds, he understands he's been in the lobby's corner with his penis hanging outside his pants (and occasionally flicking it) - because he's having a nervous breakdown. His life and business, as he knew them, are over.

"I want to rewind the last bit where it went up the stairwells," he says, voice cracking.

"Don't, Yapo," Tom warns. "You're a cool guy and a cool guy wouldn't do that."

Yapo tucks it back inside and zips up.

"Nobody's going to feel sorry for me one bit."

"Oh, no, Yapo, don't worry," Tom reassures him.

"Lots of people will feel sorry for you. Lots."

King Solomon's Sword

Mark Silcox

"Look," said Ambassador Welb of the Muloumi delegation. "I'm not saying I don't *personally* enjoy eating your species' larvae. But culinary fashions change quickly on my homeworld."

She held up her shaggy forepaws in a gesture of resignation.

"If you want us to keep on digging up uranium at the same rate, you're gonna have to find us something new to snack on."

"Repulsive, molting parasite!" chittered my boss, Second Viceroy Pttk Kllya Z. "The mere act of speaking to you fills my mouthparts with hot spew!"

Welb just shrugged. The Muloumi are an easygoing race, for all that they're sharp negotiators. I suppose she figured Pttk's outburst was part of our normal bargaining routine. But other variously-shaped alien faces around the reverberant hall were turning toward us, with expressions ranging from wary to downright irritable.

"There's also the matter of your lawsuits concerning the third moon of Velda, in the A-3a1 system," Welb continued. "We think it's about time you guys quit claiming you have mineral rights there. You haven't sunk a mine on the surface for three decades, and dealing with all the litigation is a huge time-waster."

"You speak like the lice-ridden meat-sack you are," Pttk remarked, clicking his mandibles imperiously. "However, we have had an excellent harvest of brown Gloryfruit on our home planet this year. Perhaps if our surplus larvae are too rich for your degraded palates..."

202 · That is SO Wrong!

"Gloryfruit? Are you serious? Look, you guys need to do better than that." The hirsute diplomat rose from her chair. "We wouldn't feed those nasty things to our domestic pets! Really, if the Tzekket are at all serious about doing business, you need to find a way to…"

"Akakakakakakakak!" The Viceroy lurched up onto his back legs and flung himself across the marble partition that separated the Muloumi delegation from our own. With an agile snip of his jaws, he severed Ambassador Welb's head, then shoved his proboscis into the open wound and slurped out a couple of pints of her blood.

Most of the other diplomats, scattered around the Temple of Trade, did their best to ignore this spectacle. This was an ancient room and its graceful polished balconies and scores of hidden cameras had witnessed lots of strange behavior over the centuries. But a few nearby observers shook their heads and briefly grimaced, shuddered, or clicked their disapproval.

I bowed my antennae. Just the second day of the convention and already our species were singled out as pariahs. It wasn't the first time this sort of thing had happened, either.

Something had to be done to avert further catastrophe. I gathered my wits and took a slow step over the partition, past the podium Welb had been speaking from a moment before. I retracted my jaws to show I wasn't a threat. Second Viceroy Pttk drew his head back from the corpse he'd been sucking on and glanced around dazedly, his prothorax spattered with gore. The remaining Muloumi were huddled together, sobbing and casting sulky looks in my direction.

"On behalf of all the Tzekket Trade Delegation, I hereby express my most profound regrets for what has just transpired. I solemnly pledge that the Ambassador's family will receive personal condolences from our glorious Emperor, as well as full compensation for her demise. We hope that the flatulent, unwashed degenerates of the Muloumi diplomatic corps" - I felt I had to slip in a few epithets, just for the sake of form - "will not view this incident as an impediment to further negotiations."

"What the hell is *wrong* with you?" squalled Welb's second-in-command, pounding his rear paws against the floor, while his colleagues howled and shuddered. "Do you guys understand what the word 'diplomacy' even *means*? Do you think this place would exist at all?..." He gestured with one forepaw at the high walls of the Temple around us. "If it was considered *okay* for different species to devour each other on a whim?"

"Inexcusably arrogant, parasite-ridden monkey-face..." the Second Viceroy began, but I patted him gently on the back. His incipient rant petered out into inaudibility. The musky scent of the mammals was making me a bit hungry myself, and it was hard to take them seriously while they were exhibiting such mawkish sentimentality about their dead comrade. But the shaggy creature telling me off really did have a point. And we still badly needed that uranium.

"I'm sure if we all just settle down and try to..."

As soon as I spoke again, the Muloumi turned their backs and filed out of the building in a huff. I watched them go without making any further efforts at pacification. I figured they would probably return the following day when brokering sessions resumed. But I was sure that my race would have to pay in more ways than one for today's disaster.

As I headed back to my suite on an upper floor of the Temple, I felt a chill pass through my carapace at the thought of having to report back to High Command. Aristocrats like Pttk, who have earned their titles via interstellar martial exploits, don't have to worry about official censure. But bureaucrats like me are the beneficiaries of recent experiments with meritocracy in the Tzekket Imperium and, as such, are always just a step away from termination.

"Ah hell, Cryyvtt," my old friend King's Counselor Rrkttl Yzzyn K, muttered, after I had updated him. He shot me a baleful look from the wall-mounted com screen, his antennae aflutter with annoyance. "That's the third time Pttk has slaughtered an alien right in the middle of negotiations."

"I know," I said. "I was present during the first incident, remember? This time wasn't as messy. Apparently, mammals don't, um, *explode* in quite the way that medusae do."

"Useful to know," Rrkttl remarked drily. "Think they'll come back to the table?"

"With a little gentle nudging, perhaps. They do seem very worked-up about those puny mines of theirs on the Veldan moon."

"Small mercies. It's obviously no good sending the Second Viceroy back into the fray, though. We'll have to ship him home and find a way to ease him into dignified retirement. I'm afraid you know what that means, my friend."

"Oh blast, I suppose I do. You're suggesting arbitration?"

"Indeed."

During big conventions like this one, major trading species who were unable to make it to the Temple, would often hire members of other parasite races to represent their interests. It was considerably more unusual to use such agents as neutral third parties when you'd already gone through the trouble of shipping in your own delegation. But it was probably our only realistic option at this point.

"Should I propose the idea to the Muloumi tomorrow?"

"We might as well start looking around right away for somebody to suggest to them. There are quite a few different flavors of parasite lurking around the Temple these days, so I'm optimistic we can find one sympathetic to our interests. Let me chat with a scholar I know at the Department of Xenology. See if she has any recommendations. Why don't you go get a drink, Cryyvtt? You've had a trying afternoon. Take your tachphone, just in case I need to get back in touch."

The Temple of Trade did have a really excellent bar. One thing most of the galaxy's dominant species have in common is an appetite for intoxication. All of the famous drinks that were also legal were available on tap, served by a good-natured AI named Vloot P-715, who was fluent in seventy-nine languages. When I arrived, reps from at least two dozen other species were already relaxing after the day's bartering, amid a thick fog of diversely exuded chemicals and synthetic deodorizers. Before long, I was nursing my woes over a tall Qualoone-Venom cocktail flavored with sugary leaf matter.

Given the reputation of my species, I don't get a lot of fellow diplomats sidling up to me at these sorts of venues, trying to make small talk. But I can spend hours just quietly watching, as the strangely-shaped, fragrant horde gather to slake their exotic thirsts and force themselves to unwind. Some provoke momentary surges of disgust or hostility when they pass too close. And a few of the older species have been dread enemies of the Tzekket during former, less civilized eras. But all of them are there to represent the most ancient, time-tested of species, who've triumphed over huge biological odds to arrive at the political apex of our overcrowded galaxy.

I had just ordered myself a second drink when my tachphone chimed. Counselor Rrkttl's face appeared on the screen, his antennae curving outward just a bit smugly. I took a deep draught of syrupy venom before meeting his gaze.

"Wow," I said to him. "That was fast."

"No point in wasting time. We're pretty sure we've picked out a good candidate for arbitrator. His ship arrived at the Temple two hours ago but he says he can meet you in the bar later this evening."

"Species?"

"They call themselves 'humans.' I doubt you've heard of them. They've never been major political players, galactically speaking. They registered as parasites less than half a century ago so, at this stage in their career, they are understandably eager to please."

I actually did barely recall the word 'human' from a few of the historical chronicles I like to read during long interstellar voyages. Nothing very specific was coming to mind but my curiosity was piqued. Parasite-grade species usually don't make it into the history books unless there's something a bit vivid or quirky about them.

"OK, I'm game," I told the sly old courtier. "You'd tell me if you had anything up your sleeve, wouldn't you, Rrkttl's?"

His jaws slid out a tiny bit, then retracted quickly.

"I don't want to induce any prejudices in you, my friend. Why don't you have a quick chat with this guy, then call me afterwards, so we can compare notes?"

The human envoy stumbled into the bar a few minutes later. When I first saw him, I was totally astonished. He was a mammal! A fairly exemplary one, at that - straight-backed, muscular, bilaterally symmetrical - though the absence of hair anywhere other than his face was an anomaly.

This wouldn't do *at all*, I thought to myself. The whole point of this exercise was to find a species that *wouldn't* have an automatic bias against us! Asking another mammal to adjudicate between us and the Muloumi seemed like a suicidally bad decision.

The creature looked predictably drowsy and star-sick from the day's travel. He walked straight up to me, exhibiting obvious signs of aversion, but doing a decent job of masking them with formal gestures of deference. He was wearing a ridiculous, shiny outfit with a patch sewn on the front that read 'Space Squad'. Obviously a shallow ploy to restore his species' desiccated self-esteem.

"I salute you, your great people, and your extraordinary civilization, Consul Cryyvtt," he recited in heavily accented Galactic Standard, muffing the pronunciation of my name, but not too badly. "I hope that I may prove the worth of my own, inferior species by serving the glorious Tzekket in some tiny way."

I could have chosen not to sully myself with personal contact by addressing him via an AI translator or a perceptual veil. But the intoxicating venom had taken the edge off my sense of propriety. I patted the vacant barstool beside me with the tip of one foreleg.

"Sit down, human," I said. "Let me buy you a drink."

His comically ugly name turned out to be 'Larry Hobart.' After a few sips of Lamphalian bile tincture, his wan, half-hairless visage started to take on some color.

I called up the video record of that afternoon's fiasco on my tachphone. I figured I might as well see how Hobart reacted to the spectacle before asking him any subtler, more probing questions.

Predictably enough, he reared back in his seat and shuddered violently when Ambassador Welb's head flew into the air.

"Mother of Mercy!" he shouted. "I mean, ah, was that strictly necessary, sir?"

I shrugged my antennae.

"My species do have some unorthodox folkways."

"God," the human murmured to himself. "There's so much *blood...*"

My audition-enhancers detected a palpable quickening of his heartbeat as he rewound the recording and watched it again, then a third time, from start to finish. These mammals, with their hyperactive empathy! 'Space Squad' indeed! What the hell was Rrkttl up to, sending me this warm-blooded sad sack when there were so many other hardy parasite races to choose from? Perhaps the real problem wasn't just the Second Viceroy and his kind. Perhaps even the meritocrats of my species were starting to lose their grip on the nuances of diplomacy. The thought made me inexpressibly sad. I signaled over to Vloot and ordered my own glass of frothy, inebriating bile.

Professional diligence required me to learn at least a bit more about this critter's psychological profile. When I was sure he was done with it, I took back my tachphone and watched his face as he sat for a moment in pensive silence.

"So tell me, Larry," I eventually asked him, "how did you humans get into the mediation business?"

Hobart explained that his own conspecifics hadn't had the chance to explore much of their own neighborhood before they were assimilated into the Galactic Commonwealth. That struck me as unusual - first contact is usually reserved for species that have managed to colonize at least a few dozen exoplanets.

"The annual stipend of fossil fuels and fissile minerals granted to all parasite species is an enormous boon to my people," he added.

"Aha. So you guys stripped the resources from your homeworld while you were still pre-interstellar?"

He lowered his head just slightly.

"It's a common enough story, I suppose." Then he looked me in the eyes and continued with a bit more confidence. "It turns out that we do have something of a *gift* for diplomacy, though. In less than fifty years, we've already earned considerable renown in this capacity."

"I see." I was amused by his puny boast - we Tzekket are well-known braggarts ourselves. "Why do you think that is, exactly? What is it about you humans that makes you such effective intermediaries?"

"Let me tell you an ancient story from one of my people's holy books."

Hobart's voice had already gotten louder and a bit slurred. There's nothing like Lamphalian bile for provoking fits of tipsy eloquence. A goggle-eyed Saurian ambassador from the Blewt Federation glanced over at us, scowling, then quickly looked away when I caught his eye.

"There was once a great King on my homeworld, named Solomon," said Hobart. "And he was, uh, *super*-famous for his *wisdom*. And one day…"

He stopped and glanced upward at my antennae, perhaps a little worried he was addressing me too informally. I twitched them in an encouraging way. The sacred literature of failed civilizations fascinates me - it's always full of such magnificently bad advice. He took another draught of his cold bile before continuing.

"…One day, King Solomon was approached by a pair of angry women. The two of them were quarreling over a human infant child - each one said she was the kid's mother."

This tale was already starting to drift into the surreal. But I remembered that mammal species tend to have small litters and sometimes develop a sense of morbid proprietorship over individual spawn.

"I see. So what did this King do about it?"

"Well, after listening to each woman's argument, he had a servant bring him his *very sharpest sword*." Larry paused to belch softly into one hand. "Then he said, 'Look, ladies, tell you what I'll do. How 'bout I cut your kid in half with this sword, see? Then you'll...'" - another quick burp - "then you'll each have the same amount of him! Won't that, um, resolve your dispute?"

"Hang on," I interjected. "When you say 'infant child,' what you mean is a larval human, right? Surely not?..."

"Um, no, my species don't have a larval stage," Larry replied. "Just picture, y'know, a smaller version of me."

I found I was genuinely shocked by this horrid yarn.

"So you're saying this is part of your species' *wisdom* literature?"

Hobart nodded. "Pretty smart guy, Solomon, right?"

"And these women and this non-larval child - they really were themselves, *humans*, just like your ancient King? Not some sort of domesticated food creatures or alien foes?"

Larry was starting to look a bit worried now.

"Well, it's just folklore - doubtful that it actually happened. But it worked! The two women totally backed off, or whatever."

I shook my head.

"Stories like this make me glad I'm not a Xenologist."

I decided I'd had enough to drink for the evening. I couldn't imagine what I was supposed to glean from this gruesome narrative about a human monarch menacing autonomous members of *his very own species* with some primitive instrument of death.

The crowd in the bar was beginning to thin out. There were a couple of improbable interspecies flirtations going on at corner tables, and a fierce philosophical argument playing out between two fish-like diplomats near the exit door. I exchanged a few more neutral pleasantries with Hobart as he guzzled the rest of his bile. Then I said goodnight and went back to my room.

Rrkttl's face was already on the wall screen when I returned. Apparently, he had been waiting for me.

"So, what'd you think?" he asked.

"Well, he seems agreeable and passably civilized," I replied. "But... he's still a *mammal*, Rrkttl."

"I know!" My old friend could no longer disguise his excitement. "Isn't it brilliant? Those hairy Muloumi idiots you were dealing with today will take one look at him and think the arbitration's in the bag!"

"I guess they will." I was totally lost now. "You'd tell me if there was some larger political reason why we want the Muloumi to do better than us here, right?"

Rrkttl's antennae quivered briefly with impatience.

"Of course not! You spent close to an hour with the human, didn't you? Didn't *anything* about his behavior strike you as a little...you know...*off*? Compared to the other mammals you've dealt with?"

I sighed. "To be honest, I found him pretty inscrutable. He got drunk on less than half a liter of Lamphalian bile, then told me a revolting folktale about some deviant monarch from his species' primeval era, who went around cutting children in half. He seemed to think the story represented a repository of diplomatic insight. Not really an inspiring performance."

Rrkttl was practically bobbing up and down in his seat now, and his antennae had gone curly as spiral nebulae. He was obviously enjoying some private joke.

"That story he told you is just the tip of the iceberg, Cryyvtt. Tell you what. If you're not too sleepy, why don't you tap into the Temple's historical library with your phone and glance over some of the data they have on Mr Hobart's species? Skip all the dull biological stuff and go straight to the material on their pre-assimilation history."

I groaned inwardly. It was late, and I felt like I had served my species' diplomatic corps too honorably over the years to deserve this kind of pranking. But I told Rrkttl I would do as he said.

I scavenged a nodule of sobriety nectar out of my luggage and sipped the greasy, flavorless ichor while I searched the Temple's archive for the relevant documents.

A couple of hours later, my mind was reeling. When I'd first started reading, I had been temporarily enthralled by the tales of the earliest, primitive human empires - Greeks, Romans and whatnot - though it took me a while to work out that all their fussing and fighting actually *hadn't* arisen from interspecies rivalries. Then, just when I thought I was getting the hang of this playful but over-excitable little species, I came across the artwork and photography from certain subsequent festivities.

The 'Armenian Genocide'. The 'Red and Blue Conflict' - and something their species referred to with demure mysticism as 'The Holocaust.' I'll spare you the hyperbolic details. Let's just say it was a good thing I hadn't eaten as well as drunk earlier that evening.

I called Rrkttl back.

"I'm not one hundred percent confident I understand what I've just read." I could hear a slight tremor in my voice. "They did all of this stuff to *themselves*? Not some exotic invaders or a troublesome local insurgent species? Mightn't there be some sort of translational error in the…"

"No, no, no," said Rrkttl. "Though I totally understand your disbelief. When I first got the lowdown about these guys, I called up Xenologists at three different universities just to be positive I wasn't having my legs pulled. Apart from the intermittent orgies of violence, these 'humans' haven't achieved much else of note. But they're a legend amongst students of alien life who relish a certain flavor of perversity."

"I'm still not sure I see the wisdom of having them mediate. Based on what I've just read, I wouldn't be surprised if this Hobart were to suddenly start gnawing off his own foot during negotiations."

"Why is that? Did he say or do anything while you were talking to him that struck you as oversensitive? Erratic?"

"Not at all. Rather a shy, well-mannered creature, really. And he seemed to have all the standard mammalian affects. He was clearly horrified by what Pttk did to Ambassador Welb."

"Hmm." Rrkttl's composure faltered for a moment. "That does concern me a little. If there's any chance at all of that unfortunate spectacle inclining him against us…"

"Hobart watched the film of it *three times*, Rrkttl! Once in slow motion. It was almost as though he…"

But another glance at Rrkttl's antennae was enough to detect he'd quickly returned to a mood of smug superiority. And then, at last, I understood.

"Great God Ygnyyttllyzykk! Watching the Muloumi's death *aroused* him! He *liked* it!"

"That does seem like the most plausible hypothesis, yes. Some day when you're feeling sturdy, Cryyvtt, you should take a look at a few of the films and sporting activities these critters indulge in on their homeworld, when they think we're not paying attention. To say nothing of their pornography! I bet your friend Hobart is back in his room right now, watching your video on a 3D projector. Probably dancing around naked or something."

"Thank you ever so much for that image, Counselor." The mere thought of an aroused Hobart minus his ridiculous *Space Squad* outfit was enough to make me want to exit this conversation as swiftly as possible. "So, tomorrow…"

"Make the Muloumi an austere but equitable offer. We still have our long-term reputation with other more rational species to consider. But don't act too conciliatory. The occasional little snap of your jaws, or an oblique reference to recipes for mammalian organ meats, should put our new arbitrator right in his comfort zone."

I tiled my upper thorax forward very deeply, in acknowledgement of my colleague's wisdom and foresight.

"As long as you're still running the game back at home, Rrkttl, I know the Tzekket's fate is in secure hands. Even after days like today."

Rrkttl gave a modest twitch of his right foreleg in acknowledgement, then signed off for the night.

It just goes to show you. A person can trace the most exotic of paths between the stars for the length of a whole career. But there's always something new to learn about the delicate art of diplomacy.

A Horror Triptych

John Grey

AT THE WAX MUSEUM

Sure, you've been sculptured
to the point of madness,
with your crazed bulging eyes,
mordant slug-like mouth.
But, to be honest,
you're not the least bit frightening.
Maybe it's knowing that
you're nothing but wax
and not the beast that roamed
the dismal streets of fog-gripped
late nineteenth century East London.
Sure, art is long and life is brief so they say
but it's the briefness of that latter,
sometimes curtailed by
a scalpel-wielding demon
that piques the nerve ends,
puts the brain on nervous watch.
I could reach out and touch
this statue of you, Jack,
scratch your cheeks,
poke your chest,
even run my fingers down

215

that blood-stained blade.
You've been tamed.
You're just another Michael Jackson,
Elvis Presley - a neutered image,
an insipid reminder of the real thing.
A woman even has her picture taken with you -
a smile to match your scowl.
No way to slash her,
cut her open,
send her liver in an envelope
to the police.
So what if, just like me, she wasted good money
on a lousy tourist trap.
That's hardly disemboweling, is it?

ON A NIGHT IN SERBIA

Procession below
my second-floor rooms.
A line of torches
out of one darkness,
on the way to another.
Hooded figures
in white robes,
heads bent over,
chanting softly.
I poke my head
out the window,
cry, "Excuse me,
but do any of
you have the time?"
Much muttering follows.

That wasn't the effect
they were aiming for.

THE CELLAR GARDENER

Another body dragged down
the basement stairs.
One more corpse to plant
like a flower in my cellar garden.
No watering needed.
No fertilizer.
For not a stalk will sprout.
Nothing will bud.
No blossoms can be expected.
There's more life in one tiny seed
than ten unfortunate strangers.
But where's the fun
in strangling seeds?

Moving in A Mysterious Way

Jan-Andrew Henderson

People are being exposed to a daily cocktail of pollution that may be having a significant impact on their health
BBC News

I survived the apocalypse cause I was in Sunnyvale prison canteen, waiting to visit my cousin Dave. I didn't want to talk to the other sad sacks, so I put on wraparound sunglasses and noise-cancelling head-phones.

That's what saved my life.

Nobody knows what happened to the air. All we're sure about is that human beings suffered an instant and complete sensory overload.

Suddenly, sunlight blinded people and burned their skin to a crisp. Every noise was amplified to a deafening roar. Each smell, sweet or sour, became an overpowering stench.

The end of the world came with a whimper that felt like a bang.

Out of nowhere, the prison sirens went off. Sirens are loud by defi-nition but this was in a different league. Everyone started screaming, not the wisest course of action when you're caught up in a maelstrom of unbearable sound. Through a porthole in the door, I could see a stampede for the exits, including guys in leg irons, who had to hop. Light pouring through the upper windows turned swiftly and intolera-bly bright, as if an enormous sun lamp had been switched on.

219

I threaded my way between visitors, bumping into each other in panic, eyes squeezed shut and hands over their ears. My head was splitting, despite the headphones, so I darted into the kitchen, holding my nose. Prison food smells awful at the best of times but now the stink was stomach-churning. There was a big walk-in fridge at the back, so I got inside and pulled the door shut. Then I ate a thawing sausage roll and waited in the dark until blessed silence descended.

When I emerged, it was night and the place was deserted. No visitors. No warders. No prisoners. No Dave.

I presume one of the guards opened the electronic cell doors, as a last act of altruism, setting the inmates free. Or, maybe, he just pressed the wrong button in confusion. Either way, I doubt anyone made it more than a hundred yards outside the main gate before they got toasted.

Everything happens for a reason, mum used to say. Then again, she was electrocuted by faulty Christmas tree lights and was obviously no expert on fate.

Everyone has different theories but shit happens and I don't see the point in dwelling on it. After all, the Bible has God creating the whole universe in seven days, without actually saying how he did it. And the whole shebang only takes up half a page.

But I've always been lucky and it turned out jail was the best place for me - which is something else my mum used to say. Sunnyvale's male and female wings were subterranean, joined by underground tunnels, while metal shutters could be brought down on any windows above ground. The place even had its own emergency generator and I'd say the end of humanity definitely counted as an emergency.

For a while, I thought I might be the last person on earth. Then, one by one, I came across Corrine Telford, Floyd Peterson, WTF Hartley, Div and Doob. I still don't know Div and Doob's last names. Or their first names, for that matter. There's no real need to inquire when your universe only contains six people.

We get along well enough. Each of us has staked out a little bit of turf but everyone chips in to keep things running. Like vampires, we only come out at night and there are solitary confinement cells on the lowest levels, where we can sleep the day away without being assaulted by sounds, smells and piercing light.

All in all, it's not a bad existence, considering the circumstances.

As I said, I've always been lucky.

WTF Hartley and I are a couple. He isn't really called WTF, of course, but now he can have any handle he wants. Personally, I would have gone for something like Dirk Manly or Rupert Hyphen Poshhouser. Still, it kind of suits him.

He also wears a dress most days. Not in a feminine way, because he has a shaved head and a face that looks like it vacuumed a gravel driveway. WTF just doesn't see any reason to conform to old stereotypes. Then again, he has a broad Scottish accent so, perhaps, it's the closest thing he can find to a kilt.

He also has the most important and hazardous job in Sunnyvale, foraging for supplies in town once a week.

We've developed a routine. I lather his face with sun cream while he distracts us both from the dangers he faces with a stream of meaningless banter. He keeps his voice low, as everyone does, so it's no more than a murmur. I don't mind, as it sounds quite sexy.

"I ever tell you about going tae the wildlife sanctuary in Lone Pine?" he says. "I had mah picture taken with a koala called Monica. Grabbed mah bare arms with claws that could open a safe door, then peed on me. Close up, I saw she had beady eyes and wuz incapable of any kind of expression. Like a psychopath."

He puts on several prison uniforms, each bigger than the last. It's fortunate some of the inmates were built like garden sheds.

"In the gift shop were photographs of famous people holding Koalas. President Clinton. Pope John Paul II. Even Bono. If aliens landed, they'd probably think Monica wuz some kind of world leader."

He sticks on a riot helmet, skiing goggles, rubber gloves, earplugs and nose plugs.

"Koalas. The wee bastards hae everybody fooled."

I help him into a leather flying jacket and white silk scarf he found in a vintage store. He likes to be stylish. I unbent a wire coat hanger and threaded it through the collar of the jacket, so now it stands up and protects his neck. It looks pretty cool too. Being civilized is all about keeping up appearances, WTF insists, and I agree.

"You take care out there," I warn, as always.

"I am putting myself to the fullest possible use, which is all I think that any conscious entity can ever hope to do." He gives me a thumbs up. "That's the killer computer HAL, from the movie *2001*. Douglas Rain did the voice."

WTF is a film buff.

I gently slap his butt and retreat while he opens the door to the compound. In the distance, I can see silhouettes of redundant guard towers. Even with nose plugs in, I get a whiff of a thousand odours, sharp as Gorgonzola. Thank goodness the sun has turned the corpses to dust, or we'd be eternally throwing up.

WTF blows me a kiss, steps into the night and is gone.

Time to do my rounds.

I'm officially head of security, prison nurse, health inspector and entertainment officer. Always liked to keep busy. I'm also Mayor of Brisbane and Duchess of Queensland, though those are honorary titles. I've pushed to be addressed as Queen of Royal Britain Land and Its Associated Colonies but nobody has taken me up on it.

First stop on my route is Corinne Telford.

Corinne is our cook, garbage collector and spiritual advisor. She's also a born-again Christian and thinks what happened is God's punishment on the wicked - which completely fails to explain anything. Whatever floats your boat, I suppose.

Corrine survived by hiding inside an empty coffin in the prison chapel and, out of gratitude, made it her domain. It once had beautiful stained-glass windows, telling the story of Christ rising from his tomb and suchlike, but we've boarded them over. Now they're hidden behind cheap plywood facades, which would probably make a good parable, if I could be bothered thinking one up.

Corinne spends most of her time reading the Bible and waiting in vain for the rest of us to come seeking guidance. I suggested she become a Jehovah's Witness so she could be more proactive and knock on doors. We can't exactly pretend we're not at home. She called me an unholy blasphemer, so I added that to my list of titles.

And she's obviously not too dogmatic, as she followed my advice. Sure enough, everyone claimed to be out.

Since none of us have rushed to be converted, I like to keep Corinne's holy spirits up. Each day, I present her with a theological question to ponder, hoping for a satisfying discussion.

"How's trick's, Coz?" I stick my head around the door.

"Please do come in. Mo." She beckons to me. "Would you like an Anzac biscuit?"

I accept and sit on a pew. I imagine it's a bit like communion, not that I've ever been to one.

"Right, Corrine." I launch straight in, as she isn't the type for idle chit-chat. "God is supposed to be all-powerful, yeah?"

"That is what I believe, Mo. Certainly."

Corinne has taken to speaking in a formal manner she probably considers saintly. It actually makes her sound a bit like HAL, which WTF finds hilarious. I don't know why she doesn't go the whole hog and throw in a few 'thous' and 'beholds'.

"Then here's my question, Coz. Is God able to build a wall so high, he can't jump over it?"

"Yes." No hesitation there.

"But if he can't jump over it, he's not all-powerful, is he?"

"He moves in mysterious ways, Mo."

"There's nothing very mysterious about jumping."

"It is not for me to question the Lord," she replies serenely. "We are simply here to serve."

I bristle a little at this. As far as I'm concerned, the only people put on earth to serve are waiters. But I know she'll think about it. Maybe pause, before that wall she's building around herself gets too high to jump over.

"You remembering tomorrow is the big night?" I cajole. "You gotta do something for it."

As entertainment officer, I have organised a talent show. In case that isn't enough of a challenge, I've given it a theme. Air.

Why not? I think it's funny and so does WTF.

"I have cleared my calendar." Corinne licks crumbs from her fingers and I wonder if she just made a joke. "I shall be there, never fear."

"You're not going to give a sermon, are you?" I wince.

"Everyone has their own area of expertise," she replies haughtily. "It would be foolish not to use mine."

"Of course." I try to sound enthusiastic. "Looking forward to it."

I back out the door, crouched low and waving both hands in front of my face. Corrine looks suitably puzzled.

"What on earth are you doing?"

"God's not the only one who can move in a mysterious way."

Corrine sighs.

Next stop is Floyd Peterson. As always, he's in the prison education centre, lost in thought. On the wall is a whiteboard, where some unknown dead guy has written *You can't buy happiness, so steal it,* along with a drawing of a crab on a bike. Try as I might, I can't get the connection.

"Evening, professor."

He appreciates it when I call him professor. In the old days, he was a prison janitor, saved by being in the lowest level, cleaning toilets when real shit hit the fan. He thinks our predicament is the result of mass quantum entanglement, set off by particle smashing in Switzerland.

I sit at a desk near the back of the room, like a naughty pupil, while he stands at the front.

Floyd Peterson tilts his head down whenever he looks at me. He must have worn glasses once, but nobody needs them anymore, as our sight is crystal clear. The rest of us often sport sunshades but I guess he was pretty myopic and relishes having 20/20 vision.

I think I understand why people lose their eyesight as they age. When they study themselves in the mirror, they're pleasantly blurred and it hides the wrinkles. That's why, the older you get, the less inclined you are to have photographs taken. Nobody wants a portrait of their own Dorian Gray.

It makes me appreciate WTF even more. Though I'm getting on in years, he looks at me as if I'm the last ham sandwich at a weight watchers convention. Which, in metaphorical terms, I suppose I am.

"Whatcha pondering today, Prof?" I inquire.

"I was thinking that there are billions of stars and planets out there." He points in the direction of the roof. It is a mass of white splodges made by bored inmates chewing paper and throwing them upwards till they stick. It reminds me of the night sky but I don't think he's ever noticed.

Floyd Peterson is determined to live in his own head.

"In the good old days, we were unable to reach any of those myriad wonders. Didn't bother us in the slightest, did it?"

To be honest, it always did, but I let the comment slide.

"Ever been to Venice?" he continues. "Or Amsterdam? Moscow? Krakow? Munich? Edinburgh? Tokyo? Rhodes? Chicago?"

"I went to Bundaberg once," I venture. "But it was Sunday, so everything was shut."

"All those fine places," he says wistfully. "Yet, when we had the opportunity to visit them, we never took it."

He spreads his hands.

"Why should we care, now that we can't?"

Actually, I *have* been to most of those places, Venice being my favourite. But that doesn't fit with his theory either, so I stay mum.

"It's simply a process of adjustment. See, all experience is filtered through the prism of our own perceptions and feelings, so it doesn't really matter where we are."

"The prison of our own perceptions and feelings?" I raise an eyebrow.

Floyd Peterson stares at me and I instinctively put a hand to my face. These days, if I've got a bit of food on my chin, it can most likely be spotted from another planet.

"Prism, Mo," he scolds. "Don't take the piss."

"Sorry." But I still think my interpretation is more accurate.

"Thanks for the lecture, Prof." I get up, careful not to scrape my chair on the tile floor. The noise would be teeth jarring. "You always give me a lot to think about."

But, mostly, I am thinking Floyd Peterson needs a hobby. Live in your own head long enough and you stop being comfortable anywhere else.

"Ready for tomorrow night?" I change the subject. "The big show?"

"Not really. But I'll give it a try."

Next on my rounds are Div and Doob, who live in the gymnasium. They're our mechanical wizards, keeping the generator and other geegaws running. They were sleeping off massive hangovers in a disused lead boiler when Armageddon came along and, most likely, didn't notice. Their theory is some big conglomerate invented a formula to remove pollutants choking our atmosphere and it got out of control.

Both are in their early twenties and I suspect they're in love because the rest of us are too old to be of consequence. They quite like me, though. Most people do.

I believe they're suffering from SMWD or Social Media Withdrawal Symptom, a condition I completely made up but sounds about right. They've even created a homemade Facebook page, writing post-it notes and sticking them to the wall. Visitors can tick the ones they like with a red pen on a string.

When I slide in, they are opening a box of wine.

"G'day, mates." I plonk myself between them and give both a peck on the cheek. Even that small gesture tingles as if I've rubbed my lips along sandpaper.

"Hi, Mo." Div passes me a drink. "Heard you coming, so we broke out the best glasses. The foggy ones with decorative soap rings."

I take a slurp. It's like swallowing turpentine in this new atmosphere, but all booze tastes horrible until you get used to it. Ask any teenager.

"Hope you've been practising your act," I splutter, trying not to cough.

Div and Doob regard my talent show as akin to a Victorian get-together, singing psalms around the pianoforte. But they're also bored out of their minds and welcome any distraction.

"Don't you know it!" They grin at each other. "We're gonna win for sure."

"There are no winners or losers, you know."

"Spoken like a true loser. We demand a prize."

"I'll see what I can do."

We shoot the breeze for a while and drink more wine, grimacing with each sip, until it's time for WTF to return. Then I make my excuses and leave.

I help WTF out of his clothes and he goes for a shower, which takes a long time. Anything more than a trickle of lukewarm water is painful. In the meantime, I take out the contents of his rucksack which, as usual, consists mostly of tinned food.

"Baked beans," I say brightly. "There's a surprise."

"Aye, but these are low sodium."

There are also two bottles of port, some cheese crackers and six pairs of oven gloves.

I look quizzically at him but he just taps his long nose.

I found WTF sitting calmly in a padded solitary confinement cell, with the door unlocked but closed. The only inmate smart enough not to make a run for it.

I don't know what he did and I've never queried him about it. I'm not a curious type, nor one for emotional sandblasting. We've all been given a second chance and he has made the most of his. I wish there was a parole board around to witness it.

WTF's theory is that the air is exactly the same as always - it's us who have suddenly become intolerant to it. He says it's proof people can change.

"Want me to make you dinner?" I ask. This is our little joke, as heating food would require an asbestos suit. We have to eat everything cold.

"When I originally came here," WTF talks carefully over the noise of the water. "I went tae a restaurant in Apollo Bay and ordered my first proper Aussie burger."

He turns off the faucet and I hand him a towel.

"It took three members of staff to lift onto the table. It had lettuce, tomato, pineapple, a fried egg, watercress, bacon, some kind of hairy plant I didn't recognise but might be cactus, a cigarette butt, ketchup, mayo, more pineapple, cotton, ice cream and a Bush Turkey sitting on top, in case I couldnae finish it. There may have been meat in there as well, but I gave up the will tae live halfway through and had to be rolled back to mah car."

He chuckles roguishly. But his eyes are sunken and his skin is puckered like a prune.

"How come you guys put pineapple on everything?"

That's why I like WTF. He makes me laugh. Or he tries, which is just as good.

"You go to your cell and get some rest," I command sternly. "Those trips outside are taking a real toll."

"I've seen things you people wouldn't believe," he quotes. "That's Rutger Hauer as the killer replicant Roy Batty in *Blade Runner*."

"Let me put everything away." I hang up the towel. "Need you on top form for tomorrow night, baby."

"I won't let you down." He smiles resignedly and plods off.

Though we are lovers, I don't sleep with WTF. The touch of flesh on flesh is too extreme to stand in more than small bursts. And if one of us started snoring, it would end in fisticuffs.

Instead, I go to my own cell, take a bottle of wine and a strip of Diazepam from under the mattress and down both.

We each cope in our way. This has always been mine.

The next night, everyone files into the prison hall and sits in the back row. They are certainly dressed for the occasion, sporting finery WTF brought back from his last trip to the mall. Corrine has on a full-length fur coat. Floyd Peterson is in a dinner suit and bow tie. Div and Doob have on pork pie hats and striped braces over white T-shirts. WTF is resplendent in a red mini skirt and silver spangled halter top. He hands each of us a pair of oven gloves and I finally understand.

It's so we can clap without making too much noise.

The stage is basic, just a raised wooden platform with one metal flagpole at either side, minus the flag. Not exactly the Sydney Opera House, but it'll have to suffice. I appear from the rear door, clutching a sheaf of computer paper.

"Good evening, ladies and gentlemen," I announce softly. "And welcome to the first annual Sunnyvale talent contest. I've prepared a small speech for the occasion."

I let the perforated paper unfurl and spill across the boards for several feet. The audience gives a stifled moan.

"Tough crowd, eh? In that case, without further ado, let me introduce Div and Doob - the gruesome twosome."

Div and Doob spring up and move along the line of bemused participants, shaking hands and patting them gently on the shoulders. Then they scramble onto the stage and stand at opposite ends.

"Check this out," Div chuckles. "I will now make some shit appear from thin... air."

Going with the theme. Well done, Div.

He runs one hand up his leg and produces a large piece of dried fruit, seemingly from nowhere. On his wrist is a small gold timepiece that wasn't there before.

"Hey! That's my snack," Floyd Peterson frowns. "It was in my pocket."

"And he's wearing my watch," Corinne adds. "I shall be wanting that back, young man."

Div puts the fruit on his head and stands perfectly still.

"Oooh, what a lovely pear," Doob says appreciatively.

"You took the words right out of my mouth," Div shoots back and the audience groans again. They *are* a tough crowd.

"That's fae the movie *Carry on Doctor*," WTF stage whispers. "Stop nicking jokes, you wee shits."

Doob pulls a knife from her sleeve, twirls it round her fingers and grins at him. WTF pats his top, suitably impressed.

"You've got mah shiv," he whistles appreciatively. "Well played, lassie."

Before anyone can object, Doob tosses it in the air, catches the blade and throws. It shoots across the stage, imbeds itself in the pear and tumbles into the wings.

Every jaw is open. Div and Doob take this as a positive sign, mime high-fiving each other and return to their seats. I begin to suspect they might not have been part of the maintenance crew after all. But the show must go on.

"Next up is that master of mirth and purveyor of puns, WTF Hartley." I beckon to my partner, expecting him to do some sort of stand-up routine. Instead, he grabs a basket from his feet, bounces up the steps and opens it.

It is filled with balloons, long thin and multicoloured.

He blows them up, turning bright red in the process and everyone grabs their earplugs. One pop will send us into a coma. But he begins to fold them expertly into each other. They have been lubricated with cooking spray so the rubber won't squeak - we can smell it, even at a distance. Within a few seconds, a sculpture begins to take shape, a donkey or perhaps an alligator. Either way, I'm impressed he's made an effort to stick with the subject matter. I should have known he'd try hard to please.

He lets go and the animal whizzes over our head, deflating as it twists, producing a seemingly endless wet fart. In the amplified atmosphere, the sound is exaggeratedly comical.

Everyone starts giggling.

"Thank you. I'll be here all week. Probably all year." WTF holds up a trembling hand. "Try the veal."

He glances nervously at me as I regain the podium and my heart goes out to him.

"And now, Professor Floyd Peterson," I say. "No idea what he's going to do but it's bound to be intellectual. Take it away, Prof."

Floyd Peterson brings his folding chair to the stage and sits on it. Takes a homemade carved recorder from his jacket. He puts the instrument to his lips and blows as softly as he can. It is *The Lark Ascending* by Vaughn Williams.

He plays it perfectly.

The thin, reedy tune floats around us and up into the rafters. One by one, we remove our earplugs. Amplified by the clear air, the sound becomes as full-bodied and moving as any orchestra.

We are rapt. From my position in the wings, I can see tears running down upturned faces. Floyd Peterson finishes and we wait until the last echoes have died away before clapping. He smiles gratefully and returns with his seat.

I wish I hadn't decided to let Corrine go last. Unless she can turn water into wine, she'll ruin the moment for sure. Unfortunately, it's too late now.

"Finally, we welcome Corrine Telford." I try my best to sound keen. "Who, I'm certain, is going to give us all something divine."

Corrine makes her way hesitantly into the limelight. She takes a deep breath and I wait for her to launch into some diatribe about the glory of God.

Instead, she unfastens her fur coat and lets it fall. Underneath, she is wearing nothing but a silver, two-piece bathing costume. Her body is lean and muscular, the kind of physique you only get after years of push-ups and crunches.

What the hell?

Corrine grabs one of the metal poles at the side of the stage and effortlessly flips upside down. Begins to slowly revolve, her long blonde hair brushing the floor.

The silence is palpable.

She lets go with one hand and curls into the pole, spinning faster. What the sensation of cold metal is doing to her skin, I can't imagine, but it makes my toes curl.

The audience's eyes are on stalks.

There's no way she can pull off what I think is coming next. Yet she does.

Corrine removes her other hand and draws up her knees, holding on with only her stomach muscles. I put a hand to my mouth and the others give a collective intake of breath.

Eventually, Corrine slows to a stop and pirouettes back onto the stage, as casually as if she were dismounting a bike. Her face is flushed but she is barely out of breath.

"There's moving in a fucking mysterious way for you, Mo," she hisses.

The applause is thunderous. Or it would have been if we weren't wearing oven gloves.

"That is bloody art, so it is!" Div removes his hat and salutes. "Respect, woman."

Corrine puts her coat back on, comes down and sits next to Floyd Peterson. She is shivering, so he puts his arm around her and she nestles into his shoulder.

This certainly is a night for surprises.

"I want to thank you all from the bottom of my heart." I wrap things up with a curtsey. "There's port and nibbles in the foyer. Well... that table at the back."

My voice is choked with emotion.

"Tonight has been such a success that, next year, we're putting on a musical."

"I vote for *Godspell*," Corrine says and all of us laugh, loudly as we dare.

The cast party is a happy affair. We are all a bit in awe of each other and there is a sense of camaraderie that wasn't there before. Each of us knows it takes a long time to perfect tricks like these, not just a few days.

More like years surviving on the streets than rotting in a cell.

For the first time, they begin to talk about the future. Floyd Peterson floats the idea of irrigating our prison yard and planting vegetables under a homemade sail. Corinne offers to help, admitting she grew up on a farm. Div and Doob mention casually that they used to grow marijuana and know a lot about fertilizer.

When the rest have retired, WTF takes me onto the roof because that's our place. The sky is damp with glittering stars and the world is mostly silent. Occasionally, we hear the chirp of an insect, far in the distance.

"Not everything is dead after all." I cup my ear. "There might even be other people out there."

"Life, uh, finds a way." WTF does a passable American accent. "That's Jeff Goldblum in *Jurassic Park*."

He opens a tin of peaches and the bottle of port he saved for us.

"I think you'll find this a cheeky wee number," he deadpans. "It has overpowering notes of barbecue sauce and a kick like a prostitute with epilepsy."

I take a sip and wrinkle my nose.

"Well done tonight, Mo." He hands me the can. "But I was looking forward tae your effort. How come ye didnae do something?"

"I was the compere. Wouldn't have felt right, joining in."

We each try to eat a slice of fruit, but the taste is so strong and sweet it stings our mouths. We spit them out, smirk at each other and I wait for him to launch into one of his funny stories.

Instead, WTF gazes out over the vista.

"Look at this view," he remarks. "It's beautiful but kind of sad and empty."

He glances sideways at me.

"When I was younger, I used tae think the right person for me wuz someone who'd sit by my side and feel exactly the way I did about a scene like this."

He frames me in a little box, shaped by his fingers.

"But no. The right person is really someone who fits *intae* that picture."

He sighs and it reverberates loudly over the roof. The sound is unexpectedly heartbreaking.

"Thing is, just cause someone is perfect for one scene, it doesnae mean they'll be right for the next, eh?"

I've underestimated WTF Hartley.

"Why exactly did you come to Australia?" I break my rule and finally ask him a question.

"Land built by convicts, eh?" he yuks. "Maybe I thought I'd fit in-tae *that* picture."

"I love you WTF." I stroke his cheek.

"I love you too." He tries to stifle a yawn. "Why don't you come downstairs?

"I told Div and Doob the show wasn't a competition. Didn't say there weren't prizes. I want to leave them out while everyone is asleep."

"You are most definitely the bee's knees." He clasps his hands together in an imitation of the scene from the film he's quoting.

"Andy Garcia." I pick up the thread. "The killer turned hero from *Things to do In Denver When You're Dead*."

"Clever lassie. What am *I* getting, then?"

"Stay awake long enough?" I nudge him. "You'll find out."

"There's no way I'm nodding off now."

He kisses the top of my head and leaves with a spring in his step.

I sit for a long time, wrapped in soft-skinned silence. Then I go downstairs, unlock the storage cupboard of level three and retrieve a stash of goodies.

Time to make my rounds.

I raided the prison library for the Quaran, the Tripitakas and the Torah, which I stack outside the chapel door. Corinne may as well keep her options open.

Next, I go to the education centre and set down a telescope I took from the guard tower. Floyd Peterson can use it to look at the stars, though he'll finally have to put sunglasses on. It won't bring them any closer but it might seem like they are.

For Div and Doob, I leave a couple of hazmat suits, which took me ages to find. They were once used for scrubbing cells, when inmates smeared faecal matter on the walls. Floyd Person would have known they existed if he really had been a janitor.

WTF has done enough. It's time Div and Doob started putting their light-fingered talents to better use. Anyway, they need to get out more.

Then I enter WTF's cell and take off my clothes.

We have sex quietly and gently because there's no other way to do it. It's very intense and also rather uncomfortable. Forced intimacy turning something that used to be fun into a bit of a chore.

Afterwards, we lie, side by side, fingers entwined. It's all we can manage.

"You're the glue that keeps this lot together, Mo. Know that?" Though it is dark, I can see WTF has on a serious face. "You've turned us intae a family."

"Like the mafia?"

"Nah. I mean it."

He closes his eyes and I wait until his breathing is deep and regular before getting dressed. Wisps of my white hair remain on the pillow.

I spot the basket in the corner and sigh. Making balloon animals is not something you learn in jail. More like the props a failed entertainer would use if he was performing for a bunch of convicts.

It's nice to know we have something in common.

"You don't have to pretend anymore." I softly kiss his cheek. "You're one of them."

Me? I had a family once and sure as hell don't need another. I was bored enough with my last life. Besides, I've used up all the pills in the pharmacy, WTF has emptied the local bottle shop of wine and I can't stand spirits.

WTF will understand, I hope. He knows how exhausting it is, pretending to fit in.

I go upstairs and struggle into the prison outfits. Stick on the riot helmet and glasses. Insert the nose and earplugs. Take the leather flying jacket and white silk scarf from a coat hanger and wrap them around myself. They smell strongly of WTF and, I imagine, always will. But, unlike him, my armour is for defence - not crusading.

Everyone will have their theory as to why I left. But, in the end, I put on a great show. That's what they'll remember.

I edge open the gates and step outside. I was hoping for a sense of freedom but, inside this getup, everything is muffled and dark.

I'll travel by night and hide in cellars during the day, though the air could still get me in some unguarded moment. I console myself by imagining, for a fleeting second, it might feel like being born again.

I'd love to go to Venice, as I could afford to live there now, but Sydney will have to do. I'll move into a suite on the top floor of the Waldorf Astoria with a balcony overlooking the opera house. Watch the stars, drink champagne and dine on tinned caviar, even if it tastes like crap.

There won't be anyone to share the view or feel the way I do about it, but I'm used to that. I'll survive, as usual.

To be honest, the end of the world hasn't really made much difference to me.

As I say, I've always been lucky

About the Authors

A Monster Circles The Wreckage.

Jan-Andrew Henderson is a Scottish author of 36 children's, teen, YA and adult fiction and non-fiction books. His novels have been shortlisted for 15 literary awards and he is the winner of the Royal Mail Award and Doncaster Book Prize. He now lives in Brisbane.
www.janandrewhenderson.com

I Know What You Did Last Trimester

Sara Corris resides in Brooklyn with a dog from London and a spouse from Buffalo. Her work has been performed by Liars' League in London and appeared in *Trembling With Fear, The Chamber, Horror Sleaze Trash, Bending Genres* and others. She is a lifelong horror devotee and sluttishly embraces its many varied subgenres. Find on Twitter her at @sara.corris.

Hell Is…

Keith Gray is the winner of The Smarties Book Prize and the Angus Book Award and his novels have been shortlisted for the Guardian Fiction Prize (twice), the Booktrust Teenage Prize (twice), the Scottish Arts Council Book of the Year Award, the Catalyst Book Award, the Costa Children's Book Award and the Carnegie Medal.

He lives in Vienna.
www.booktrust.org.uk/authors/g/gray-keith

My Year With The Perfect Family

Mark Nutter grew up in a motel near Joliet, Illinois, which is not as glamorous as it sounds. He acquired a taste for absurd comedy in the womb. Mark is the author of *Giant Banana Over Texas: Darkly Humorous Tales* and *Sunset Cruise on the River Styx: Dark, Absurd Tales*. He has been published in *Jokes Review, HAVOK Magazine, Mystery Weekly, Dear Leader Tales* and *The Daily Drunk*.

He is the winner of the Los Angeles Drama Critics Circle Award and the LA Weekly Theater Award, for the music & lyrics for *ReAnimator: The Musical*.

Mark wrote the music and lyrics and co-wrote the book for The *Bicycle Men*, named Outstanding Overall Production at the New York International Fringe Festival. He has also written for television (*SNL, 3rd Rock from the Sun*) and film (*Almost Heroes* starring the late Chris Farley).

www.marknutter.com

The Night Hank Came Back

Maxwell Price is a former music journalist from the deep south now living in Los Angeles. His novella *The Rockabilly Singer* has been published by 18th Wall Productions, with short stories published by Grey Matter Press and featured on the *Pseudopod* podcast.

Instagram: Thee That Thats's (@thee_that_thats)

Composters

Anita Sullivan is a multi-award-winning playwright (BBC Radio Drama. Race in the Media. Writers' Guild) with over 60 scripts performed and broadcast in the UK and internationally. Her work includes radio, site-specific theatre and digital/interactive storytelling. She is currently growing oyster mushrooms in her garage. www.anitasullivan.co.uk

The Magic Tea Pot

Mike James is the Canadian writer of *The Hotel at the End of Time*. His work has been featured in several anthologies, including *Executive Dread* by Jolly Horror Press, *Horror Library v7* by Dark

Moon Books, *Cossmass Infinities* and *Reservoir Road Literary Review*. You can connect with him on Twitter @mikejamesauthor
www.michaeljamesauthor.com

The Brentford Wives

Jen Mierisch's dream job is to write *Twilight Zone* episodes. Until then, she's a website administrator by day and a writer of odd stories at night.

Jen's work can be found in *Horla, Dark Moments, Sanitarium* and numerous anthologies. Jen can be found haunting her local library near Chicago, USA.

www.jenmierisch.com

The Nature of My Game

Mike Deady is a lifelong resident of Massachusetts. After retiring from a forty-two-year career in engineering, he started writing horror fiction at the urging of his brother, Bram Stoker Award-winning author Tom Deady. Mike's work has appeared in *Totally Tubular Terrors* and *Supernatural Drabbles of Dread*. He is a member of the New England Horror Writers.

Nunavut Thunderfuck

Dale L. Sprule has had more than 50 stories published, including two story collections: *Psychedelia Gothique* and *Psychedelia Noir* and two novels, *The Human Template* and its sequel *Escape from the Carnivorous Forest. Nunavut Thunderfuck* was nominated for a Pushcart Prize.

www.dalelsproule.com

Wamid!

Nathan Cromwell (Ken Hueler) teaches kung fu in the San Francisco Bay Area. With fellow members of the Horror Writer's Association's local chapter, he gets up to all sorts of adventures (only some involving margaritas). His work has appeared in *Stupefying Stories*, *Another Realm* and *Strangely Funny III*. As Ken Hueler, he appeared in *Space & Time*, *Weirdbook*, *Weekly Mystery Magazine* and *Tales for the Camp Fire*.

https://kenhueler.wordpress.com

Manny

Anthea Middleton is a software engineer, originally from Ireland but living in Edinburgh. She is the winner of the Henshaw Prize, has been published in Horla and is working on her second novel *Downward Facing Doug* - about a murder at a futuristic yoga retreat.

You can see her blog at www.antheamiddleton.com

In Our Own Realm We Are Lords

Cliff McNish is a best-selling children's and YA author, winner of The Salford Book Award, The Calderdale Book Award, The Hillingdon Award and the Virginia Readers' Choice Award His fantasy *Doomspell Trilogy* was translated into 26 languages and sold several hundred thousand copies worldwide. His novel *Breathe* was voted by The Schools Network of British Librarians as one of the top adult and children's novels of all time. His adult horror has appeared in the *2nd Spectral Book of Horror*, Hellbound Books and Nightjar Press.

www.cliffmcnish.com

Burden To Bear

John Mahoney's short stories have been published by *The Yard: Crime Blog*, *Pinky Thinker Press* and *Etched Onyx Magazine*. *Highlights Magazine* published a joke he wrote before he knew Santa Claus wasn't real.

Murder Mommy

Eric Laber is Professor of Statistical Science at Duke University. He has published two books and more than 80 peer-reviewed articles.

His writing has been praised by critics as 'technically correct', 'acceptable after minor revision' and 'containing a lot of notation'.

Live Chat

C.M. Barnes lives and writes in New Mexico. Barnes' work has appeared in *American Short Fiction, Digital Americana, Booth* and elsewhere.

https://silenceoncebroken.com

Ars Amatoria

Katie McIvor is a Scottish writer and library assistant. She studied at the University of Cambridge and now lives in England with her husband and two dogs.

Her short fiction recently appeared in *Mythaxis Magazine, Etherea Magazine, The Nashville Review, Three-Lobed Burning Eye* and is forthcoming from *Silver Blade*.

You can find her on Twitter @_McKatie_

Yapo's Magic Pintle

Shelly Lyons is a Los Angeles townie who writes screenplays and weird fiction. One of her great delights is discussing made-for-TV horror and thrillers - from 1970s satanic panics to recent for-ladies' stalker potboilers.

Her fiction has appeared in the *Wight Christmas* horror anthology, in the upcoming *Planet Bizarro* anthology, *Peculiar Monstrosities* and in *The Dead Unleashed* anthology. She is the author of the sci-fi/humor/horror novel *Like Real*, to be published by Perpetual Motion Machine later this year.

www.shellylyons.com

King Solomon's Sword

Mark Silcox was born in Toronto, Canada and has worked as a security guard, a short-order cook, a freelance writer in the video game industry and a philosophy professor. He currently lives in Edmond, Oklahoma. His novel *The Face on the Mountain* was published by Incandescent Phoenix Press in 2015.

https://www.amazon.com/Mark-Silcox/e/B01F2KS4JQ/ref=dp_byline_cont_pop_ebooks_10

A Horror Triptych

John Grey is an Australian poet, US resident and winner of the Rhysling Award for genre poetry. He has been published in *Leading Edge, Salzburg Review* and *Hollins Critic.* His latest books *Leaves On Pages, Memory Outside The Head* and *Guest Of Myself,* are available through Amazon and he has work upcoming in *The Fifth Dimension, Space and Time* and *Holy Flea.*

Moving In a Mysterious Way

Yeah. It's Jan-Andrew Henderson again. He's the editor, so he gets to put in two stories - no matter how bad they are.

ABOUT THE EDITOR

Jan-Andrew Henderson is a professional member of the Institute of Professional Editors, an industry assessor/mentor for the Queensland Writers Centre, an ambassador for Australia Reads, a peer assessor for the Australian Council for The Arts and a convenor for the Aurealis Awards. He runs the Green Light Literary Rescue Service, offering advice and editing to writers.

He has been published in the UK, USA, Australia, Canada and Europe by Oxford University Press, Collins, Hardcourt Press, Amberley Books, Oetinger Publishing, Mainstream Books, Black and White Publishers, Mlada Fontana, Black Hart and Floris Books.

www.janandrewhenderson.com
www.greenlightliteraryrescueservice.com

CPSIA information can be obtained
at www.ICGtesting.com
Printed in the USA
BVHW040401190522
637488BV00024B/46